W9-CCD-742

"Kenzie?"

She glanced over her shoulder to find Stephen watching her from the corner of the building. Was a man supposed to look that sexy with a scowl on his face?

"More trouble?" she asked, coming back to the bottom step. Why couldn't Murtagh be satisfied wrecking her career with the lawsuit?

"No." Stephen crossed to her with a few ground-eating strides and the light from the camper window washed over his face, revealing the depth of concern in his gaze. "You're safe here with me behind this fence. I promise."

He looked so earnest, so determined to tolerate her invasion of his space until everything in her world was back to normal. "I appreciate that."

Leaning forward, she brushed her lips to his cheek. A light, friendly, platonic gesture was all she intended. Instead, he caught her as if he thought she'd lost her balance, his hands hot on her waist. Then his lips touched hers. Bracing her hands on his strong shoulders, she wanted to sink a little deeper, explore his taste as his masculine scent and the summer night enveloped her.

* * *

Be sure to check out the next books in this miniseries:

Escape Club Heroes—Off-duty justice, full-time love

* * *

If you're on Twitter, tell us what you think of Harlequin Romantic Suspense! #harlequinromsuspense

Dear Reader,

Welcome back to Philadelphia, PA, and the Escape Club! This riverside hot spot is *the* place to find both great music and a safe haven if you have a problem that doesn't fit within the framework of typical law enforcement.

Stephen Galway first appeared in *Safe in His Sight*, my debut book for Harlequin Romantic Suspense, and though I've written several novels in between, I've never been able to put this brooding man out of my mind. I've wanted him to have a happy-ever-after since the first moment he showed up on the page, grumbling at his brother.

Kenzie Hughes, a PFD firefighter, is in trouble and her options are dwindling when help comes from an unlikely source: Stephen. For some reason he sees right through her independent nature, which is currently propped up by little more than bravado and a big smile. Time after time he listens and then quietly steps up and does what's needed and all without trampling her pride.

Life has dealt Kenzie and Stephen some serious challenges and alone they found unique ways to cope and compensate. But now that they've met, it's time to make some hard choices about who they are, what they really need and how those revealing answers will shape their future.

Live the adventure,

Regan Black

BRAVING THE HEAT

Regan Black

HARLEQUIN® ROMANTIC SUSPENSE

Recycling programs
for this product may
not exist in your area.

ISBN-13: 978-1-335-45649-6

Braving the Heat

Printed in U.S.A.

Regan Black, a *USA TODAY* bestselling author, writes award-winning, action-packed novels featuring kick-butt heroines and the sexy heroes who fall in love with them. Raised in the Midwest and California, she and her family, along with their adopted greyhound, two arrogant cats and a quirky finch, reside in the South Carolina Low Country, where the rich blend of legend, romance and history fuels her imagination.

Books by Regan Black

Harlequin Romantic Suspense

Escape Club Heroes

Safe in His Sight
A Stranger She Can Trust
Protecting Her Secret Son
Braving the Heat

The Coltons of Shadow Creek

Killer Colton Christmas
"Special Agent Cowboy"

The Coltons of Red Ridge

Colton P.I. Protector

Harlequin Intrigue

Colby Agency: Family Secrets (with Debra Webb)

Gunning for the Groom
Heavy Artillery Husband

The Specialists: Heroes Next Door (with Debra Webb)

The Hunk Next Door
Heart of a Hero
To Honor and To Protect
Her Undercover Defender

Visit the Author Profile page at Harlequin.com for more titles.

For my friend Sam, a man who consistently stepped up as a sheriff's deputy, as an author and as my inspiration for Stephen's dad, Samuel Galway.

I am forever grateful for the light and laughter you added to my world.

Chapter 1

Standing at a prep counter in the Escape Club kitchen, Kenzie Hughes stuffed the last bite of her sandwich into her mouth and added her plate to the rack loaded for the dishwasher. She thanked the cook and slipped the strap of her backpack over one shoulder. Pausing at the doorway to the main floor, she scanned the empty stage, looking for Grant Sullivan, owner of the establishment.

The extra personnel Grant had brought on for the summer concert series were resetting for the evening show. Leaving them to cover her workload through the afternoon changeover didn't sit well with Kenzie, but her landlord had called. She had only a few more hours to clear out whatever she didn't want exposed to termite fumigation and the dust and debris from the repair process.

If she hustled she could get to her apartment and back again before the doors opened for the evening session. That would please her as much as it would please Grant. It wasn't as if she had anything better to do with her time, other than finding an affordable place to crash for a couple weeks.

Though her pay from the Philadelphia Fire Department had continued during her current administrative leave, storage units and short-term room rentals added up fast. She'd asked both her union representative and her lawyer if she could visit her mom in Delaware while her apartment was out of commission, and been told she had to stay in Philly. Both the union rep and her lawyer implied that her leaving town could be perceived as an admission of guilt.

"Can't have that," she muttered to herself.

If there was anything Kenzie dreaded more than the potential outcome of her current legal trouble, it was having nothing productive to do while she waited out the process.

She had, in fact, been cleared of any wrongdoing during a PFD investigation that followed a complaint from a man she'd rescued from a fire. He'd claimed her incompetence had resulted in minor injuries that could have been avoided. Just when she thought she'd be back on the job, the victim had filed a civil suit against her personally. She knew she wasn't guilty of any error in the process of saving his life. The victim disagreed. Loudly, publicly and constantly.

Stop, she ordered herself. Dwelling on the negative situation only fouled up her mood. The jerk didn't have a case at all. If he had, the PFD would have fired her outright weeks ago. Her lawyer assured her most civil cases settled out of court; it was simply a matter of working the case and being patient with the system. Oddly enough, the only place Kenzie successfully exercised patience was while working emergency calls and fires.

Unable to find Grant, she tracked down Jason Prather at the bar. The latest full-time addition to the Escape Club, Jason was the closest thing Grant had to an assistant manager. Tall and wiry, bordering on skinny, he, too, had a few years with the PFD on his résumé. Whenever she looked at him, she thought he could pass as a front man for one of the bands that came through if he'd let his thick black hair grow out.

"If Grant asks, will you remind him I went to clear out my apartment? I should be back in time for opening tonight."

Jason gave her a long look over the tablet he was using to record inventory. "You need any help? I can send—"

"No, thanks. I've got it," she managed to reply. If she said anything else, she'd probably break down in a puddle of frustration. Grant was doing enough for her already, keeping her busy with this job. She refused to impose on anyone else.

Hurrying out of the club and across the street, she cringed at the sight of her road-weary compact sedan. Though the primer-and-rust color scheme was a fright, it ran, and that was the important thing. And it was paid for. She'd sold her car and paid cash for the rust-bucket sedan so she could redirect her previous car payment to her legal fees for the civil case. When she didn't have those extra expenses anymore, she could go back to a better car. One with a powerful engine and serious sex appeal, she thought, indulging in a quick fantasy of a classic American muscle car.

As if. Although owning a classic Camaro was on her

bucket list, this case meant it would be a long time before she'd be able to make that kind of investment.

After unlocking the driver's door, she tossed her backpack into the passenger seat and slid behind the wheel. She turned the key in the ignition, expecting the sputter and catch of the small engine, but hearing silence instead.

"No." She dropped her head to the steering wheel, almost ready to give in to the threat of tears she'd been fighting off all week. Her apartment closing, if only temporarily, the civil suit claiming she was unfit for firefighting, and now a car that wouldn't start.

Crying over this heap of metal was pointless, but it was one obstacle too many right now. She ruthlessly swiped away the lone tear rolling down her cheek. It wasn't the potential expense of repairs, though cash was currently tight. No, what upset her more was the idea of asking another friend or family member for more help. Her independence had taken enough of a beating lately. Here she was at thirty years old, feeling less self-sufficient now than when she'd crossed the stage for her high school graduation. Unlike so many of her peers, back then she'd had clear goals and a clear path planned to reach them.

"This is not happening." She tried the ignition again, got the same result.

With a colorful oath, she removed the key and pulled the hood release. After slamming out of the car, she raised the hood and stared into the filthy engine. Her father, a car aficionado and passionate weekend race car driver, might have wept at the sight. He'd taught her everything he knew about cars and engines, and when she'd bought this one, it had been functional, if ugly.

The new battery she'd installed after the purchase was the only clean thing in view. With a critical eye, she assessed the rest of the machinery, looking for an obvious problem.

"It has to get better," she said aloud, willing herself to believe the words.

Life hadn't been perfect. She'd experienced her share of sorrows to offset the celebrations and happy milestones of being an independent adult. Overall, she'd been content through both the highs and lows. Until the last fire she'd worked, three months ago, turned into a difficult rescue and ongoing nightmare. Though she tried to ignore it, a small voice inside her head wondered again if that would be the last fire she ever fought.

"All of this will pass." Just like every other pain, challenge and setback she'd faced. She calmed herself with the assurance that she'd be back at the firehouse, back with her crew on the truck soon. She couldn't afford to let her mind wander away from anything less than her ideal outcome.

Returning to the driver's seat, she turned the key again, listening for clues. Was it the alternator or starter? It couldn't be a broken fuel gauge. She'd just filled up with gas yesterday. "Come on, baby, tell me what's wrong," she said to the car. "We've got things to do."

If she didn't figure this out, she'd leave Grant shorthanded during what was sure to be a packed house tonight. She shook the steering wheel. Sure, Grant might understand, but that wasn't the point. Letting people down, shirking commitments wasn't how she operated. Besides, working at the Escape Club distracted her, filling all the empty hours while the PFD kept her off the job.

As tears threatened again, she jerked the rearview

mirror around and glared at her reflection. "*You* are a firefighter," she said to the moody face in the mirror. She pushed the wisps of hair that had escaped her braid behind her ears. "You're one of the *best*," she said, willing away the doubt in the blue eyes staring back at her.

And if you lose the case and your career is over, who will you be?

She was really starting to hate that pesky negative voice that kept sounding off. Shoving the mirror back into place, she tried to start the car once more. Instead of getting anything out of the engine, she heard a knock on the window. She jumped in the seat, startled to see Mitch Galway on the other side of her open door. Her friend, part-time Escape Club bartender and fellow firefighter, Mitch had suggested she ask Grant for a job to help her through her current crisis. *Momentary* crisis.

"Car trouble?" he asked, tipping his head to the exposed engine.

"It won't turn over."

"Let me hear it." He signaled her to try again. Mitch knew cars and often helped his older brother with custom restorations at the Galway Automotive shop over in Spruce Hill. At the lack of response, he frowned and walked out of sight behind the open hood.

She silently prayed he could help as she checked the time. If she didn't make it to her apartment soon, all her belongings would be out of reach for at least two weeks. The last thing she needed was the expense of buying a new wardrobe.

"Any ideas?" she asked as she joined him. "I know it has gas in the tank."

He frowned at the engine. "In that case, my first guess is an alternator," he said. "You need a good mechanic?"

"I am a good mechanic," she reminded him. Or she had been when her dad was alive. With the right tools and time, she could probably sort this out on her own. Too bad she didn't have either.

"True." He dropped the hood back down and dusted off his palms. "You know I can hook you up," he said with a quick smile.

"What I need is a good car." She explained the dwindling time issue to Mitch. "I never should've waited until the last minute to do this." She didn't share the still more embarrassing fact that she had no idea where she would stay tonight or any night until she could go back to her apartment. Mitch had offered his spare room to her last week, but she'd turned him down. Newlyweds, he and his wife didn't need her underfoot.

Mitch tossed her the keys to his truck. "Go get your stuff," he said. "I'll call my brother and get your car towed to the shop."

Dollar signs danced through her head. Maybe she could trade labor for parts or something if his brother was amenable. "I'm not sure—"

"We'll figure it out," he said, waving off her concerns before she could name them all. "Get going."

"All right." Arguing with him to save a smidge of pride only robbed her of more time. "Thanks."

She grabbed her backpack and dashed over to Mitch's truck. She appreciated his generosity as well as his gracious acceptance of her circumstances. Everyone on the PFD knew she was in over her head with the civil suit and working every available hour at the Escape Club to pay for a decent lawyer to defend her.

A former firefighter himself, the plaintiff, Randall Murtagh, knew better than most people what *should* be done during a rescue. That he'd made it nearly impossible for her to save him didn't seem to have any relevance to his injuries, in his mind. A card-carrying member of the old guard who believed only men were capable of pulling people out of burning buildings, he made no secret of the fact that he wanted women drummed out of the ranks. If he couldn't get all the females off the PFD with this case, he seemed hell-bent on making her a prime example against equal opportunity employment.

And there she was dwelling on the negative again. She couldn't control his issues, only her response, and she wouldn't let a jerk like Murtagh take any more chunks of her life.

Fortunately, she was soon distracted, packing all the belongings she cared to take as swiftly as possible. She crammed clothing and linens into two suitcases, boxed up her stand mixer and kitchenware, and filled two more boxes with family pictures and hand-me-downs that were irreplaceable. Per the instructions from the landlord, she labeled her bed and dresser, the only furnishings she'd added to the apartment when she moved in, and locked the door.

An intense, inexplicable sadness came over her as she secured the last box in the truck bed. This wasn't an ending. It wasn't as if she'd been evicted. That would come later, if she lost her job. This was one more untimely circumstance in a life that had suddenly been filled with high hurdles.

With a final glance at the lovely old building she'd called home, she headed back to the club and a long shift that would keep her mind and body busy for the rest of the night.

* * *

At Galway Automotive the phone rang, a shrill sound interrupting the throbbing pulse of the heavy metal music filling the garage. Under the back end of a 1967 Camaro SS, Stephen Galway used the voice control to lower the volume on the music. At an hour past closing on a Friday, he wasn't obligated to answer the phone, but a heads-up for what problems might be showing up tomorrow never hurt.

"Pick up, Stephen. It's Mitch." His brother's voice wasn't nearly as soothing as the heavy metal had been. The oldest of Stephen's younger siblings, Mitch was the one who consistently refused to let him stay off the family radar for too long.

"I know you're there," Mitch pressed.

Where else would he be?

"He'll come through," Mitch promised in an undertone to someone on his end of the call.

"Not your job to make promises for me, little brother," Stephen muttered.

"Pick up," Mitch said, bossy now. "I've got a friend here at the club with car trouble. Tow it out of the employee parking lot and we'll come by and look it over when I have time tomorrow." He gave the make, model and license plate number of the car.

Huh. Stephen rolled out from under the Camaro, wiping grease from his hands. His brother knew as much about cars as he did. If Mitch couldn't get his friend's car rolling, there was a serious problem. Still, he didn't pick up, waiting to see if his brother would sweeten the deal.

Mitch swore. "Come on, Stephen. The club has your kind of group onstage tonight. I'll buy you a beer and help you hook up the car."

Stephen picked up the handset. "I'll head over." He glanced down at his stained T-shirt and jeans. The customer waiting on the Camaro wasn't in any rush, preferring this rebuild and restoration be done perfectly rather than by a specific date. *If only they could all be that patient*, Stephen thought. "Give me an hour or so."

Dropping the receiver back into place, he scowled at his stained hands and T-shirt. Promised beer or not, if he wanted inside the Escape Club during business hours he had to clean up. He put his work space to rights and lowered the bay door. The Camaro would be waiting when he returned.

He walked through the office and around to the refurbished camper he'd parked behind the building. Not that long ago, he would've headed to the house he once shared with Mitch, but his brother and Julia, his recent bride, had eventually settled there after their honeymoon.

Stephen had promised his mom he'd find a decent house somewhere near the shop. It was a good neighborhood. Instead, he kept taking on more work, limiting his time to search. The last time he'd gone house hunting had been with his fiancée, Annabeth. Even after three long years he still couldn't walk a property without hearing in his head how she'd react.

Last year, when his parents had suggested he move back home with them, he'd bristled. He hadn't taken it any more gracefully when Mitch and Julia swore he wouldn't be in their way. The newlyweds didn't need a big brother crowding them. His parents didn't need him returning home when they could all but taste the empty nest. His youngest sister, Jenny, was almost ready to spread her wings.

Although they meant well, there were days when he was sure he'd drown under all the love and good intentions of his family.

Losing Annabeth before they'd had a chance to experience the life they'd dreamed of didn't make him an invalid. He maintained a successful business and supported the PFD and other causes in the community that mattered to him. Stephen continued to give special attention to the after-school program where his fiancée had worked, and where three years ago she'd been shot and killed for having the audacity to help kids avoid gangs and drugs.

He'd long since given up on shedding the melancholy that hovered like a storm cloud over his life. What his family wanted for him and what he knew he could handle were two different things. He didn't bother trying to convince them anymore. Work was all the sunlight he needed. Cars and engines he could understand, fix and make new again. People were too fragile, himself included. In his mind, that was all the rationalization necessary for the old Airstream trailer he'd purchased. After months of work, inside and out, he considered it home, though he wasn't yet brave enough to use the word within his mother's hearing.

As the oldest, he really should get more respect for his good judgment, if only by default.

Having washed off the pungent smells of the shop, he debated briefly about clothing. He'd prefer shorts on a summer night, but since he was going to hook up a car, he opted for jeans and a red polo shirt. When he finally reached the club, he found room for the tow truck near the back of the employee parking lot across the street. With the Escape Club perched at the end of the pier, few cars were granted the prime spaces on busy nights. No one emerged from a parked car or otherwise expressed any interest in his arrival, so he walked down to the club.

On the rare occasions his brother got him here, Stephen couldn't help but admire what Sullivan had made out of his forced early retirement and an old warehouse. He'd never heard anyone question Sullivan's choices, or express worry over what he was or wasn't doing with his life. Though admittedly, a club naturally was a more social environment than an auto shop. People came from all over for the bands the Escape Club drew to Philly.

Striding straight to the front of the line, Stephen realized maybe he had more in common with Sullivan than he thought. Galway Automotive was building a solid reputation and people were calling from all over the region to get their cars on his restoration schedule.

"Unless you hire a female mechanic, you'll never meet a nice girl under the hood of a car." His mother's voice broke into his thoughts. Myra Galway had a way of saying things that slid right past his defenses and lingered, mocking him with her maternal logic. If only his mom would admit there was more to life than filling lonely hours with pointless chatter with women who sneered at his stained fingernails and the rough calluses on his palms.

At the burly doorman's arched eyebrow, Stephen gave his name and was quickly waved inside.

The bold, heavy sounds of the metal band onstage slammed into him and battered away at the discontent that persistently dogged Stephen since his fiancée's death. He leaned into the music, weaving through the crowd until he reached Mitch's station at the service end of the bar, closer to the kitchen.

His brother eyed him and popped the top off a bottle of beer, setting it in front of him between serving other patrons. Good. Stephen wasn't in much of a talking mood. The delayed conversation was no surprise, considering the sea of humanity supporting the band from all corners of the club.

"Took you long enough," Mitch said at the first lull between customers. "You might be here awhile."

Stephen checked his watch. He'd said an hour or so and had hit the mark precisely. "How come?" he asked, though he didn't care about the time, since the band was as good as Mitch had promised.

"No way I can get out there right now. This set just started."

Stephen shrugged and swiveled around on the bar stool to watch the band. They were good, from the sound to the showmanship. He was enjoying the music, the process of being still and people-watching. Waitresses in khaki shorts and bright blue T-shirts emblazoned with the Escape Club logo brushed by him with friendly glances and quick greetings as they exchanged trays of empty bottles and glassware for the fresh orders Mitch filled with startling efficiency. From Stephen's vantage point everyone in the club seemed to be focused on excellent customer service. Sullivan had definitely created an outstanding atmosphere.

"Do you always ignore the signals?" Mitch asked when another waitress walked off, tray perfectly balanced.

"What are you talking about?"

Mitch shook his head. "Signals from *interested* women," he said. "If you'd pay attention, you'd see it for yourself."

"Please. Not you, too." Stephen glared at his little brother. "You know I've got too much work to spare time for dating."

"Uh-huh." Mitch slid another city-wide special across the bar to a customer and marked the tab. "Then I'm sorry I called you. Another beer?"

"Water," Stephen answered, then checked his watch again. The band would probably take a break soon. He drained the glass of water Mitch provided and pushed back from the bar. "Tell your friend I'm waiting out in the truck. No rush. Thanks for the beer."

"Stephen, wait."

Not a chance. What was it with married people? His parents and married siblings were ganging up on him lately, and being relentless about it. Was there some statute of limitations on grief he didn't know about? He'd tried believing that crappy philosophy of it being better to have loved and lost, and couldn't pull it off. He'd loved, he'd lost everything and it sucked.

They kept wanting him to be happy, checking in on him week after week, never letting it rest. Was he happy? He didn't know. At this point he wasn't sure he cared about happiness. Business was good. Booming, in fact. If that was enough happiness for him, his family should back off. Not everyone got a happy ending. He'd accepted that hard truth; why couldn't they?

"Hey! Stephen Galway?"

Nearly to the truck, he turned at the sound of his name. Recognizing the waitress uniform, he was tempted to ignore the slender blonde jogging his way with a long, ground-eating stride. His brother earned points for tenacity. Stephen made a note to punch him at the earliest opportunity.

"You are Stephen, right?"

"That's right. And you are?" The lamp overhead cast her features in shadow, illuminating pale hair pulled back from her face. He remembered seeing her in the bar. She was the one with the long braid that fell to the middle of her back, and great legs anchoring that willowy body.

"Kenzie Hughes." She stuck out her hand, then let it fall when he didn't reach out to meet her halfway. "You probably don't remember me."

"Should I?" The name wasn't ringing any bells.

"Guess not. I was in the same high school class as Mitch."

Stephen was ready to march back into the club and punch his brother right now for orchestrating this elaborate setup. He had work to do without dragging the tow truck out on a wild-goose chase. What bad idea or wrong impression had Mitch planted in her head? He stared at her, struggling for a polite way out of this. It wasn't her fault his brother was an idiot.

"Um, anyway," she continued, "I didn't mean to keep you waiting." She pulled keys from her pocket. "The car's right over here."

Now he felt like a complete jerk. Stephen had assumed he'd be helping out one of Mitch's male buddies. "Great." He fell in behind her and put his mind back in car mode. "Let's take a look."

He tried not to wince when he saw the vehicle. Not his business what people chose to drive, and people who drove rust buckets like this one made up a core segment of his business. He let her explain Mitch's opinion of the situation while he listened to a whole lot of nothing going on in her engine. Something didn't smell right under the normal scents of oil and gas.

"If Mitch couldn't get you running here, we're better off hauling it in." He dropped the hood, checked the latch. "Do you have a way to get home?"

She climbed out of the car and he noticed the interior was packed with boxes and suitcases. He couldn't imagine Sullivan allowing any of his employees to live out of their car, and if she was doing so, she hadn't left much room for herself.

"I'll be fine," she said, her gaze sliding to the crammed interior. "Here." She handed over the keys. "I'll get your number from Mitch and call you tomorrow."

"One second." *Hughes, PFD, female.* It all clicked into place and embarrassment flooded through Stephen. "You're Mackenzie Hughes."

Her entire body went on the defensive in one fluid movement. "Yes. Is that a problem?"

"No." He couldn't believe he didn't recognize her in the club. Her name was at the center of a public debate about the ability of female firefighters. In person, her height and poise were evident and she looked far more capable than she did on television, where the images provided focused on her photogenic and fine-boned, feminine face.

"Of course not," he reiterated, when she cocked an eyebrow at his long perusal. He'd heard his brother rant more than once in Kenzie's favor. Like most people of his acquaintance, Stephen thought the gender bias was in the past. "I'll take good care of the car," he promised. "What's with all the boxes?"

Now her shoulders slumped. "Do I have to unload them for you to tow the car?" She looked around as if a storage shed would appear out of thin air. "I didn't think of that."

"If you don't have a problem with it, I don't. Things might get jostled as I load and unload the car."

"No. My stuff will be okay." She backed away. "Thanks so much. I'll pick up the boxes tomorrow."

He trailed after her as if someone had set him on automatic pilot. "How?"

She skidded to a stop. "Pardon me?"

"If I have your car, how are you getting around?"

She gave him a weak smile. "I'll figure it out."

He blamed it on having sisters. Only her car was his business, but he still felt compelled to get a better answer from her. "What time are you off tonight?"

"Two."

"Have Mitch bring you over to the shop."

She gaped at him. "You can't be serious. At two in the morning?"

Something about her response had him changing his mind. "Good point." His brother had a wife waiting at home. "I'll bring over a loaner car for you."

"At two in the morning?" she repeated, incredulous.

He rolled his shoulders and resisted the urge to shift under that intense blue gaze. "That's when you need it, right?"

"Well, yeah, but—"

"Then I'll be here. Unless you won't have time to drop me back at my shop on your way home?"

She snorted. "No, I can do that."

"Good. We're all set." He turned away before she could argue, and went to load her car onto the flatbed tow truck. Being near her put an odd pressure in his system, as if his heart was a half-beat too slow. He glanced back over his shoulder and caught her staring at him.

Couldn't blame her; he barely recognized himself in his actions since she'd caught up with him. For his own peace of mind, he chalked up his uncharacteristic behavior to Mitch's frustration on Kenzie's behalf. According to his brother, she'd had a rough time of it since the PFD put her on administrative leave after a victim blamed her incompetence and weakness as a woman for his minor injuries.

She hadn't looked the least bit weak to Stephen, and if Mitch vouched for her, she could handle the job. That must be why he was so determined to do more than the bare minimum of towing in her car for an evaluation and repair.

Kenzie worked the rest of the night with a little more spring in her step. Hope flashed bright and hot though her system at odd and unpredictable intervals. It was nice to feel a genuine smile on her lips. Maybe the recent circumstances hadn't permanently smothered her courage and optimism, after all.

As she cashed out and split her tips with the rest of the staff, she realized she'd earned enough on this shift to cover an economy motel for the night and give Stephen some money for the tow and repair. Every penny left over would go to the lawyer fund.

"Grant's looking for you," Mitch said, as he walked into the break room. "And I have a text for you." He held out his phone.

"For me?" Who would text Mitch to reach her?

"About your car," he said.

Belatedly, she realized she'd been in such a hurry to

get back to the club that she'd forgotten to give Stephen her cell phone number. The text message asked Mitch to tell her he was waiting outside. Kenzie replied with her cell phone number and let him know she needed only a few more minutes. She rolled up her apron and shoved it into her backpack, then headed for Grant's office.

Rapping a knuckle on the open door, she stepped inside when Grant turned from his computer monitor. He smiled and waved her in, asking her to close the door. His constant energy belied the gray salting his hair. She suspected the creases bracketing his warm brown eyes were a result of laughter as much as the challenges he'd faced in his career as a cop and a nightclub owner. He reminded her of her dad, she realized with a prickle of nostalgia. Not in appearance—Grant had a barrel-chested, stocky build and her father had been tall and slim. The similarities were in the general demeanor of both men. Grant cared for his club and his employees with the fatherly affection and protectiveness she remembered her dad exhibiting every day of his life.

The chair squeaked as Grant leaned back. "Was it a good night?"

"Yes. Thanks again for giving me so many shifts."

"I prefer employing people who are willing to work," he said. "You know, you remind me of your dad in that way."

"I didn't realize you knew him." She knew she was overtired and overstressed when tears stung behind her eyes. Fifteen years had passed since they'd buried him, and she usually didn't feel melancholy anymore unless it was the anniversary of the warehouse fire or Christmas. Her mother had been determined her daughters would smile with hearts full of happy memories when they remembered their father. She insisted living well was the best way to affirm all the love and gifts he'd given them.

Grant nodded. "There are few circles in Philly tighter than those of us who worked the front lines." His thick eyebrows drew into a frown over his assessing gaze. "I heard about your car trouble."

The swift change of topic helped restore her composure. "Mitch called his brother for me. Stephen came out and towed it to his shop. He, ah, offered to loan me a car until mine is fixed." She still wasn't sure how she was going to cover the extra expenses.

"That's good." Leaning back in his chair, Grant drummed a quick rhythm on the edge of his desk. "Here's the thing. I just got off the phone with Stephen."

"About my car?" That didn't make any sense. "Why?"

"You may not know it, but he likes to stay busy," Grant said. "He took a look at your car as soon as he got back to his shop."

"Did he find the problem already?" She braced herself for the worst, assuming Stephen had mentioned parts, labor and prices.

"Yes. He says he can fix it fairly quickly, though he's not sure that's the wise choice since the car's a rolling wreck. His words, not mine." Grant sat upright suddenly and the chair squeaked a protest. He ignored the grating sound, massaging at the scar tissue in his shoulder, the way he often did when he was thinking. "Any chance you forgot how your dad taught you to care for a car and accidently dumped sugar into your gas tank?"

What? "Of course not."

Grant's intent brown eyes turned weary from one blink to the next. "Didn't think so." He blew out a breath and rubbed his temples. "Stephen can explain all the details, of course. I just wanted to be the one to give you the big picture."

"Which is?" she prompted when he hesitated.

"Everything Stephen found suggests that someone sabotaged your car."

"Sugar in the gas tank is hardly the problem people think it is," she said, latching on to the one factor she could comprehend in this bizarre situation. It was a fairly affordable fix to change the clogged filters and flush the tank and fuel lines. "Maybe the previous owner pissed off someone who didn't know keying a car was a better form of revenge."

"Maybe," Grant allowed. He looked as if he wanted to believe her theory as opposed to the evidence that contradicted it. "How long have you had the vehicle?"

She gripped the straps of the backpack, resisting the logic and implications he was forcing on her. "Three weeks." He arched an eyebrow. She didn't need him to say it for her. "If I'd bought the thing with sugar in the tank it would have given me problems long before now."

"So you bought the car at the same time you had to hire an attorney for the civil suit?"

"Yes," she replied, grudgingly.

"Then whoever dumped sugar in the tank was targeting you."

"Unless they didn't realize the car had been sold." She rushed on when Grant rolled his eyes. "It's an inconvenience, that's all." She could do the repairs, assuming Stephen would let her borrow space and the tools.

Grant glanced at the clock over the office door. "You need help, Kenzie. Support."

She understood it wasn't a question. Help was what Grant did. He'd never been able to depart from his inherent need to get involved from his days on the police force. He probably hadn't tried too hard.

She gathered the fraying remnants of her pride. "My attorney has it under control," she said. "He assures me it's a matter of wading through the system."

"I'm glad to hear it." Grant stood up, ending the meeting. "It's okay to remember you have friends willing to help, too."

"Thanks." She hated the idea of dragging her friends into her problems. Besides, there wasn't anything to *do* except let her lawyer handle the case.

She escaped the office and the club, relieved and troubled in equal measure. Outside, she paused and breathed deeply. The air at this hour was clear along the river and as cool and pleasant as Philly could be in the summer. The stars in the inky sky above were faint, the lights from buildings on both sides of the river offering more sparkle.

Only a few cars remained in the lot, and she assumed the small SUV parked next to Mitch's truck was the car Stephen had brought for her. Standing between the two, the Galway brothers turned to her as she approached. She sensed she'd interrupted something important.

"Hi," she said. "Sorry for the delay."

"No problem." Stephen opened the passenger door of the SUV for her. "I'll drive to the shop and you can take it from there."

"Okay." She glanced at Mitch. "Thanks for loaning me your truck today."

"No problem." Lines of tension bracketed the stern set of his mouth. It wasn't a look she often saw on his face. "Be careful, Kenzie."

"Always," she promised, before sliding into the seat.

He couldn't be warning her about his brother. "You told him about the clogged fuel filter?" she asked, as Stephen slid behind the wheel and started the car.

"Saves him a trip to the shop tomorrow," Stephen replied, pulling away from the club.

"That's…thoughtful." So why did Mitch seem aggravated?

Stephen's gaze slid from the nearly deserted streets to her and back to the road. "Practical. I've got your car in pieces already, easier for me to put it back together. If that's what you want."

"It's what I need," she replied. When the case was settled she would take great delight in buying a better car. "You didn't have to give me a loaner this nice."

"This was what I had available." He shifted in the seat as if he wasn't comfortable with the conversation. "You needed something with better security."

She could argue the point, though the irritating sabotage spoke for itself. "We don't even know the prank was aimed at me. It could be someone who thought the car still belonged to the previous owner." A weak argument was better than none.

He snorted, clearly not any more convinced of that than Grant had been. "Better not to tempt fate again. This one has a tamper-proof tank and hood."

"Guess that limits someone to cutting the brake lines, slashing tires, rerouting exhaust, planting a GPS tracker or even an explosive," she said. She'd meant it all as a joke, but the list unnerved her.

"Your safety isn't a joke. Did you ask Grant for protection?"

"No." The idea was absurd. She could take care of herself. She leveled her toughest stare at him, the one she saved for those who aimed sexist comments at her when they heard she was a firefighter. There had been far too many opportunities to perfect the expression since Murtagh went public with his complaint and civil suit. "While I'm dressed as a waitress at the moment, you might recall safety is an essential aspect of my career."

"I only meant—"

"I'm an adult," she interrupted. "As a firefighter I'm trained to cope with any number of crises, including saving people and property. It's my job to put out fires." At least she put out fires whenever lawsuits didn't keep her on the sidelines. "I'm merely pointing out there's no way to prevent all forms of trouble. That, too, is an element of my career."

He didn't reply and in profile she noticed his jaw set in a hard line. She imagined if the radio were off she would have heard his teeth grinding.

"I'm sorry," she said. "That was really rude." Embarrassed, she toyed with the straps of her backpack. "You've gone above and beyond to help me today. Despite the rant, I do appreciate it."

"Forget it," he said. "I understand irritable."

He stopped in front of a wide gate barring the entrance to Galway Automotive. Plucking a key ring from the cup holder, he pressed a button on a fob that must have been connected to his security system. The gate slid back, rolling along the inside of the tall fencing surrounding the business. Rather than put the car in Park, he drove through the opening and the gate slid closed behind them. She caught the cameras mounted at the gate, assumed there were more around the property.

She wasn't sure what she'd expected, but it wasn't the well maintained blacktop pavement surrounding an

L-shaped building. What must serve as his office jut-
ted slightly forward from the line of bays stretching to
the side. Several cars were parked on a strip of gravel at
the far end of the building and the tow truck had been
backed into a space near the gate where Stephen could
leave quickly if necessary.

Bright security lights mounted around the property
were aimed at the building and they came on as he drove
by. The manufactured sunlight smothered any hope of
shadows. Made of metal rather than stone, the garage
didn't have much in common with a fairy-tale castle, yet
Stephen had definitely created a fortress. The only things
missing were a moat and a vigilant dragon.

A dragon? The whimsical thought was a clear sign
the late hour had taken its toll. She felt a bizarre wish to
stay right here in this sheltered place until her troubles
went away. Too bad lawsuits didn't disappear if they
were ignored.

He parked next to the office, away from the other
cars, and the headlights glanced off the gleaming silver
siding of a sleek, bullet-shaped camper.

"It's bigger than I expected," she said.

"The trailer?"

"No." She laughed now, giddy and definitely overtired. "The business."

He gave her a long look. "I own the block now."

Impressive. She managed to swallow several prying
questions about the man and his work that were none
of her concern.

"Do you need anything from your car?" he asked.

Feeling unsettled, she ducked away from his gaze
and nudged the backpack with her knee. "I'm set for tonight. Is there a good time for me to swing by and pick

up everything tomorrow? I guess I mean today?" The clock on the dash showed it was already past three. "I can help with the repairs to my car, too."

He didn't jump on her offer. "Where will you take your things?" He cut the engine and held on to the key.

She had no idea. "I'll figure something out." Although she couldn't leave town, maybe her belongings could. Her mom had extended the offer. Kenzie just needed to make time to drive up there.

The burnished gold eyebrows flexed over his eyes. "You don't have anywhere to stay, do you?"

She was too weary to fib or bluster through. "I figure there's an available motel room somewhere in town." She waved a hand at the clock. "I only need a few hours of sleep. Tell me what time to come by."

His lips pressed together and he nodded once as if an internal debate had just been settled. "I didn't think so. You'll stay here tonight."

He got out of the car and walked to the camper. She gawked at him through the windshield, trying to make sense of his statement. Trying to catch up as her pulse went racing ahead of her at his abrupt declaration.

When he noticed she wasn't behind him, he came around to the passenger door and opened it. "Come on."

She gripped the edge of the seat. "No thanks. If you'll give me the car key and open the gate I'll see you tomorrow."

"As you said, it's already tomorrow," he said, completely ignoring the salient point that she would leave and handle her troubles on her own. He reached past her for the backpack, his forearm brushing across her bare knees.

"Hey, that's mine. What are you doing?" She shifted

her leg, pinning his arm. *Mistake*, a small voice warned her too late. His skin was warm against hers and in this position his handsome face was close enough that the security lights sparked in the dark blond stubble shading his jaw.

The tough, callused palm of his free hand landed on her leg and he extracted his trapped arm and simply lifted her out of the car. He handled her as if she weighed nothing. Worse, he behaved as if he had the right to move her about at will. Where was her fight?

"You'll stay here tonight," he repeated, setting her on her feet. "I'll stay on the couch in the office. We'll sort out the rest in the morning."

She dug in her heels as he opened the camper door and waited for her to go inside. "Stephen, this isn't right. It's too much," she added, when he refused to agree with her.

He tipped his head. "Go on in and make yourself at home. We've both lost enough sleep as it is."

Nothing else he could have said would have convinced her to cooperate. Fully aware she'd been a big imposition already, she obediently walked up the steps. She glanced back before he could close the door. "Stephen, why are you doing this?"

He shrugged. "Good night, Kenzie."

She watched him disappear into the office, bewildered by his unexpected kindness.

Emotions she'd rather not examine churned inside her as she stood in his camper. It was neat and clean, and the evidence that he lived here was everywhere. The plain, heavy white mug stationed near the coffeepot on the narrow counter. The mail tucked into a slim wire basket next to a laptop computer on the shelf behind the table. She passed the bathroom and caught a whiff of the crisp, green scent she'd noticed on his skin.

Why would Stephen give his home to her, even for a night?

Her pride had taken a hard tumble in recent weeks and she'd been so consumed with the lawsuit that she couldn't ask her friends to let her crash on couches or in spare rooms. Requests like that left her too vulnerable. Her friends, with lives and concerns of their own, didn't need to hear her worries and fears about her future.

Her backpack slid from her grasp and hit the floor with a soft thud when she spotted the stack of clean towels at the foot of the perfectly made bed. He must have found the trouble with her car and then cleaned up in here, turning his home into a guest house. For her.

Gratitude swamped her. Everyone but Stephen had let her get away with her small fibs about having things under control. He didn't even know her. They were basically strangers. How had he seen through her defenses so easily?

It was a question she would never answer while she was exhausted. She stripped away the Escape Club uniform and readied herself for bed. As she slipped between the cool, clean sheets, she decided none of the whys and hows of Stephen's actions mattered as much as figuring out what she could do to make it up to him.

Chapter 2

Almost three hours later, Stephen woke with the sun and a colorful vow to find something to cover the bare window on the back wall. He supposed he could board it up, but that seemed extreme for a temporary situation. He squinted at the window and considered planting a tree. That would have a lasting benefit even if it didn't help in the short term.

Short term, he reminded himself. Kenzie wouldn't be in his trailer for long. She gave off independent vibes as bright as the sunshine glaring in his eyes. He sat up, scooping his hair back from his face as his bare feet hit the cool vinyl flooring. At least it wasn't winter, when the freezing temperatures tried to climb right through the heavy-soled boots he wore in the shop.

With no hope of more sleep, he decided to get to work. He grabbed clean clothes from the pile he'd brought over last night and headed into the bathroom wedged between the office and the storage room. The cramped space didn't have an ounce of aesthetics, since clean, efficient and functional were all the design elements he'd cared about when he made the improvements.

Back in the office, he punched the button on the machine to brew coffee, and checked phone messages. Disappointment crept in when none of the callers asked about the restored Mustang he'd listed for sale last week. It had been in rough shape when they found it at an auction. He'd warned his brother that particular car would drain time and money. At least he had a better distraction today.

Turning, he opened the cabinet over the coffeemaker and pulled a foil-wrapped toaster pastry out of the box. Filling a stainless steel mug with fresh coffee, he carried it and the pastry into the shop and circled Kenzie's disassembled car while he waited for the caffeine and sugar to kick in. The poor excuse for transportation put a knot in his stomach as he debated where to start. So many options, and the best choice might be scrapping it for parts. Couldn't move forward on any of it until they discussed what she wanted. *Please scrap it*, he thought. It would be a public service.

He drank more coffee, savoring the jolt of caffeine, and shifted his focus to the far more appealing 1967 Camaro SS. This was the car that got Stephen out of bed every morning since the client, Matt Riley, had dropped it off. A total rebuild, inside and out, and despite the need for fresh paint, about as far from Kenzie's nondescript junker as a car could get. He'd cleaned every inch of the engine until a person could practically use it for a dining table, and now that the muffler was installed the Muncie four-speed transmission was ready for a second test drive.

Inside the Camaro, the upholstery was in decent shape, with only a few repairs and touch-ups needed. Same with the body. Stephen wondered where Riley had managed to find such a gem and if he'd share the source.

The Camaro wasn't the only thing waiting on him, just the most fun. Finishing the pastry, he dusted the crumbs from his fingers and trashed the wrapper. Time to get busy. With a sigh, he turned to the car parked in the last of his four service bays. His sister Megan had dropped off her minivan for new brakes and fresh tires. Naturally, she was hoping he'd deliver it when they were all at family dinner tomorrow.

Did none of them realize he could smell these setups a mile away? Megan and her husband could pick up the minivan as soon as he was done this afternoon. By insisting on making the exchange tomorrow, they made sure he couldn't skip the dinner. He supposed he should be grateful for Megan's willingness to go without her beloved minivan for nearly forty-eight hours. Given half a chance, she'd tell him to appreciate her devoted-sister sacrifice, but he recognized his mother's influence at work. No one was better at keeping family together than Myra Galway.

With more affection than gratitude, Stephen turned up the music and put the vehicle on the lift to knock out the single straightforward job on today's agenda.

Kenzie came out of the recurring nightmare riding the hard wave of adrenaline and confusion. It always started with the same call to the row house fire. The same search protocol. When she found the victim, the nightmare shifted on her. The man was too heavy for her alone and the fire was burning too hot and fast, blocking every route as her team tried to reach her. The victim shouted at her, berating her until his throat went dry, yet none of his ideas was remotely plausible. Huddled in a corner, surrounded by smoke with flames marching toward them, she would wake up with the unbearable pressure of failure in her chest and the sheets tangled around her legs.

She had not failed that victim. Randall Murtagh was alive because she'd done the right things. She'd pulled him out of a terrible fire with minor burns that were probably healed already.

She tried to wriggle free of the sheets, nearly ripping them away before she remembered they weren't hers. Her skin clammy with the sweat of the nightmare, she found herself registering other details. This wasn't her bedroom. The space was too bright, the mattress too firm, and the scent of the laundry detergent on the linens was wrong.

Scrubbing at her face, she felt the rest of her situation crash over her like a bucket of ice water. At least the last wisps of the nightmare were gone. She untangled her legs from the sheets and paused as a variety of sounds and smells drifted by her waking senses.

For a moment she wallowed in the comfort and familiarity of clean motor oil, grease and new rubber tires. She heard the pulse of heavy metal music underscored by the whirr of power tools. All of it mingled with the promise of another hot and humid summer day in Philly.

She straightened the bedding and then headed for the bathroom, which was almost roomy, considering the limits of the camper. Fifteen minutes later she emerged refreshed and feeling human again. Dressed in denim cutoff shorts and a T-shirt sporting the logo of a local microbrewery, she made a cup of coffee and tried to figure out what to do with all the hours between now and her shift at the club tonight.

Her stomach growled, but she didn't feel right about helping herself to Stephen's groceries, despite his hospitality. Of course, with the loaner car he'd given her, she could restock his supplies easily. It still felt weird going through his cabinets for a bowl and cereal. She added milk and found a spoon in the basket of utensils on the counter. At the table she ate her cereal and used her cell phone to scroll through travel sites, looking for the best prices on decent motels near the club.

She knew she was hiding from Stephen, and life in general, when she'd washed her dishes and caught herself reorganizing her backpack. Stephen deserved better from her. For that matter, she deserved better. The sooner she got out there and helped him with her car, the sooner she could be on her way. She shoved her bare feet into her tennis shoes and headed over to the garage to say thanks again and refine her plans to get out of his hair.

The music crashed over her as she approached the garage through the open bay door nearest the office. Though her car was in pieces, she grinned, recognizing one of her favorite heavy metal bands doing a cover of one of the recent pop chart hits. She was about to follow the sound of an impact wrench to the other side of a champagne-colored minivan on a lift when the phone rang.

Stephen didn't seem to hear it over the tools and the music. Kenzie assumed he had a machine or service that answered calls for him. He might even have his calls forwarded to his cell phone during business hours. The phone kept ringing and, following impulse, she picked it up. "Galway Automotive."

"Hello?" a woman said, clearly startled. "Where's Stephen?"

Is this a girlfriend? "His hands are full changing a tire at the moment," Kenzie improvised.

"Who are you?"

Not as much jealousy as speculation in those three syllables. "I'm Kenzie," she replied, using her best polite-receptionist voice that she'd refined during her first week of administrative duty for the PFD. "May I take a message for him?"

"*Umm,* sure. This is his sister Megan. I was checking on my minivan."

Kenzie smiled. She'd heard a few typical big-brother stories from Mitch, but never met Megan. "If you can hold a moment, I'll see if I can get an update for you."

"Great."

The curiosity and confusion came through loud and clear and Kenzie had to stifle a chuckle. Stephen must not keep a receptionist around. The place did have the feel of a one-man operation. Accustomed to working with a team and having people around constantly, she couldn't imagine so much solitude. She didn't want to risk making a mistake with the hold button and cutting off Megan's call, so she placed the handset gently on the desk and hurried into the garage.

She saw her little rust-bucket in pieces, but her gaze locked for a long, reverent moment on the classic Camaro SS. A 1967, she knew. Oh *my.* Her hands tingled to peek under the hood. It would benefit from fresh paint and oh, that pure American muscle cried out for a touch. This was as close as she'd come to a car like this since her dad died. She hoped Stephen would be willing to show it to her and fill her in on the details later.

A classic Camaro was her dream car, if money weren't an object. It was a pipe dream at the moment, and likely would remain so for the next decade. *One day*, she promised herself, exerting significant willpower to stay on track with the minivan, when she would've happily gone exploring the Camaro.

From her vantage point only Stephen's legs and lower torso were visible under a minivan on the last lift. She failed in her attempt to ignore the appeal of those long legs and the T-shirt lifting to reveal toned abs when he stretched for something. *Whew.* She tucked away that little buzz of attraction.

Kenzie had no chance of getting his attention over the blaring music. It wasn't hard to find the speakers, but she didn't see the controls. She shouted. He didn't flinch. There were too many things in a working garage that might catch a finger or hand wrong if he was startled. She came around the front corner of the car and shouted his name again.

This time he froze. Slowly, he turned in her direction, and she could see the wire brush he was holding in hands darkened by brake dust.

He stared at her as if he couldn't figure out why he wasn't alone. "Kenzie."

She started to shout, pausing when he held up a finger and lowered the volume with a voice command. "Your sister Megan is on the phone," she said. "She's asking about her minivan."

He rolled his eyes and then glared down at his hands. "Give me a second."

"I can handle the call for you. You're doing both front and rear brakes?" she asked, when he didn't volunteer any information.

"No. Just rear brakes, and new tires all around," he replied.

Kenzie glanced about, judging his progress. "Do you want her to come by this afternoon?"

"Not really," he muttered.

Kenzie laughed, understanding the sibling dynamics. "When works for you?"

"She's such a nag," he grumbled. "When she dropped it off, she made me agree to deliver it for her at Sunday dinner tomorrow."

"No problem. Leave it to me." Kenzie returned to the office and picked up the phone. "Megan?"

"Yes."

"Thanks for waiting." Kenzie smiled as she explained Stephen's progress and his confidence that the minivan would be delivered on time to Sunday dinner.

"Great. Thanks, um, what was your name?"

"Kenzie."

"I'm so glad you're there. It's about time he hired good help," Megan said. "Have a good day," she added brightly.

"You, too." Replacing the phone in the cradle, Kenzie sat back in the chair and swiveled side to side gently. Maybe she could give Stephen some time in the office or the garage while she waited to return to her normal schedule at the firehouse.

"Was she rude?"

Kenzie smothered the reaction as the deep burr of Stephen's voice skimmed over the nape of her neck. He stood just outside the door frame, wiping dark streaks from his hands with a shop towel. Something about him sent her heartrate into overdrive. This was not the time for her hormones to take a detour.

"Not at all," she replied, she managed in a steady voice.

His eyebrows arched in disbelief. "She didn't do any wheedling to get her minivan back today?"

Kenzie shook her head.

"Huh. Thanks."

The man was pretty cute when he was baffled. "No problem." She was about to ask about her own car when the phone rang again. Stephen's face clouded over with a scowl. "Go on back. I'll handle it," she told him.

"Really? Thanks. Just take messages," he said, practically running back to the shop.

She handled the various inquiries for the rest of the morning. When her stomach was rumbling around noon, she wandered back into the shop with the intent of picking up lunch for both of them. Stephen wasn't in the garage. The bay where the minivan had been was empty and Kenzie followed the sounds of water running outside.

She found him power washing the brake dust off his sister's tire rims, and her first thought was that he should hire someone to handle that kind of thing. It would be a great job for some high school kid. Not her business how he wanted to run his garage.

Her second thought, and those that followed right after it, were centered on the way his T-shirt, damp from the spray of water, molded to his chest. When he turned that serious, brooding gaze on her she nearly forgot she was here about lunch.

"Keys are in the loaner," he added, after requesting a meatball sub from the pizza place down the block.

"They are?"

"Well, sure. It's yours to use whenever you need it. The key fob will handle the security gate for you."

She was still processing all the implications of his easy generosity when she returned with lunch. He'd finished the brakes and cleaned up the service bay during her brief absence, and she marveled at his efficiency.

A man who obviously appreciated solitude, he didn't want her hanging around while they ate, she assumed, but she didn't want his well-earned break interrupted by the phone. He'd seemed almost afraid of the thing earlier.

"So what's with delivery over having Megan pick up her minivan?" Kenzie unwrapped her sandwich and took a big bite. "This is amazing."

He nodded, his mouth full, too. When he'd swallowed, he said, "Delivery tomorrow isn't ideal, but I'm already doing the job for the cost of parts. If I do it in record time, they'll never let me rest. Do you know how many Galways there are?"

She did a quick head count. "You have four siblings, right?"

"Yes," he said between bites. "Add in parents and cousins and in-laws, and a man wouldn't have time for anything else."

"I thought Mitch helped you out."

"He does. He prefers the custom work more than the maintenance stuff," Stephen said.

"Don't we all?" There was an excitement in restoration, in breathing new life into quality machinery.

Stephen raised an eyebrow. "To be fair, he would've handled Megan's van if I'd been slammed."

"Based on the phone calls I managed this morning, I'd say you could be slammed at any given moment. If you can spare the bay, and time with the tools, I can fix my car on my own," she said. "After hours, so I can stay out of your way."

"You know cars?" he asked.

"My dad taught me more than enough to handle that particular car."

He lifted a bottle of water to his lips and Kenzie caught herself staring at his jaw and throat. It was as if he was carved from some substance that could shift between a solid and fluid state at will. He was almost too lean and the shadows under his eyes were a sure sign he didn't sleep as much as he should.

She belatedly recalled he'd been engaged a few years back, the woman murdered before the wedding. It put Kenzie's own issues into sharp perspective. Her career was at risk thanks to Murtagh, not her life.

"You think your car is overwhelming for me?"

"I think my car is a piece of crap and well beneath your level of expertise." She found herself on the business end of that inscrutable expression. What was going on behind the hazel eyes shadowed by those burnished gold eyebrows?

"I can spare the space and tools," he said. "Thanks for helping out with the phone. I usually just check messages at the end of the day."

"I didn't realize you had an answering machine," she said, trying to contain the happy urge to bounce in her chair. Working on a car, even the pitiful rust-bucket, would be a fabulous distraction until she was back on shift. "That makes me feel better about leaving you this afternoon."

His brow wrinkled. "You're leaving?"

"Yes," she replied. "I'm scheduled on the late shift

again tonight at the club. Between now and then I need to find a place to stay." She pointed to the boxes he'd stacked for her near the storeroom. "I can't just leave all my stuff here in your way."

Stephen's hands stilled, the sandwich wrapper balled up between his palms. "You have a place to stay."

Finding herself the focus of his full attention made her mouth go dry. She felt like the proverbial deer in headlights. It took two attempts to get the right words past her lips. "Last night was too kind. I'm not kicking you out of your house."

"It's yours," he stated. "For as long as you need it." He stood up, as if that was the end of the conversation.

"But last night you said—"

He cut her off. "I said we'd sort it out today." He tossed his trash and leaned back against the counter, apparently waiting for her to say something else he could shoot down.

"That feels like way too much of an imposition."

"You're wrong." A muscle jumped in his tense jaw. "I know what firefighters make," he stated. "And I know what lawyers can charge. If it makes you feel better, keep answering the phone and taking messages when you can."

"That's hardly a fair trade for kicking you out of your home," she protested.

His fingers flexed around the edge of the countertop. The muscles in his forearm bunched and relaxed slowly. "If it's all I'm asking for, why argue the point?"

"Do logic and reason ring a bell?" Why was he insisting she stay here?

"Does *sabotage* ring a bell for you?" he countered, his gaze heating up.

This wasn't the conversation she'd planned on having with him, but it was too late now and she was too aggravated to successfully turn the topic to the Camaro. "I don't need protection."

He folded his arms over his chest. "Duly noted. Do you want to file a police report about the damage?"

That gave her pause and she took her time to think it through. As both Grant and Stephen had previously pointed out, someone had most likely targeted her with the sugar in her gas tank. At the moment she could think of only one person angry enough with her to try such a stunt. "No."

"Because you know who did it?" Stephen pressed.

"What good would it do to file a report? I have no idea when it happened."

"Based on the settling and filter damage, I would guess it happened within the last week," Stephen said, his voice as hard as his gaze now. "A police report is an official record. It could establish a time line or a pattern of behavior."

"Stop. Please." She held up a hand as she studied him. There was obviously a bigger issue on his mind than a disabled car. Filing a report would also mean suggesting Murtagh as a suspect, which could make her look like an idiot grasping at straws to undermine his credibility in the lawsuit. She had to trust her lawyer's advice that the truth would come out and clear her of any wrongdoing or errors.

"I hear what you're saying," she continued. "This was probably a prank gone wrong. Yes, the timing makes it unlikely, but it is possible this was a case of mistaken identity." Logic and odds aside, she couldn't risk giving voice to the outrageous theory that Murtagh had done it. "I've only had the car three weeks."

"It's paid for?" Stephen asked.

"Yes."

"Then I'll put it back together for you." He sighed and pulled such a grimace, she laughed, startling them both.

"That isn't necessary," she said. "I can handle the repairs, and help with the phone when I'm here."

He shot her a skeptical glance. "And you'll work at the club and jump through hoops for your lawyer, too?"

That image made her grin. "He keeps telling me he's the one jumping through hoops on my behalf."

Stephen rolled his eyes. "You've got a deal, *if* you agree to stay in the trailer."

She counted to ten. Slowly. "I don't like the idea of pushing you out of your place."

He shrugged that off. "You'll get over it."

It was such an unexpected reply she laughed again.

He pushed away from the counter and reached into the fridge for another bottle of water. Pausing at the desk, he skimmed the messages she'd taken, various expressions flitting across his stern features. He turned over one message slip and wrote out a short list.

"Can you get these parts ordered for me?"

She glanced at his neat, block-style printing. "Sure."

"Thanks." He looked her over head to toe and back up. "If you hit a snag, be sure to ask for help."

"I promise."

"I have coveralls you can borrow. What about better shoes?"

"There are steel-toed boots in one of the boxes over there." They were battered, but though she'd had few chances to use them in recent years, they still fit.

"All right." With one last look, he walked out. A moment later the music started pulsing again.

Sensations continued to fizz through her system long after he left the office. Part of it was the anticipation of getting her hands dirty and seeing the result of fixing something. Another part was pure lust over the opportunity to work near a man who was bringing that classic Camaro back to life. Both man and machine had her system revving, she thought with a wistful sigh.

She couldn't recall the last time any man as sexy as Stephen had studied her so thoroughly. Her face felt hot and her fingers trembled as she ordered the parts he'd requested.

With that task done, she rooted through her belongings and found her boots, then eyed the clock. Now that she didn't need to find a place and move her stuff, she could potentially get started flushing the fuel lines before heading to the club.

She was almost—no she was *definitely* relieved when a call came in for a tow truck and he agreed to go pick a vehicle up. Relieved. Yes. If she went out to the garage and tried to work beside him now, with all this fizz, there was no telling what kind of stupidity her hormones would talk her into.

Neither of them needed that kind of complication.

What the hell was *wrong* with him? Stephen wondered a few hours later, as he worked alone in the shop. Every time he thought he had his head on straight, the memory of Kenzie's laughter sent him spinning, the echo of the sound rattling through his head. Cranking the radio didn't help. He left the garage and went out to detail his sister's van. Spoiling her with that kind of surprise was probably a mistake and his mood soured further.

That mouth on Kenzie, he thought, so mobile and expressive. Her lips were quick with a smile and he couldn't keep the images out of his head. Her laughter astounded him, the merry sound full and loud and rich, as if she didn't care who heard her. He envied that wide-open spirit, even when it grated against the solitude he'd carefully built here.

How could Kenzie laugh at *anything* with a civil suit that threatened her career hanging over her head? He shot a glance back at the garage, fighting off the urge to get in there and just do the work for her.

She claimed she could handle it, and it wasn't a complex task to flush a little sugar out of a fuel system. If only that was all that junker needed. He was almost embarrassed to have such a sorry-looking car in the shop.

Not sorry to have Kenzie around.

The errant thought startled him and he shoved it away. He didn't like extra people milling about in his space, but having her answering calls had been a big help. Mitch was about the only other person he could work with. Even his dad got under his skin after a few hours.

At least she wasn't here tempting him into conversation just so he could hear her voice. The last time a woman intrigued him like this, he'd been engaged to her. Stephen fought back the unwelcome spark of interest. Kenzie was a temporary anomaly in his self-contained life. She needed a break and he could tolerate having her around for a few days as long as she didn't start in on him with questions about the business or why he was a loner.

Finished detailing his sister's minivan, he parked it

next to the cars he was ready to sell. While he'd been out with the tow truck, Mitch had called, claiming to have a buyer lined up for the Mustang. Stephen hoped his brother closed the deal on that one soon. The upholstery and paint alone had cost them a small fortune.

He tried to work up irritation over having it sit here and failed. The car looked amazing and they'd get their asking price eventually. The swell of pride in the work drained enough of the persistent tension out of his neck and shoulders that when his mom's sassy red sedan pulled through the open gate, he managed a rare smile.

"Happy Saturday, sweetheart," she said, drawing him into a hug. "You look good."

Her hugs never changed, no matter what was happening in his life. She must have just come from the salon, he realized, as a wave of feminine scents swept over him. Her hair was sleek and smooth and the gray effectively hidden by a perfect application of ash-blond color. "You look great, Mom."

"Nice of you to notice." A little pink warmed her cheeks as she beamed at him. "Hopefully, your father can be persuaded to take me out tonight."

Stephen didn't think it would be much of an effort. His parents were still in love after all this time and the challenges life tossed at them. While he knew that wasn't in his future, he valued the rare treasure of their relationship. "Car trouble?"

"Not a bit."

Her gaze slid past him toward the office and he realized his sister had tipped her off that a woman had been here. Answering phones and relaying messages. Stephen managed not to roll his eyes at his mother's

obvious agenda. "If you're looking for someone in particular, she isn't here."

His mom's expression fell so fast he felt terrible for
busting the bubble of hope wreathing her face. "What
do you mean?"

"Please." He walked toward the office, urging her
to come out of the heavy, late afternoon heat. "Megan
called you, right?"

Myra nodded.

"There's nothing to it, Mom. I'm just helping out one
of Mitch's friends. She had car trouble."

"You're helping Kenzie Hughes," she stated.

"Nothing gets by you," he said. It had been that way
all his life. Myra Galway had a mysterious, maternal inside track on information involving her children. Wishing he had a better explanation for the stack of boxes
near the wall and the folded linens at the end of the
couch, he offered her something to drink.

"Water, please."

He handed her a bottle of water from the fridge and
waited for her to explain her visit. It didn't take long.

"Kenzie was Mitch's classmate all through school,"
Myra told him. "You probably don't remember her at
all."

"No." He was tempted to ask what his mom might
know about Kenzie's dad, but that would only stoke her
persistent hope that he would eventually open his heart
to a relationship again. *Not a chance.* He couldn't handle
that kind of vulnerability again.

"Well, the poor girl's name has been splashed all over
the news lately."

Stephen was very selective about when he turned

on the news. Sometimes knowledge wasn't power, only more pain. "Mitch told me some of it."

"Your brother says she's one of the best firefighters around. He's convinced the suit will fall apart." His mother's gaze took in all the things that were out of place in his office. "You let her sleep here?"

He chose not to explain the precise definition of "here." "Her landlord is fumigating or something. Her stuff was in her car." He gestured toward the boxes. "Her car was here. It was late…" He pushed his hand through his hair. "Made sense to me at the time."

Her smile, a mix of maternal delight and concerned tenderness, put him on edge. "You turned out all right," she said, clearly satisfied with her parenting skills. "Here's another bit of sense for you. Bring her to Sunday dinner tomorrow."

No. "Mom." He set his jaw against the persistent lance of pain searching for his heart. "She probably has plans," he added. Kenzie at Sunday dinner was a terrible idea.

"You'll ask and find out," she said breezily. "There's always room for one more at the table."

Did she practice these careless phrases that eviscerated him? By now he and Annabeth should have been working on their first baby and joining his married siblings in testing their mother's theory about room at the table. A lousy drug dealer had decided Annabeth had done enough good in this life, and snuffed her out with a cowardly ambush at the community center.

Three years after her death there were still nights when Stephen was convinced he'd heard those gunshots. The community center was too far from the garage for that to be possible, but the sounds haunted him anyway. *I should have done more for her*, he thought, though there had been nothing within his power to do. Logic seemed to have no effect on overwhelming grief.

Stephen turned away, wishing the water in his hand was a beer or a whiskey. Conversations like this one were better with a whiskey close by. Distracted by those dark memories, he flinched when Myra touched her hand to his shoulder.

"I consider Kenzie a friend of the family," she said gently.

"Then you should be the one to extend the invitation." Though the churlish tone shamed him, he wouldn't take it back. She had to know she was asking too much of him.

"That is actually why I came by," she pointed out. "Since I missed her, I trust you'll handle it on my behalf. *Politely* and graciously as I would."

"Mom." He gazed down at her, wondering why thirty-two years hadn't been enough time for him to build up immunity to the mom voice. She wouldn't drop it until he agreed. "I'll text you if she can't make it."

His mother's eyebrows lifted and she tried and failed to suppress an amused smile. "Thank you." She rocked back on her heels. "Do you have time to show me the progress on the Camaro out there?"

He knew she was trying to put him back on his feet after dealing a blow, and he let her. "The engine is in and the transmission came together," he said, as he walked with her around the car. "It needs a test drive and I'm waiting on a few more original pieces I found from a dealer in Ohio. Then it's off for the finish work."

"Do you know what the color scheme will be?"

At some point in the past, the paint had been a metallic champagne. "Silver with black rally stripes. He's career army."

"Make sure you take pictures if I don't get over here before your client picks it up."

"Sure thing, Mom." She ignored the fact that he had a portfolio of before and after pictures online she could access anytime, insisting that he show her in person. He knew it was because she worried he spent too much time with the quiet thoughts in his head.

If she had any idea how disquieting his thoughts were she'd have real reason to worry.

Myra made a bit more small talk, and when she seemed convinced he wouldn't do something stupid like take the rest of the day off and wallow in grief and alcohol, she left him in peace.

Stephen closed the gate when she'd gone and set the emergency number to ring through to his cell phone. Too restless to work, he cleaned up his tools, gave Kenzie's car another hard look and went to move more of his things out of the trailer and into the office.

It felt rude to him to keep invading space he'd given her. Better to keep as much distance as possible between him and Kenzie. His gaze landed on the denim cutoffs and T she'd worn earlier, on a corner of the bed. A vision of her long, gorgeous legs filled his mind, followed closely by an echo of that bold laughter.

Basic human nature explained why her legs got under his skin, but the effect of her laughter baffled him. Maybe the happiness of it, a sound foreign in the shop, was what bugged him. That sound shouldn't fit in and yet something deep inside him wanted to make room for it. Damn, he needed more sleep.

He closed his eyes and brought Annabeth's serene

face to his mind. A dark beauty with generous curves, his fiancée had had a steady, pleasant outlook underscored with integrity and grit that made her someone people trusted. The kids confided in her about things they were too scared to share with anyone else. On appearance alone, Kenzie was the polar opposite, not to mention the vast personality differences, and yet he had a random, discomfiting thought that they might have been friends.

Twice he picked up his phone to text Kenzie about dinner with his family. Twice he stopped, deleting the messages before he could send them. If his mother caught wind of him taking the easy way out, he'd get a lecture and a heavy dose of that sad disappointment she wielded so effectively.

He and his siblings agreed on one thing without fail: it was always better to make Myra Galway flat-out mad than to disappoint her.

To do this right, and avoid a mom lecture, Stephen would either have to go to the club or wait up for her. Resigned, he took a shower and changed clothes to go back to the Escape Club. He considered taking the Camaro, to get a feel for the clutch and the suspension, but he was too restless to listen to the car.

Instead, he grabbed a dealer plate, put the For Sale sign in the rear window of the Mustang they needed to move, and planned a route through the city that might spin up some interest. If that particular route took him by the community center where Annabeth had worked, that was just coincidence.

Right. Not even he believed that.

The community center was a central, positive influence working persistently to keep a toehold in a neigh-

borhood framed with rough edges. The area was hard
on the eyes and residents in broad daylight. Once night
fell, those rough edges turned razor-sharp and mean.

Since losing Annabeth, Stephen continued teaching
the basic automotive class despite the vicious ache in
his chest every time he came near the building. After
her killer was acquitted, he'd picked up the habit of frequently driving through the neighborhood in various ve-
hicles. Occasionally, he parked a block out and walked
in, daring any of the local thugs to take a swipe at him.

They often did.

His walks and drive-bys were random. Sometimes
they paid off and he caught a picture of a drug deal that
he forwarded to the police, or he caught wind of a name
while he wandered past on foot. For all the good it did.
The police would pick up one dealer and another stepped
up, keeping business rolling. Once in a while he timed
his visits or ended his classes so he could walk other
staffers to their cars, as he should've done every day for
his fiancée. Sometimes he just circled the block, letting
the deep purr of a big engine serve as a warning to the
petty criminals skulking in the shadows.

So far, the man he wanted to confront, the man who
had killed his fiancée, had yet to make himself a target.
Stephen didn't have anything better to do with his life
than wait him out.

Tonight, he circled the block like a shark, generally
being a nuisance and interfering with the fast deals that
happened at the corner. The thugs tasked with backing
up the dealer showed their guns on his third pass. The
familiar dance put a kick in Stephen's pulse. He was
aware they knew who he was and where to find him
when he wasn't trying to interrupt their business. Just

one reason he kept upgrading the security at the garage. He used to lie awake at night, praying someone with ties to Annabeth's murder would come by and get caught on his cameras.

Spoiling for a fight, he parked the Mustang under the floodlights and security cameras in the community center parking lot and went for a quick stroll. At this hour the facility, church and other buildings on this side of the street were deserted and locked up tight.

He walked around to the front of the building and sat on the steps. Although the building owners tried to keep security cameras operational, anything aimed in the general direction of the dealer on the corner was repeatedly disabled. Stephen had decided he had to stand in whenever possible.

Annabeth's blood had long since been washed away from the area, but the fresh paint they'd used on the railings was peeling again after three years of weather. He knew where they stored the paint and he had a key to the center. He'd almost decided to take care of it now under the glare of the streetlights when a rusty station wagon from the nineties pulled up to the corner. It made Kenzie's sedan look good by comparison.

Stephen raised his phone and hit the record button, making sure the video light caught the driver's attention. The car sputtered and rolled away, deal incomplete. From across the street, the thugs shouted a warning at him.

Stephen lowered the phone and gave them a wave without leaving his post. He scared off another two cars before the enforcers stalked across the street with orders to make him leave.

Finally.

He waited for them, his weight balanced and his knees

loose. They could just shoot him. Luckily for him, they knew as well as he did that two innocent people dead on these steps might inspire someone to actually come through this neighborhood and clean it up for good.

"Get the hell outta here," the first kid said. He couldn't be more than twenty, probably younger. His T-shirt, emblazoned with a classic arcade game character wielding an AK-47, was partially tucked into dark jeans. Stephen noted the bulging biceps and the brands seared in faint patterns on the kid's dark skin.

At Gun-shirt's nod a second man walked to the base of the stairs to face Stephen. Bald, his pale head lit by streetlights, he wore a white undershirt and faded jeans that rode low on his hips, revealing the band of his boxers. Stephen assumed the open jacket must be hot in this weather. An unfortunate circumstance for Baldy, since the jacket did nothing to conceal the gun shoved into his belt.

"You need to leave," Baldy said. He drew the gun and took aim at Stephen's midsection. "Go willingly, or go permanently, your choice."

Stephen raised his hands. "Willingly," he replied, starting down the steps.

At the sidewalk, Gun-shirt grabbed Stephen's arm and drove a fist into his gut. Although Stephen was braced for it, the blow took a toll, stealing his breath. He gasped, doubling over, hands on his knees. When Gun-shirt leaned close to make more threats, Stephen punched him in the throat. The thug staggered back into the street, bouncing off the hood of a slowly passing car before he caught his balance.

The bald man swore and aimed his gun once more,

but Stephen was quicker. He kicked out, connecting with the guy's knee. Baldy crumpled into a whimpering heap.

Across the street, the furious dealer called for reinforcements. Stephen shouted out a crude suggestion before he ran for the parking lot. He knew none of these criminals wanted to get caught chasing an innocent civilian by those cameras.

Safely in the Mustang, Stephen drove off. He was several blocks away before the pain started seeping through the adrenaline rush. He kept to the rest of his planned circuit, cruising through much nicer streets filled with people out for the evening at restaurants and posh bars. Hopefully, the sign in the rear window would attract some positive inquiries.

The sooner they moved this car the better. He had other builds in mind and more plans to keep himself busy through the summer.

Chapter 3

Things were hopping at the Escape Club tonight and tips were already weighing down Kenzie's apron pockets. It was a good feeling, although waitressing wasn't nearly as much fun as fighting fires. Here, no one seemed to care about her gender or build as long as she kept the drinks coming. The lively atmosphere and the pulsing music were a bonus, filling the space with an energy that made the hours fly.

Onstage Grant was taking a turn on the drum set while the band's real drummer stood back, grinning and working the crowd. Kenzie laughed, enjoying the sight of her boss having a blast as she weaved through the crowded dance floor to call out her orders at the bar. Mitch was on duty at the firehouse tonight, a fact she did her best to push to the back of her mind as she waited for Jason to fill her tray with longneck beers and two fancy cosmopolitans.

The PFD was a typically tight-knit community and Kenzie had first met Jason when he was teaching at the academy. He couldn't be much older than her, and she'd never heard what had led him to the academy so early in his career. Now, he was a full-time assistant to Grant. As much fun as she had with most of her shifts here at the Escape, she couldn't imagine choosing this over the real challenge and sense of accomplishment that came with fighting fires.

"Any word from your lawyer today?" he asked, as he added curls of lemon peel to the pale pink cosmopolitans.

She shook her head. "The last email claimed no news is good news. I just have to be patient."

"Easy for him to be patient—he's doing his job while you're stalled out on the sidelines. Not that we aren't happy to have you here," he added with a friendly wink.

Kenzie hefted her tray to her shoulder and gave him a warm smile. "Thanks. Not many people understand that."

She moved through the crowd, delivering drinks and taking more orders in her section. The summer concert series was a huge success, padding the bottom line for the Escape Club as well as the rest of the businesses along the river. It helped that Grant made a habit of pairing local bands on the rise with established regional groups vying to get onto this stage in front of music lovers.

When she approached the bar again several minutes later, Grant and Stephen were talking near the doorway that led to the kitchen. She felt that sizzle at the sight of the oldest Galway brother. The sensation was quickly followed by curiosity when she realized the men were embroiled in an intense conversation. Pressure simmered through the air as Grant crowded Stephen.

She called out her drink orders and told herself the two men had better things to discuss than her. Besides, she was stable now that Stephen had insisted she stick around, and had given her time to fix her own car. Though it couldn't possibly be any of her business, she kept sneaking glances at them.

Stephen turned slightly, blocking her view of Grant's face. A moment later, Grant was all but hauling Stephen back to his office. Kenzie stared after them for a long moment.

"What's all that?" she asked Jason.

"Don't know. I get the impression Stephen has a few issues," he replied. "Grant's been in his face for a few months now."

She swallowed the urge to ask why. If Stephen wanted her to know something about him, he would share. She wouldn't abuse his hospitality by snooping around for details like a high school gossip girl with a crush on the star quarterback.

Crush? Her mind locked on the word and wouldn't let go as she kept up her circuit between her customers and the bar. Sure, he was attractive and he added plenty of sex appeal to that intense broody look. Huh. She hadn't realized she was into that. Maybe it was just his proximity to that soon-to-be-stunning Camaro.

By the time her break rolled around, she was more than ready for a breather from the crowd and noise in the club. She grabbed a bottle of water from the kitchen and a power bar from her backpack and went outside for some fresh air.

The muted sounds on the river always fell over her like a silk curtain. Though she was only a few paces from the club, with businesses thriving up and down the waterway, the immediate peace and dark enveloped her, tempting her to linger well past her allotted fifteen minutes.

"What are you doing out here?"

The gruff demand startled her as she sipped the water and she choked. Sputtering, she turned to face Stephen. Oh, the man had broody and sexy in spades. Kenzie made a mental note to use some of this unexpected free time to find a date. This was a big city. She could find some neutral and friendly guy to hang out with, someone who didn't dare her hormones to rise up and take control of her common sense.

"I'm on my break," she said, when her throat finally cooperated.

"Alone." Stephen glared at the dark river behind her. "Out here."

"Not alone anymore," she said, with as much patience as she could muster. Until this particular moment, the man had shown her remarkable kindness. She supposed it was his turn to be rude.

"It isn't safe out here," he said, shoving his hands into the pockets of his jeans.

"For who?" she asked carefully.

"For you." He glared across the river as if New Jersey was on the verge of launching a fleet to invade Pennsylvania and take her captive.

"You'll notice I'm fine," she replied, deliberately taking a step closer to the river, distancing herself. Something was troubling him and she felt compelled to draw

out an explanation if possible. She watched him lingering at the blurry edge of the shadows near the building.
"You and Grant were intense. Everything okay?"

"You'll notice I'm fine," he replied.

Normally having her words tossed back in that bored
tone would irritate her. Stephen made her laugh. "So
we both have things we don't want to talk about." She
turned her back on the river, preferring the view he offered. That stoic, immovable stance dialed up the fizz
factor in her system whenever he was near and she rev-
eled in it. "That's fair. I'm surprised to see you here two
nights in a row."

"I'd rather be at the garage."

She understood that perfectly. She worked to hide
her grin. "I bet. Please don't tell me you're here to keep
an eye on me." Grant had a tendency to call in favors or
hand out orders as needed, with the idea of protecting
people he cared about. Still, a pleasant, happy warmth
slid through her to be a person Grant wanted to keep
safe. He was one of the world's good guys.

"Not exactly." Stephen crossed his arms and then un-
crossed them, shoving his hands into his pockets again.
He took a deep breath and met her gaze. "I came by tonight to let you know my mother would like you to join
us for Sunday dinner tomorrow."

Wow. The darkness hid the scowl on his face, but she
heard it in his voice. Through Mitch, she knew Mrs. Galway expected her children to gather once a week unless
they were on shift or out of town.

"Thought it would be better to do it now, rather than
after your shift," he added under his breath.

He would have waited up for her two nights in a row?
No one other than family had done that for her. She

wanted to assign some significance to it, though she really didn't know him well enough. She studied him as closely as the dim light allowed. What did he want her to say?

He shuffled his feet. "You can think about it and let me know in the morning."

"Your mother's worried about me feeling left out?" A trademark Mrs. Galway move. She'd always been one of Kenzie's favorite parent volunteers when she and Mitch were in school. The woman had a way of making everyone she met feel as if they mattered.

"That's my guess," he said.

"Thanks." The idea of sharing a meal with the Galways sounded like fun. "The invitation is a thoughtful gesture."

"Is that a yes?" he asked.

"Would you like me to refuse?" Thanks to Mitch, Kenzie was aware that when the Galway kids brought a guest to Sunday dinner, it was assumed that person was significant. That wasn't the case for her and Stephen and she didn't want to make the situation difficult for him. "It wouldn't bother me at all to have Sunday to myself."

"Do you have something else to do tomorrow afternoon?"

"No," she answered. "I'm off tomorrow. I was going to work on my car."

He stepped back, as if he found that news distasteful. "Then I'll tell her you'll join us."

"Only if that's okay with you," she insisted.

"It's fine." He pulled out his cell phone.

She didn't quite believe him, but she didn't want to argue the point and make this conversation any more difficult than it was. "Great. Thanks."

Family dinner hadn't been a regular occurrence with Hughes women, even before her mother and little sister had moved to Maryland. In recent years, the three of them tended to do more family bonding over spa days, shopping trips and the occasional beach weekend.

Stephen slipped his phone back into his pocket and stood there. As awkward moments went, this had to rank in the all-time top ten. "I should get back to work," she said. "Did you enjoy the band?" she added.

"They're a local favorite."

She was about to call him on the evasion when he reached to open the door for her and grimaced. She recognized pain when she saw it. "What's wrong?" She shifted, taking the weight of the door off him.

"Nothing," he said, following her into the club.

"Liar." She looked him over, head to toe, not seeing any obvious injury. "Something's hurting you," she pressed.

His eyebrows shot up. "It's not a big deal. I slipped on a step."

"Landing on your side?" On reflex, she reached for his rib cage, then pulled back, curling her fingers into her palms.

"Pretty much," he replied. "Nothing's broken," he added before she could ask.

"You're sure about that?"

"I've had a broken rib before," he told her, without elaborating on how it had happened.

"All right." Pain would explain the general discomfort he projected, though she sensed there was still something more lurking under the surface. "If you're sticking around, have Jason pour you a beer. My treat."

"I'll just get going. Unless you have another break coming."

She grinned. He seemed determined to keep an eye on her. "I'll be safe," she said, backing toward the club noise spilling into the hallway.

"Have someone walk you out tonight," he called after her.

"Yes, sir."

Kenzie decided Grant must have asked Stephen to keep an eye on her, after all. No other reason for Stephen to make that request. Rather than getting bent out of shape about it, she welcomed the sweet sensation that life was giving her a little upswing, a boost to help her over the other muck she was trying to navigate.

Hours later, as she closed out the shift and waited for Jason to walk her out to the car, Grant offered to take on the role of safety escort.

"I need a favor," he said, as soon as they were away from the club.

"Of course. You've certainly done plenty of them for me." She appreciated that the Escape Club had been an option for her, bridging the gap and keeping her busy while she waited to get back on shift at the PFD.

"Can you keep an eye on Stephen?"

"What?" She couldn't have heard him correctly. Grant made no secret of the fact that he helped people tangled up in difficult situations, but Stephen seemed capable of handling himself.

"You are staying at his place, right?" Grant asked.

"I am." She didn't add that Stephen had practically insisted on it. "On top of the loaner car, he's letting me stay in his camper until I can get back into my apartment."

Grant snorted. "He told me he's lending you space and tools to fix your car, so that will give you more reason to stick close. Try not to fix it too fast."

"What is this about? Stephen doesn't strike me as the type to enjoy having people looking over his shoulder."

"You're right, but someone has to do something and you're already in." Grant's bushy, salt-and-pepper eyebrows dipped low over his dark brown eyes. "Can you please try?"

She had a sudden image of Stephen's face twisted with pain. "He didn't fall down the stairs, did he?"

"Not without help," Grant muttered. "Since his fiancée was murdered and the killer acquitted, Stephen has struggled to stay on track."

A chill of unease trickled down her spine. "Meaning what, exactly?" What sort of situation was she signing on for? Grant had to know she didn't need more life complications that Murtagh's legal team could use against her. Though Stephen didn't give off the vibe of a man using drugs or alcohol, he was so reserved she couldn't be sure.

"A buddy of mine in Narcotics tells me Stephen sends in pictures, tips, and occasionally names of drug dealers near the community center where his fiancée worked," Grant said. "Tonight, they got another tip and the undercover officer in the area caught a few pictures of Stephen in the community center lot before and after the tip came in. I think he's hurting from a fight."

Stephen didn't have a substance abuse kind of habit; he had vigilante tendencies. *Great.* "Is he trying to get himself killed?"

"Can't answer that one," Grant said. "I do know if he

doesn't lay off he runs the risk of blowing a major drug bust in the area."

At the car, she shoved her rolled-up apron into her backpack and pulled her keys out of the smaller pocket. "And here I thought you'd told him to keep an eye on me."

"I did." Grant's unrepentant grin flashed across his face. "He wasn't excited about it, but I'm hoping such an impossible and unnecessary task will distract him from the troubles near the community center."

She rolled her eyes. His flattery amused her and blended with his fatherly concern into a comforting warmth that soothed her tired mind and body. "It's a tall order, but I'll do my best," she said, unlocking the car. "Does Mitch know anything about this?" She didn't want to stick her foot in her mouth at Sunday dinner.

"If he does, he didn't hear it from me," Grant said. "I've been trying to guide Stephen away from this habit quietly."

"All right." If Grant hadn't enlisted any of the Galway family's help on this issue, she wouldn't, either. It was always better to know where she stood. She opened the door and pushed her backpack into the space behind the driver's seat.

"And Kenzie?"

She glanced up. Grant was still leaning on the passenger side of the car. "Don't let Stephen run you off."

"Not a chance," she assured him. "His camper is the most affordable place in town." Keeping it light, she gave her boss a confident wink and settled behind the wheel of the loaner car.

Though Stephen valued his privacy and solitude,

working at his garage was no hardship for her. She enjoyed getting her hands dirty and had already planned to help him out as much as he'd allow just as payback for letting her stay. Now she had to rethink how to dig in deeper, and keep him closer to the garage without driving either of them crazy.

Just past noon the next afternoon, Stephen waited by Megan's minivan, wondering if he should go check on Kenzie. They had plenty of time to get to the house, but he hadn't seen her since her break last night.

When he'd returned from the club, he couldn't recall if he'd told her what time to be ready today. Frustrated and sore from the scuffle at the community center, he'd taped a note to the camper door for her. Though he'd waited up until she returned from her shift, he didn't go outside when she arrived. The note hadn't been there when he checked this morning and he had to assume she'd seen it. Or he could just go knock on the door and make sure she was up.

No. He wouldn't nag her. She might have changed her mind or decided she'd rather sleep after her crazy-late hours.

Running on fumes from lack of sleep, he might have downed too much coffee while he dealt with invoices and paperwork as the clock on the wall crept closer to Sunday dinner time. Maybe they should just take two cars over, though he didn't want her to think he would leave without her. Exasperated with himself, he tried to sigh and only managed to swear at the pain in his ribs when he inhaled.

He couldn't get past how *wrong* this felt to be taking

someone other than Annabeth to the Galway weekly ritual. Sure, his mother considered Kenzie a family friend, but she would be arriving with *him*.

His palms went damp and guilt fogged his mind as memories slammed into him from every angle. The last time he'd brought a woman to Sunday dinner he and Annabeth were in the thick of wedding plans. His mom had surprised everyone at dessert, bringing out samples from three bakeries vying for the wedding cake and reception contract. The family voted in favor of a rich berry cake, insisting it was the best choice for a summer wedding.

If he closed his eyes, he could almost see Annabeth's delighted face as she savored a bite of fluffy, light lemon cake. He hadn't had a preference between the samples until that moment. As soon as her favorite was obvious, he wanted her to have whatever made her happiest. Wouldn't settle for anything else.

It had been his job to make her life better in every way possible. *Epic fail*, he thought. And it was only getting worse. No matter what he did at the community center during or after hours, Annabeth's memory kept drifting further into the back of his mind.

He tugged at the open collar of his button-down shirt. The humidity was already unspeakable. What had they been thinking? Summer was too hot for formal occasions. Except with Annabeth, getting married in July, the anniversary month of their first date, had seemed perfect.

They'd had big plans for that summer and all the ones that would follow as husband and wife. Four days after that cake tasting, his life and all their plans were shattered when the phone rang and the cops told him she was dead.

Carefully, he took a slow, deep breath, mindful of the bruised ribs this time. He wasn't going to get out of this dinner and he needed to pull himself together or he'd be on the receiving end of pitying glances and smothering concern all afternoon.

"Hey!" Kenzie waved as she crossed the yard. "Have you been waiting long?"

"No." Mentally, he shook off the melancholy and forced a smile onto his face. She wore strappy sandals, and a dress in a blue patterned fabric that tied behind her neck and flowed over her body, down to points just past her knees. Her hair was braided differently today, across the top of her head rather than straight back. It looked softer and left her shoulders bare. She was a punch of sex appeal with a girl-next-door smile, and he struggled to find two words to fit together into a coherent thought.

"Why don't I follow you over in the loaner?" she suggested.

If it wasn't so hot, he would have suggested they walk back to the shop after dinner. "Mitch and Julia will give us a ride back. He wants to be here when the potential buyer for the Mustang stops in."

"Oh. I didn't realize you had an appointment today."

Stephen shrugged and walked over to open the passenger door for her. The fluttering fabric of the dress played peekaboo with her knees as she hopped into the minivan. He jerked his gaze away. "Mitch sent me a text message from someone curious about it after I drove it around last night. I'm hoping it's a legitimate offer."

He felt her watching him as he rounded the hood of

the car and climbed into the driver's seat. "Are you feeling all right?" she asked.

"No," he admitted, before he caught himself. He couldn't put the brakes on any of the feelings knocking around like bumper cars in his gut.

"Your family would understand if you skip dinner because you're hurt. Just give your mom a call."

Hardly. They all thought he dwelled in the past too much. Although they respected his grief, too often they suggested Annabeth would want him to move on. Previous attempts to move on had been too much like boxing up their shared memories and giving up on justice. "Not Mom. Besides, she's eager to see you." He managed a weak smile as he twisted to back out of the space.

He made the mistake of glancing Kenzie's way and the concern in those blue eyes stopped him. Looks like that should be illegal. "What?" he demanded.

"Stephen, the pain is etched on your face," she said, with far too much compassion.

"Gee, thanks," he muttered. Surely he'd gotten better at hiding his raw emotions by now. He resumed the task of driving as if his life depended on it. The sooner they got over there the sooner it would be over.

"Did you do anything helpful when you got home?" she pressed.

Stephen wasn't following the subject change, but he refused to risk another glance at her. "What are you talking about?"

"Your *ribs*. It's obvious you're sore from falling last night. Are you sure nothing's broken?"

He nearly laughed with relief, except that would hurt too much. "I'm all right."

"If you say so." She didn't sound the least bit convinced.

"Thanks for the concern," he said sincerely. He'd forgotten how it felt to have someone other than family take an interest in his welfare. Well, Grant cared enough to tell him to stay away from the dealers near the community center. It wasn't something he could stop. Annabeth deserved more than an acquittal arranged by a fast-talking lawyer.

He couldn't articulate any of that to Kenzie, not without revealing far more than she needed to know. "In my experience nothing helps bruised ribs but time," he said, as he parked on the street in front of the house he'd grown up in.

The door opened and Megan hurried out to see her minivan. "You washed it for me." She beamed at him. "James will be grateful."

"Part of the full package," Stephen replied. As he moved to open the door for Kenzie his sister got in the way.

Megan scoffed. "Since when?"

Stephen dropped the keys into her hand. "I had time." He gave her a gentle, one-armed hug with his good side.

She stepped back and glared at him. "Who told you?"

He ignored her question in favor of introducing Kenzie, pleased when his voice didn't crack in the process.

"Hi." Megan gave a halfhearted wave. "You were in Mitch's high school class."

"I was," Kenzie replied with an easy smile.

As the two women bonded over fashion, Stephen wondered why *he* didn't remember Kenzie from high school. Apparently back then being the oldest meant he'd had zero interest in his younger siblings.

"Julia and Mitch are already here," Megan said. She turned back to Kenzie. "Are you on his side when it comes to the Marburg law firm?" She pointed at Stephen.

He rolled his eyes. "Leave her alone, Megan." His family acted like he had no common sense. Just because Marburg got Annabeth's killer acquitted didn't mean he hated his new sister-in-law for working there.

"Everyone knows Marburg is representing the plaintiff against her," Megan replied in a stage whisper. "I was only going to give Julia fair warning if Kenzie turned out to be as moody as you."

"Megan." He urged them up the walk toward the house.

"I've met Julia at the firehouse," Kenzie interjected. "And no, I don't blame her that the law firm she works for represents the guy suing me."

Stephen gestured for Megan to go inside first, then pulled the door closed behind her. He held firm when Megan tried to open it again. "For the record, I'm okay with Julia, not with Marburg." He swallowed, searching for the right words. "If there's anything I can do to help you beat the lawsuit, count on me."

Her blue eyes went wide, then sparkled as she squished that big laugh of hers into a quiet chuckle. "Thanks for the offer, Stephen. According to my lawyer we just have to wait out the process, but it's good to have a friend right now. Better than good. Thanks," she said again.

Part of him appreciated being safely labeled as a friend while another part of him rebelled at the idea. The door opened before he could decide on a suitable response, and Stephen was ready to snap at Megan when he realized it was his mother. She stared him down.

"Hello, Mrs. Galway," Kenzie said.

His mom drew Kenzie inside and gave her a big hug as she aimed an "I taught you better" glare at Stephen.

Disappointing his mother was the worst and an excellent distraction from the unexpected turn his thoughts were taking with Kenzie. Being attracted to a pretty woman was normal, though not at all welcome. Why couldn't she have worn shop coveralls to dinner? He walked in and closed the door, trying to focus on tattling little sisters and the other details of life that never seemed to change.

Megan's little ones came at him first and he quickly sheltered his bruised side from their boisterous greetings. He was glad he and Kenzie had arrived last, subjecting them to less predinner chitchat. He lingered in the foyer with the kids while his mom reminded the rest of the family of how they all knew Kenzie.

He was inching toward the kitchen when Mitch and Julia walked in from the dining room, their hushed conversation cut short when they spotted him.

Stephen tried to pretend he didn't have a care in the world. He turned Julia's hug to the side as he'd done with Megan, but Mitch clapped him hard on the shoulder and caught him wincing.

"Again?" Mitch said under his breath.

Julia looked back and forth between them. "Do I want to know?"

"No," the brothers said in unison.

"All right." She slipped into the family room and joined the conversation there.

"You two probably should've finished that discussion in the car," Stephen said, "or waited until you were home."

"How much did you hear?" Mitch asked, his gaze

aimed at the family room as if he could keep an eye on his wife through the wall.

"None of it," Stephen assured him. "Trouble is stamped on your face."

"I'll fill you in at the shop," Mitch said. He forced his lips into a dreadful excuse for a smile. "Is this better?"

"Better than my version usually is."

"You can fill me in on that later, too," Mitch said.

Stephen didn't dignify that with an answer. It was bad enough Mitch had outgrown him by a couple inches. He wasn't about to relinquish his role as the oldest brother and all the perks that came with it. Not even for the duration of a conversation. He didn't need a keeper, didn't need any reminders that harassing drug dealers was a dangerous hobby. He had to assume Mitch heard about his afterhours treks to the community center from a friend on the police force, the same way Sullivan had heard about it.

Thankfully, the family gathered around the dining room table, and Stephen let the voices flow around him, blotting out the ache in his side and the thoughts of last night. He tried to stay quiet so no one heard the grief lodged in his throat or accused him of being cynical. Though he offered comments and answered questions when necessary, he preferred hearing what was going on in their lives. What could he say? His life had frozen three years ago and his existence revolved around the garage, with the same routine day in and day out, week after week.

To his vast relief his family included Kenzie in the conversation as if she were a weekly fixture without expressing any hint of pushing her at him in a personal capacity. He picked up on the details that her mother and little sister, Courtney, had moved to Maryland five years ago. She made it sound like they got together only a few times a year.

He briefly entertained the idea of that much freedom, but shut down the vision when it felt as if he'd been cut loose to float away. When his lips parted to ask about her dad, he dug into his potatoes. Not his business and definitely not smart to ask her anything personal in front of his mother and sisters.

She and Julia got along easily enough, proving Kenzie was a better person than him. He'd been rude, hating Julia simply because she was an attorney. Well, he'd wanted to hate her and couldn't quite manage it, since it was so obvious his brother had seen something more under the woman's employment with the notorious Marburg law firm.

"The lawsuit Murtagh filed against you has been all over the news, Kenzie," his father said. "How are you holding up?"

"Being sidelined is a challenge," she admitted. "The shifts at Escape Club are a great distraction. No one there seems to recognize me." She sent Stephen a glowing smile that hurt more than his rib cage. "Stephen has been more than generous about giving me time and space at the shop to fix my car."

Weakness more than generosity, he told himself. He liked her company and already he knew he'd miss her when she left."Your dad would be tickled to hear you talk like that," Samuel said with a chuckle. "The two of you were sure something."

Kenzie only nodded, as if some emotion had her choked up. Stephen swallowed more questions along with the urge to give her an outward sign of support. His mom would leap on any glimmer of interest he showed as hope for something more than a platonic association. He was surprised to realize he didn't want her to run Kenzie off too soon.

"He might have a proper guest room to offer, too, if he ever bought a house," Myra said.

The gentle reprimand underscoring her words only poured more salt in that wound. What did a workaholic bachelor need with a house? Stephen cut into his ham and shoved a big bite into his mouth, preventing him from saying something he'd regret.

"The camper is plenty comfortable," Kenzie said. "Stephen did a great job with it."

Crap, he thought, as Myra's eyebrows arched and her gaze met her husband's across the table. Kenzie seemed oblivious to the way she'd drawn full attention from every adult at the table. He caught a gleam in his youngest sister's eye and blurted out the first thing that came to mind before Jenny could open her mouth.

"Dad, you knew Murtagh. Do you think he'd sabotage her car? Someone put sugar in her gas tank."

Samuel's face clouded over, his jaw set. "Murtagh always was an a—a jerk," he said, correcting his language for the grandkids just in time. "If your lawyer wants to depose any of us who worked with him, we're every last one of us willing."

Kenzie's lips pressed together, holding back the surge of emotion welling in her eyes. "Thank you," she said quietly.

The sight of those tears she wouldn't let fall was like a metal splinter under his skin. He wanted to take her away from anything that dimmed her sparkling laughter. What was wrong with him?

From his side of the table, Stephen caught the look of concern Julia aimed at Mitch. They must have been talking about Kenzie earlier. He couldn't imagine that Marburg would assign Julia, Mitch's wife, to Murtagh's legal team. Once they reached the privacy of the garage, it would be Stephen's first question.

Conversations resumed and his dad asked him about his current project.

"I'm finishing up the rebuild of a 1967 Camaro SS for Matt Riley," Stephen replied.

"General Riley's oldest?" Samuel asked.

"That's right." Stephen nodded.

"I didn't realize that one was for Matt. We haven't seen them in years," Myra said. "It sounds like they're becoming good clients," she added, with a hefty dose of maternal pride.

"And they have excellent taste in classic American muscle cars," Mitch added. "I still want to know where he found it. It's in such good shape."

Megan's oldest asked what a muscle car was, drawing Stephen back into the conversation. He happily explained, in the simplest terms, that a muscle car earned the name because of how it was styled and built, and had an engine geared for performance. "The cars that are classics now were new when Grandpa was your age."

"Show some respect," Samuel grumbled with a grin.

Kenzie looked down the table at his wide-eyed nephew. "My dad taught me muscle cars growl when you're going slow and purr when you drive fast. I bet Uncle Stephen will teach you all about it when you're older."

Stephen gave her a long look. Classic cars were one interest his fiancée hadn't shared with him. Oh, she'd admired and respected his work, but she didn't know cars or parts and hadn't been inclined to learn. That had been fine with him. She'd traveled with him to a few car auctions, hanging out at the hotel pool while he conducted business. He thought of Kenzie answering the phone and managing the customers. Annabeth would never have been comfortable stepping into his space that way.

Stephen couldn't figure out how that made him feel. Done with his dinner, he helped Jenny clear as the others finished. As his mom served up thick slabs of cherry cobbler for dessert, he caught Megan and James exchanging cryptic glances. Happy to get even for earlier, he called her on it. "Something you'd like to share with the rest of the class, Meg?"

She wrinkled her nose at him. "Who told you?"

"You did," he said.

Her eyebrows snapped together a moment. "No, I didn't. We haven't told anyone."

James draped an arm across the back of her chair and Stephen felt a sharp pang of resentment over the gesture. He missed sharing intimacies like those looks and small touches. He checked his watch, wishing for an excuse to get out of here before the surly mood took over and he said something stupid.

"We were saving the news," James said.

"News?" Myra set dessert in front of her husband and leaned in when he wrapped his arm around her waist.

As James gave Megan's shoulder a squeeze, Stephen gritted his teeth. He knew what his sister would say before the words came out of her mouth.

"We're expecting again," Megan said at last. When

the first chorus of happy congratulations died down, she added, "It's twins."

Laughter and groans filled the room and Samuel offered James his sympathy. "Good luck with that," he said with a heartfelt sigh. "One to two is enough challenge." He nodded at Stephen and Mitch in turn. "Going from two to four overnight?" He gazed up at his wife, eyes sparkling with humor and love. "Good luck," he repeated.

"You'll have all the help you need." Myra paused to kiss the top of Megan's head as she returned to her chair.

"Meg and I weren't that bad," Andrew declared, defending himself and his twin sister.

"None of us slept for weeks," Stephen said, as if it had been agony.

"Years," Samuel said, teasing them all.

Mitch said, "I remember helping Mom all the time."

Myra cackled. "Please. You rescue people now in less chaos than I faced daily with four children. I cried tears of joy when Stephen started kindergarten. And then Jenny came along."

"And being a perfect angel, I quickly became the favorite," Jenny said with a wink.

To prove he could do something of value other than marry well and procreate, Stephen retreated to the kitchen. They tended to rotate the cleanup chores, but he needed some breathing space. He was happy for his sister. Delighted, he assured himself as he rinsed plates and loaded the dishwasher.

"You okay?"

Mitch. He kept his back to the sympathy in his brother's voice.

"Fine," he said. Anything more than one syllable would push the envelope of his control.

"I've told everyone we need to get over to the garage to meet the potential buyer for that Mustang. Julia and Kenzie are ready when you are."

Stephen finished loading the dishwasher and returned to the dining room. "Ready." When the conversation paused, he ordered Andrew and James to finish the cleanup for his mom. He made quick work of the goodbyes and finally made it through the door. Julia and Kenzie were trailing Mitch to his car.

"Hang on." Megan was on his heels, preventing a clean escape. "How did you know I was pregnant?"

"Why are you so convinced I did?"

"You only do the half-hug thing when I'm pregnant. Did I leave something from the doctor in the van?"

"Just a lucky guess," he said. Ignoring his griping ribs, he pulled her in for a real, two-armed hug and she cinched her arms tight around his waist.

He grunted. "Come on, Meg."

"Well, this one has to last, since I'll be big as a house with twins soon."

"Right." He let her squeeze all she wanted. "Love you, sis."

"Love you, too," she said against his shoulder. "Go be happy," she added, her gaze sliding toward Kenzie.

"Shut up," Stephen protested. "We're friends." Again, something unfamiliar inside him rebelled at that label.

Megan only twinkled in that way of women overflowing with happiness. "So was James."

Stephen was more than a little relieved to escape to Mitch's gleaming Dodge Charger. Only a few years old, it served as an advertisement for Galway Automotive.

Julia and Kenzie had taken the backseat, giving him more leg room up front.

"Tell me about this buyer," Stephen demanded, needing to put the family and talk of babies out of his mind. "You think he can really afford it?"

"I've told him we don't do financing, if that's what you mean," Mitch replied. "I think he can make the deal. Don't tell me you've got another buyer on the hook."

"I wish." A bidding war could be fun, although if they wanted to do that, they should take it to auction. Stephen struggled to hide the deep despair clamping around his rib cage like a vise. He wanted to blame the pervasive discomfort on the altercation last night or Megan's hug, but he knew this pain was emotional. "Is he willing to pay cash?"

"Well, I didn't ask him for stacks of unmarked twenty-dollar bills," Mitch joked.

In the backseat, Julia and Kenzie were talking in low tones. Kenzie was definitely a better person than he was. Given a choice, he'd rather see the notorious law firm dismantled and their historic building on Walnut Street removed from existence brick by brick. That little fantasy kept his mind off dinner, Kenzie and the thousand other stupid things bothering him like a swarm of bees.

"What's wrong with you?" Mitch asked, when they reached the garage and the women were out of the car. "You're grouchier than normal."

"I'm fine." Stephen reached for the door, paused. "Did you promise this buyer a deep discount or something?"

Mitch called him on it. "You're hurt again." He swore. "You ask all kinds of stupid questions when you want to smother the pain."

"Go to hell."

Mitch grabbed him before he could get out of the car. "You can't keep this up. It's time to get some help."

He didn't dignify that with a reply. Besides, he was far more interested in what Mitch and Julia had been talking about before dinner.

"Megan's pregnant and you can't dredge up any real happiness," Mitch continued. "The misery is obvious to everyone."

Stephen bristled. "I'm happy for them." What kind of jerk wouldn't be happy for them? "End of story." He glanced out the window and saw Julia and Kenzie still looking chummy. Maybe Julia was filling her in on what had upset them.

Mitch drilled a finger into Stephen's shoulder. "It's me. I was there, remember?"

Yes, Stephen remembered. How could he forget that his brother had responded to the 9-1-1 call that a woman, Stephen's fiancée, had been shot? His brother had been there while Annabeth bled out on those cursed steps, well beyond the help of the paramedics on the scene. Stephen would never forget how he'd failed to protect the woman he'd planned to grow old with. Mitch had been the one who'd called him. Mitch had held him when grief and denial dropped him to his knees in the ER.

"You're wrong. I fell, that's all," Stephen lied.

"Like hell. You need to talk with someone. You can't hide under cars alone all day and go looking for fights all night. You deserve better."

"I had better," Stephen shot back. "And you've got better things to worry about than me." His gaze drifted to Kenzie. "Plus I'm not alone." She was all the interference he could handle in his routine right now. "You're a good brother for caring, but I'm fine."

Mitch swore again. "Come on—"

Stephen swiveled around as a car pulled to a stop in front of the gate. "Your buyer?"

Mitch nodded, the scowl on his face smoothing out as he climbed from the Dodge to greet the newcomer. Stephen envied that ease his brother demonstrated, and tried his best to smile at the man, who seemed vaguely familiar.

"Jason?" Kenzie's lips curved into a grin as she hurried over to join them.

Something clicked for Stephen. This was one of the full-time bartenders from the Escape Club. A weird ripple of irritation chased through him as Kenzie and Jason fell into an immediate, friendly conversation.

Clearly, she knew how to get along with anyone in any circumstance, he decided, as she turned the conversation to the car. Had he ever been that easy with people?

Having had more than a week's worth of conversation over family dinner, Stephen let the others chat. He leaned back against the trunk of another car-in-progress and let Mitch handle the dealing. His little brother enjoyed the bargaining as much as he enjoyed the hands-on work.

Although… Stephen slid a glance at Julia. Would Mitch still want to be as involved when they started a family?

Kenzie, a smile on her face, walked over. He tried to keep his eyes on her face rather than that teasing hem of her dress.

"You're not into the art of the deal?" she asked.

"He's better at it," Stephen answered. He could smell the sunshine in her hair and something tangled with it that reminded him of a summer-ripe peach.

"What about the Riley Camaro in there? Did you negotiate that deal?"

He looked toward the bay where the Camaro was hidden by the lowered door. "That's different."

Her bare shoulder rubbed faintly against his biceps.
"Come on. Tell me more."

"It's more like a commission." He glanced down to
her shining face and knew she wouldn't let it rest. Talking was overrated and he always seemed to get tangled in
the wrong details of the conversation. He folded his arms
over his chest, the movement pressing his arm to hers.
He swallowed, holding his ground rather than jumping
away from her. "The Riley family brings us the car, a
list of priorities, and gives me the budget," he said at last.

"Interesting." She was eyeing that bay door as in-
tently as he had been.

He told himself he didn't want to know if she'd aimed
that "interesting" at the customer's methods or him. "I
need to take it out for a test drive," he said before he
thought better of it. "You could ride along," he suggested,
startling them both.

"Right now? You sure you're up for it?"

"Once we're done here." And he could drive with far
worse injuries than bruised ribs. He lifted his chin toward Mitch and Jason. "Unless you'd rather join him?"

"I'm surprised Jason's looking at a car with that kind
of price tag." Kenzie's nose wrinkled as she studied the
Mustang.

"You don't like it?" he challenged. He and Mitch had
brought that thing back to mint condition. "It's a '70."
In theory, it could get upward of a hundred grand at the
right auction. He had confidence that Mitch would work

a profitable deal. Stephen was eager to get it off his lot and churn the profits into another project.

"I know," she said. "I can *appreciate* the car," she added quickly. She did her best to suppress the smile and failed. "And it's excellent workmanship. Still, there is something about the lines of a classic Camaro."

Her soft murmur of longing gave him a jolt, as if he'd touched a loose live wire. Stephen couldn't reply. His passion for cars ran the gamut from classic to quirky to cutting edge. He loved them all, and the challenge and ongoing learning kept him sharp. Cars didn't need conversation. Engines and tires and mufflers didn't demand he talk about feelings. The garage was a place to get things done. In a world that had frozen three years ago, the night his fiancée died, the garage gave him tangible progress and rewarded honest efforts equitably.

The Mustang's beefy engine roared to life and Jason, Mitch and Julia took the car for a short test drive. When they returned, the deal was settled in the office, payment and delivery arranged, and at last Stephen was alone again.

Well, almost alone.

He changed from the button down to a Galway Automotive T-shirt and joined Kenzie in the bay where the Camaro waited. She'd changed into denim shorts, a faded red, sleeveless cotton top and canvas shoes. She'd redone her hair, the thick braid falling straight down her back. He told himself he didn't miss the dress.

"My dad would have loved this one," she said, her voice soft and wistful.

He recognized the nostalgic nuance in her tone. "How long ago did he die?"

"I was fifteen," she said, her hand sweeping over

the rise of the rear fender. "Our dads worked together," she added, caressing the tail fin. "Did you know that?"

"Vaguely." She was thirty and death had neatly divided her life in two parts, yet she remained so vibrant, completely alive. For the first time in recent memory Stephen wanted to ask how to manage that full recovery. Watching her, he realized the sorrow was still there, deep in her eyes, the tug at the corners of her lips. He wondered how her dad had died. He couldn't recall any deadly fires around that time. "Back then, the fire department was low on my list of priorities."

She met his gaze, her blue eyes sparkling. "Girls, right?"

"Cars." *Girls followed*, he thought, with an inward smile. "Engines made sense to me, and to my mother's dismay street racing was my preferred adrenaline rush."

She stopped at the front of the car, her eyes wide. "Seriously?"

"Young and stupid." He flipped the Camaro's keys around his index finger. "Sure you want to be seen with me in this?" The lines and body of the car were in decent condition, but although the factory color had once been crisp champagne, the years and a little rust gave it an unsightly coppery patina.

"That could be embarrassing," she teased. Stepping back, she planted her hands on her hips. "Better let me hear the engine first."

Mechanically, the car was nearly done. He needed to test the suspension and make sure the manual transmission was good to go. Curious how she'd react, he kept his gaze on her as he reached in and turned the key.

The engine roared to life.

Her expression absolutely lit up and she threw her

head back in one of her big laughs. If he'd felt sucker punched earlier, seeing her in that dress, her reaction to the car might as well have been a knockout.

He had no idea how to cope with all the reactions she stirred inside him. Thankfully, she wouldn't be sticking around more than a week or two.

Chapter 4

Settled into the passenger seat, Kenzie could tell her heart was still running a little fast as Stephen drove the Camaro away from the shop, and not just because of the big block engine under the hood. Oh, that sound had been like magic, sending her straight back to those days of helping her dad in the garage. Just like her father always said, in the lower gears, this kind of motor growled, ready to leap at the first opportunity to open up.

Sure, the car had given her pulse a jump start, but it was the man behind the wheel that kept her system amped up. His hard jaw set in concentration made her want to reach out and see what kind of touch would soften him up. The flex and motion of his working hands and forearms as he shifted gears posed a ridiculous temptation to reach out, to feel that sinuous movement under her fingertips. Not smart to go there just because she was feeling lonely.

Keeping her mouth shut and her thoughts and hands to herself, she sank into the experience of watching Stephen handle the car. He needed to listen to and feel what the car was doing under him. She made her own mental notes, just in case he asked her opinion later.

As they cruised through the neighborhood, she tried to divert her attention with the Sunday evening activities around them. Summertime in this part of town was a throwback to an idyllic era. With the car windows rolled down, the scent of burgers and hot dogs on backyard grills drifted through, backed by the soundtrack of delighted shrieks of children dashing through sprinklers.

"What was your favorite part of summer as a kid?" she asked abruptly.

"Catching fireflies," he replied, the stern line of his mouth easing with the memory. "Though burying my little brothers in the sand when we went up to Ocean City in Jersey is a close second."

"They really let you do that?"

His lips twitched, though he didn't smile. "Let's just say they always managed to draw the short straw."

She chuckled. "Being oldest does have its advantages."

"A few," he agreed.

He wound his way out of the neighborhood and let the car open up a bit more, then picked up Interstate 95 and aimed north, away from the city. She didn't care where they were going because the driving was plenty of fun. Shedding the city and her recent troubles gave her a sense of relief, despite knowing she'd have to go back and ride out the lawsuit.

Once he was in fourth gear the engine sounded good to her, but she felt a lag in the clutch whenever he shifted from second to third. She didn't mention it; this was his project, and he had to be feeling it more than she did.

The low purr of the engine filled the space where most people would want to talk, and she enjoyed the companionable silence as the miles slipped by. She'd been doing so much talking, defending and justifying her decisions in the Murtagh fire, that Stephen's quiet tendencies were a refreshing reprieve. So focused on the professional ramifications, she hadn't realized how the case was consuming her personally. The only thing no one wanted to discuss with her was what she was going to do if Murtagh won his case against her.

She glanced at Stephen again. It wasn't as if firefighting was the only thing she could do. She was a quick learner, tenacious, good with her hands, and she had decent skills with computers, too. If Stephen hired her to manage the office, she could build on that, giving him a hand with the basic maintenance tasks. Combined with waitressing at the club, she could make ends meet.

She sighed, frustrated and more than a little discouraged by how that life looked in her mind. Her career as a firefighter couldn't be over. Not like this. She had turned her gaze to the passing scenery. Positive thinking was essential. She had to keep a strong vision of the result she wanted.

"What do you think about the car?" Stephen asked, drawing her away from the less pleasant thoughts.

"The engine loves the highway," she said.

His lips tilted into a faint smile. "Riley will have his hands full keeping her in check in town."

"About that," she said.

He shot her a quick glance.

"Is there a hiccup between second and third gear or do you enjoy abusing a clutch?"

He laughed, a rusty sound that seemed to surprise them both. "I took an oath as a mechanic not to abuse any machinery."

The joke made her smile. "What a relief," she teased.

"I think I know what to look for when we get back," he said. "I'm glad you noticed it, too. But you weren't thinking about the car."

She didn't appreciate his observation skills. "I wasn't *only* thinking about the car." It was as far as she wanted to go on the subject. They barely knew each other, and though he wasn't the only person trying to help her though this rough patch, something in his quiet intensity slipped past her defenses. She wasn't sure she could deal with that kind of invasion. Not now, anyway.

Before she could ask what he'd meant by the earlier offer to help her beat the lawsuit, he was turning off the interstate to a less-traveled side road.

"Would you like to just think about the car?"

She stared at him, almost afraid to hope. "Are you offering to let me drive?"

"Yes."

That single word sent a thrill of anticipation rolling through her. It was all she could do to sit still when she wanted to bounce in her seat like one of his siblings' children had done at the sight of him.

He stopped to fill the car with gas, but didn't turn over the keys when she hopped out and held out her hand.

"Five minutes," he told her.

She took in the trees lining the road and something clicked. She hadn't been up this way in a long time. More than fifteen years, in fact. Her weekend trips out of Philly had come to an abrupt halt when her dad died. "Where are we going?"

"Be patient." His lips twitched again.

That bemused expression made her want to tease him for hours and hours with more than words. She pulled herself back from that slippery slope. Neither of them was in the market for a fast fling. He was doing her a big favor letting her stay in the camper, and she didn't dare screw that up by letting her hormones call the shots.

He continued down the access road until the trees cleared away to reveal an old oval racetrack. She sat a little forward in her seat. "I have been here."

"You have?"

"Yes!" The grandstands looked weary and forlorn now. She remembered when bright racing team flags had flown from the poles along the top rail. She could almost smell the popcorn blending with the pungent scents of hot tires, oil and gasoline. "Ages ago when my dad did some racing on the weekends," she replied. "I was probably twelve or thirteen the last time."

"How did I not know about that?" Stephen asked.

"It's not like he was some racing celebrity or anything," she pointed out. "He had to give it up when he got sick."

Stephen parked the car and climbed out, to punch a number into the security panel at the gate. She was reminded of the security measures at his garage when the fence rolled back. Once they were through, he waited until the fence closed behind him.

"Did you buy this track?" She couldn't believe her good luck. "Are you going to open it up again?" All the wonderful memories with her dad came rushing back. This evening just kept getting better and better.

"No. I couldn't quite justify that, but I know some of the right people."

"I can't believe I'm about to drive this beauty on this track."

"Me first," Stephen said.

"Right, right. Of course." As he worked through the lower gears, she sat back, getting a feel for the track, impatiently waiting for him to open it up.

Then he did and she laughed again as the engine responded, the vibrations coming up through her feet on the floorboards, surrounding her in a delicious sensation. He leaned into the corners, weaved back and forth on the straightaways, testing the Camaro's responses. Then he opened it all the way for a few exhilarating laps.

As he slowed down, she nearly begged him for one more lap before she remembered it was her turn to drive. Her palms went damp when he stopped at the start/finish line, and she swiped them across her shorts. Releasing her seat belt, she scrambled out of the car.

The moment the car stopped she raced around the hood, reaching the driver's door before he was all the way clear. She skidded to a stop before colliding with him and instantly regretted it, imagining what those strong hands would feel like on her.

"Eager?"

"You have no idea," she admitted. Stephen had her fired up more than the car. She didn't bother trying to contain her excitement. At one time she and her dad had dreamed of her doing the driving, racing her way up through the ranks from tracks like this one to bigger venues.

"Promise me one thing." He stopped her with a light touch at her elbow.

Her skin warmed all over under his touch and the intensity in his hazel eyes sent an extra spark through her system. One question answered. "I'll be careful." He had to know she would never do anything stupid with someone else's car. Or with him.

"That's not it."

"Then what?" Impatient, she rocked up on her toes and back again.

"Give me time to buckle in before you hit the gas?"

She laughed, the only outlet for so much excitement. "I promise." His hand slipped away. "You'd better be quick about it."

Kenzie adjusted the seat and took a few calming breaths before she placed her hands on the wheel. When they were both ready, she familiarized herself with the clutch, shifting and accelerating and then slowing and downshifting, as Stephen had done when they started out.

"This is smooth as glass everywhere but second to third."

"Just drive," he muttered.

She spared him a long glance as she came up on the start/finish line again. "You ready?"

"Eyes on the road," he said.

"Yeah, the traffic is awful out here." She goosed the gas, watching his face.

"Kenzie."

"No worries," she assured him. "I've got it under control." Thanks to her dad, driving was as natural to her as walking or breathing.

Stephen made a noise loaded with skepticism.

She accelerated on the next lap, familiar now with

the track surface, the car's responses. "This track is in great condition," she said.

"Better to maintain it than let it rot and then have to rebuild if they decide to open it again," he replied.

"True." She pushed the speedometer past eighty. "Re-opening here would be amazing."

She knew better than to push a new engine too hard too soon, and she behaved herself, though the motor would have given her more. At just over ninety miles per hour, the rush was incredible. The Camaro hugged the turns and prowled over the front and back straight-aways. It was almost as much fun as watching her dad win races when she'd been a kid.

"You've got skills," Stephen said. His voice was full of clear admiration and far more relaxed than it had been on the short drive to dinner.

"Thanks." She shifted through another turn. "If only I'd been a boy I might've done more racing."

"Girls can drive," Stephen pointed out.

She grinned when she wanted to melt into a wistful puddle. For a quiet guy, he had a knack for knowing just what to say. "Fifteen years ago, without Dad in my corner, it was an uphill battle I wasn't ready for. There were too many other details to handle."

She took the next lap slower, and when she finally rolled to a stop, the melancholy of missing her father had her heart in a crushing grip.

"Need a minute?" He rested his hand on the back of the seat and his thumb brushed lightly across her shoulder. "Or another lap?" he teased.

Shaking off the unexpected sadness, she climbed out of the car before she begged him to hold her and gulped in the evening air mingling with the heat of the car.

"Thanks, Stephen," she said brightly, when she trusted her voice again. "That was a blast." It was good to make new memories in an old, familiar place. Careful to keep her distance so she wouldn't do something dumb like hug him, she moved back to the passenger side.

"You're welcome." His eyebrows were flexed in a thoughtful frown as he resumed his place behind the wheel.

They'd topped off the gas tank and were back on the highway when he finally spoke. "You decided not to race cars, but you followed his footsteps and became a firefighter?"

"That was also a bit of an uphill battle," she said. "Though there was more support in place. The gender bias decreases every year." It would be nice if someday she and other female firefighters wouldn't have to cope with people who shared Murtagh's outdated views.

"Racing is really how I got interested in firefighting," she continued. "Dad was an inspiration, of course. Watching the safety crews and the pit crews in action really convinced me," she added, thinking of the time when her father's engine had roared to life and promptly exploded into a ball of flame.

Inexplicably content, she watched the evening light fade to dusky blue velvet over the river as they returned to the city. Summer twilight always left her nostalgic for dirt racetracks with her father and camping trips with the family.

"Thanks for a great time," she said, when he'd parked the Camaro back inside the bay so he could make the adjustments to the clutch. She knew it hadn't been a date, though it had been one of the best evenings she'd had in recent memory. She stretched her arms overhead, wishing it could last just a little longer. Still, rejuvenated and relaxed, her body thrumming from the car and the man, she walked over to the bay where her car waited.

Beside the classic muscle car, her disassembled compact looked more pitiful than ever. If only she could buy the loaner car from him, she'd tell him to scrap the weary car for parts, assuming there was anything of value left in it. Murtagh's mottled face flashed into her mind and she fought back a wave of resentment over his frivolous lawsuit. Refusing to let trouble creep in and spoil her mood, she started toward the camper.

"Kenzie, hang on."

She suppressed the little shiver that went through her at the sound of his low voice as she turned back toward him.

"I like the way you drive and the way you listened to the car. If—" His cell phone rang, cutting him off. "Hold that thought," he said, before he answered.

She knew something was wrong when what she'd come to consider his normal scowl deepened into a troubled expression, shadowing his hazel eyes. Concerned, she took a step closer to him.

"She's fine," Stephen said to the caller. "Yes, I'm *sure*. I'm looking right at her." Another pause. "Consider it done." He ended the call and tucked his phone into his back pocket.

"That was Grant," he said, as he moved to lower the door on the open bay, closing them in the privacy of the shop.

"What happened?"

"Someone vandalized a car in the Escape Club parking lot. The customer was naturally upset and called the cops."

"Good," she interjected. "Was there more?" she prompted, when he didn't move or explain anything else about the call. "Was he phoning for a tow truck?"

Stephen ran his hand through his hair, mussing it, and her fingers twitched as if she had a right to smooth it back into place. She forced her eyes away from the way his T-shirt rode the flex of his biceps.

"Yes, they needed a tow truck, but Grant called someone else." Stephen's gaze locked with hers and a chill slid down her spine.

There was more. "Just say it."

"The vandalized car is nearly identical to your loaner."

Her knees wanted to buckle, though she refused to show it. Her stomach twisted. "Murtagh."

Stephen's chin jerked in a brief nod. "Grant's thinking the same thing. He wants you and me to stay alert."

She shuddered at the idea of Murtagh following her and watching her so closely. No amount of willpower or resolve could restrain her reaction. Stephen reached out and rubbed the goose bumps from her bare arms.

"What if…?" She stopped herself a half second too late. All the ways Murtagh could hurt someone, thinking he was getting even with her, flashed through her mind in a blur. As a first responder, she'd seen plenty of the mishaps, accidents and deliberate injuries people suffered. She covered her mouth with a hand, trying to regain her composure. Stephen didn't need her going to pieces.

"No one got hurt," he said. "Grant says it was only property damage."

Kenzie stepped back from him and tucked her hands into her back pockets before she could give in and lean into all his quiet strength. "No witnesses?"

"He didn't mention anyone coming forward. You can ask him next time you're over there. But you won't be going to and from the club alone."

"Stephen, you have a business to run. You can't trail after me everywhere I go." That kind of hovering would give Murtagh's threats too much validity and erode what was left of her confidence. Where was her spine? What had happened to the courage and defiance that had gotten her over every other hurdle life dropped in her path?

"Fine." He leaned back against a workbench. "You can take a different car every time you leave."

"Stop." She waved off the offer. "The vandalism at the club might very well be a complete coincidence. You know the loaner is a fairly common model."

He rolled his eyes and folded his arms over his chest. "Right. Grant Sullivan is known for jumping to outrageous conclusions."

Her temper spiked and she swallowed the rude retort on the tip of her tongue. Stephen wasn't the problem. He was only trying to help. "That's not it. I don't want to be more of an imposition. The depositions don't even start for another week," she managed. She glanced again at the heap of parts that were once a car. "I'll take care of that between my shifts at the club this week and find a different place to stay. You don't need my drama in here."

"This is the safest place for you and you know it."

True. "Hotels have security," she pointed out.

"For a price," he shot back.

Frustrated, she wanted to kick something. There had to be some way to get control of the mess that was her life. *Temporary mess.*

"I could take care of your car in my sleep. Let me."

"No." She couldn't handle more of his kindness right now. "It's my responsibility. Let me know what else you need me to do around here in trade for the time and space. Something more than the phone."

"Fine." His gaze narrowed.

He didn't sound all that fine about it. "Thank you," she whispered, through the tangle of emotions. Anger at Murtagh, gratitude for Stephen's unflagging generosity and concern for some unknown person who'd been caught in the crossfire of her troubles twisted her up inside.

"Your car, your repair," Stephen said. "But you're staying in the trailer. That part isn't up for further discussion."

"Okay." She turned away and headed to the camper. If she stuck around, she'd start crying. Stephen did *not* need that.

It had been such a wonderful day with the Galway family, topped with the treat of her first time taking real laps on the same track where she and her dad had enjoyed themselves all those summers ago. Did Murtagh's actions have to poison everything? For the first time she gave serious consideration to leaving town against legal advice. It might be worth risking the "appearance of guilt" to get away for a few days.

Her nose stung and for a split second tears blurred her vision. Give up Philly and her place in it because some whiny jerk didn't like the way she'd saved his life?

No. She yanked open the camper door and turned on the lights. She would *not* give Murtagh that kind of power over her life. Although he might take her career, he couldn't have a single one of the intangibles that made her the Kenzie Hughes her family and coworkers respected.

"Kenzie?"

She glanced over her shoulder to find Stephen watching her from the corner of the building. Was a man supposed to look that sexy with a scowl on his face? Studying him, she realized she couldn't just leave. Not after Grant had asked her to keep an eye on Stephen. She'd given him her word and she took that type of promise seriously. Besides, it would be so much better to think of something other than her problems.

"More trouble?" she asked, coming back down the steps. Why couldn't Murtagh be satisfied wrecking her career with the lawsuit? Petty behavior like vandalism didn't make any sense to her.

"No." Stephen crossed to her with a few ground-eating strides and the light from the camper window washed over his face, revealing the depth of concern in his gaze. "You're safe here behind this fence, with me. I promise."

Standing on the bottom step, she was eye level with him. His words smoothed over all her prickling nerves. She almost gave him those same words back, except her protecting him wasn't supposed to be obvious.

He looked so earnest, so determined to tolerate her invasion of his space until everything in her world was back to normal. "I appreciate that." Knowing how much he preferred his solitude, she felt the gesture unravel something within her.

Leaning forward, Kenzie brushed her lips to his cheek. A light, friendly, platonic gesture was all she intended. Instead, he caught her as if he thought she'd lost her balance, his hands hot on her waist. Then his lips touched hers. By accident or design, the spark of contact set her body humming. She braced her hands on his strong shoulders, wanting to sink a little deeper, explore his taste as his masculine scent and the summer night enveloped her.

It would be reckless to fall into that sweet fantasy. She eased back, forced her hands to come along with the rest of her. "Thanks again, for everything today." She darted into the camper on quivering legs.

Whoa. That had been an eye-opener.

She moved away from the door and clapped a hand over her mouth before the nervous laughter bubbling up could burst free. Her lips felt as though she'd tasted something too spicy. She'd had plenty of real dates in the past that didn't end with a kiss as enticing as that one. There was some *serious* heat simmering under all that calm, cool and collected that Stephen projected.

Heat that ignited a tantalizing jolt of desire in her bloodstream.

Don't go there, she scolded herself. That kiss had been a happy accident. She had to put it, and all the hot-summer-night fantasies the feel of his lips on hers stirred up, out of her mind. It was the only sane way forward.

Stunned, Stephen felt his feet grow roots, holding him in place as Kenzie disappeared behind the trailer door. She'd kissed him. No. He'd kissed her. Did it matter who'd started it? He licked his lips, catching the faint taste of her strawberry lip gloss. *Strawberry.* That was a surprise.

When his feet were finally ready to cooperate, he turned and walked away from the trailer, if only because he wanted to climb those steps, throw open the door, pull her into his arms and kiss her again.

Not the best move after he'd just told her she was safe with him here on his property. What had he been thinking? He hadn't been thinking at all, obviously, but acting on impulse.

He wasn't supposed to be kissing Kenzie or anyone else. Reality doused him as effectively as a cold shower. His last first kiss had been with Annabeth. Kenzie hadn't meant anything romantic by the gesture. She'd aimed for his cheek and something inexplicable had him taking advantage of the moment.

Back in the office, he closed the door but didn't lock it, just in case she needed something in the night. His conscience demanded to know what he thought she might need. Did he expect her to run in and ask him to comfort her after a nightmare? Yeah, that would happen. Maybe she would need shelter from an intruder? Not a chance. His security system would alert him long before a trespasser could cause any trouble.

He glared at the dead bolt and couldn't make himself turn it to lock her out.

For the first time he thought maybe his mom and sisters had a point about him needing to dive back into the dating pool. Unfortunately, that didn't feel right, either.

Kissing Kenzie was proof he wasn't ready. He'd chosen the wrong response to a friendly gesture and now he was overreacting and overanalyzing the mistake. He could only imagine the blunders he would make on a real date.

So why was he still reliving those few seconds of her lips on his as if he'd never been kissed before?

"Man up," he muttered, double-checking the status of the security system at the desk.

She's a friend of the family, he reminded himself as he changed into a T-shirt and gym shorts for the night. She might as well be another little sister. As if the two sisters he had weren't enough to worry over on any given day. When he added in the two sisters-in-law, even he could see the last thing he needed was another woman in that category.

Yet thinking of Kenzie in any other type of relationship held far more risk. He wasn't ready to date, wasn't looking for a receptionist or even a tenant for the trailer. Draping a sheet over the couch, he squeezed the pillow between his hands, trying to wedge Kenzie into the sister category.

She just wouldn't go.

Maybe it was the big blue eyes or the soft lips or that ironclad willpower that kept her going forward no matter what bombshells life dropped on her. Stretched out on the couch in the darkness, he could admit part of his attraction to her might be tied to the way she'd handled the Camaro on that track. The woman could *drive*. Her delighted grin had been infectious and the way her small hands worked the gearshift and steering wheel slid right under his defenses.

He caught himself rubbing his shoulder where her hands had touched him, and punched the pillow under his head. Dwelling on any aspect of her as a woman was the wrong thing to do. He should be working on regaining some sense and perspective.

Logically, he knew she wasn't over there in the trailer savoring the feel of that kiss the way he was. She was probably annoyed—and rightfully so—that he'd taken advantage of the moment. Then why did the taste of her hold him with such an unbreakable grip?

Because he never planned to leave himself open to that kind of longing and need again.

His mother had tried a couple times to set him up with someone new. That last attempt had been a miserable night, he recalled, with some regret for the woman involved. He suspected his mom frequently sent single women and their car troubles his way, with her fingers crossed that one of them would break through the grief that kept him locked up in his work.

Her well-meaning attempts to see him happy again only made him feel more broken inside, drifting further beyond repair.

Desperate for sleep, he forced his mind back to what he'd felt and heard while test-driving the Camaro. He wasn't satisfied with the clutch performance from second to third. He suspected the most likely root of the problem and would tweak it tomorrow. Any other concerns and solutions evaporated as the memory of Kenzie's dazzling happiness when she took the wheel played across his closed eyelids.

Letting her stay here was a mistake, yet he was committed now. Instead of taking her to Sunday dinner and kissing her, he should have been asking why she didn't have a boyfriend helping her out. He'd sat up and reached for his phone to text Mitch and ask about Kenzie's personal life when he realized there was no good way for his brother to interpret that kind of question.

She didn't strike him as a woman who would let him steal a kiss while she was in a relationship with someone else. Kenzie radiated integrity and loyalty.

No. Just like everything else lately, he'd have to deal

with his hang-ups on his own. Mitch worried about him enough already. No sense giving his brother more cause to come around and pester him. He was being an idiot, and he'd given Kenzie his word that she could stay. If she felt inclined to answer the business phone and repair her car by herself, he should shut up and let her.

Attempting to get comfortable in his makeshift bed again, he closed his eyes and kept them closed until he fell asleep.

All too soon, sunlight through the window brought him awake and he dragged himself to the shower to face Monday. If he was working, with the music amped up and power tools running, maybe she wouldn't bother asking him what he'd meant by kissing her. He could hope. And if he was working he'd be too preoccupied to do something dumb and try to kiss her again.

Thankfully, when Kenzie walked into the garage with her coffee and an easygoing smile, she didn't seem annoyed or inclined to hold that kiss against him. She didn't seem inclined to chat, either. He noticed the dark smudges under her eyes, but kept his concern to himself as she pulled coveralls over her tank top and shorts. After lacing up her steel-toed boots, she started in on her pitiful junker, pausing whenever the phone rang.

Over the next several days they fell into a surprisingly comfortable routine. In the mornings they worked side by side. He found and fixed the clutch issue on the Camaro and sent it off for the interior and exterior work, returning to the more typical maintenance tasks. Kenzie booked service appointments, searched for and ordered parts, did an inventory on a whim and fielded calls for the tow truck, as well as potential restoration clients.

He stayed away from the community center, telling

himself the neighborhood would survive his absence for a few more days. Without a good reason for leaving, he couldn't take the chance she would discover his unpredictable and unpleasant hobby. Instead he worked late or researched cars he might want to restore. Although he was tempted to do his drive-bys while Kenzie was working at the club, he resisted the urge. Security system or not, he didn't want Kenzie coming home from a shift to find the garage empty.

When she wasn't scheduled early at the Escape Club, she ordered lunch and they would sit down in the office and eat together before she headed to her evening shifts. Although Kenzie's sunny demeanor was usually at odds with his perpetual solitude, he found himself enjoying those conversations more than he anticipated. She loved sharing stories about working on cars with her dad, and she never lectured him about his lacking social life. He eventually realized she was deftly avoiding the topic of anything related to Murtagh or the lawsuit, and Stephen found himself happy he could help her, even if it was only to serve as a small distraction.

Happy in any capacity wasn't something he'd ever expected to feel again.

Though she was eager to return the loaner, he'd convinced her not to stop with a new fuel system, but to go ahead and take care of the long list of potential troubles with her car. During her shifts at the club, Stephen hustled to get the parts she would need into his storeroom, for her to find at the right time.

She had excellent skills as a mechanic, and if he needed extra hands around the shop, she would have been at the top of his new-hire list. He told himself it wasn't just because it was pure pleasure watching her peel off the

oversize coveralls whenever she had to leave. Though he
tried, he couldn't kick that fascination of her long-limbed
body out of his head, not even when he reminded himself Kenzie needed a friend more than a pseudo boss hit-
ting on her.

Between the GPS tracker on the loaner car and the
constant communication between him and Grant and
Jason, Stephen didn't feel the need to tail her to and from
the club or blow up her phone with check-in requests.
If Kenzie had any idea how many text messages were
exchanged regarding her safety on any given day she'd
be furious with all of them.

It wasn't that they didn't believe in her ability to hold
her own, but rather a general unease about the guy suing
her. They hadn't heard anything out of him after the car
had been vandalized at the club, and though the security cameras hadn't offered a conclusive ID, everyone
assumed the vandal had been Murtagh.

As Stephen finished up an oil change service for Mr.
Cartwright, a faithful customer from the neighborhood,
he was waiting for the phone to ring with a Kenzie update. She'd put in two hours at the shop before her mid-
morning appointment with her lawyer. Apparently he
wanted to give her an update on the deposition process
and schedule. After that she was supposed to go straight
to the Escape Club for a double shift.

"That's a sorry excuse for a man right there," Mr.
Cartwright said from his typical waiting place, near the
doorway between the shop and the office.

Stephen glanced up from the tire pressure gauge.
"What's that?"

"Old" Mr. Cartwright had lived in the neighborhood,
a block down from his parents' place, for as long as

Stephen could remember. His hair had gone white and wispy and his shoulders were stooped, but his mind was sharp as ever. One of Stephen's first customers, he brought his car in for maintenance every three months like clockwork, had a cup of coffee and shared his opinion on everything from the weather to global politics. With a wry chuckle, he always claimed waiting while Stephen tended to the car got him out of his wife's hair and saved their marriage.

He raised his paper coffee cup toward the television Stephen had installed in the small customer waiting area he'd carved out of the office space when he'd bought the place. "That man is alive and walking around thanks to the Hughes girl. He should be on his knees thanking her, not suing her."

That brought Stephen to his feet and he hurried over to the television. The cameraman chose that moment for a close-up shot of Randall Murtagh's red-cheeked face, while a ticker at the bottom of the screen ran a summary of how he'd come to file a civil suit against Kenzie.

Stephen couldn't hear anything Murtagh said because Mr. Cartwright had hit his stride, rattling off a litany of opinions about trial-happy lawyers, community heroes and bitter old men until at last the interview was over. As soon as he had a break, Stephen meant to ask Julia why Murtagh's legal team allowed him to do public interviews before the case even got rolling.

His concentration fractured, he turned to the checklist posted on the wall to help him tick through the last details of Mr. Cartwright's service. He sent the older man on his way with a hearty handshake.

Alone in the garage, Stephen sent Grant a text message as a heads-up. He didn't want Kenzie getting blindsided by this while she was on shift. She was popular among the club staff and probably equally liked by regular customers. He knew someone would mention it to her.

With time to spare before his next appointment, he closed the driveway gate and retreated to the office to search the web for a replay of the interview. He decided it was a good thing Mr. Cartwright had talked throughout the interview because Stephen wouldn't have been able to control his language.

The accusations and outrageous claims Murtagh aimed at Kenzie and the PFD had to qualify as slander. Someone needed to give the jerk a serious wakeup call. As Mr. Cartwright said, the man was alive and well when he might just as easily have been dead.

Stephen groaned when the interview showed pictures of the man's burns. He wouldn't presume to judge another man's pain, but those burns were mild enough that they had to be completely healed by now.

"Vindictive bastard, aren't you?" he said to the monitor when the interview finished.

Stephen pushed back from the desk as a familiar wave of helplessness surged through him. Other than quiz Julia or send a sympathetic text message to Kenzie, he couldn't do a damn thing for her. His temper reared up and he slammed his palms into the metal file cabinet, rocking it back against the wall. With an oath, he stalked out to the shop to find a better release valve before he did something irreparable in the office.

Mad as hell on her behalf, he cranked up the music as he debated his options. He could cruise by the community center, for all the good that would do around noon on a weekday. It was much easier to strike back at those useless drug dealers from the shadows, though reporting a few drug deals wouldn't help Kenzie. He sent a text to Mitch asking what the PFD was doing to protect Kenzie and their own reputation. No telling when his brother would have time in his shift to reply.

Stephen picked up a wrench, spinning it repeatedly in his hand, desperate for some kind of action. There had to be something to bleed off this pent-up frustration. He'd failed Annabeth. He wouldn't fail Kenzie, too. Staring at her car, he decided to start with that.

She might get pissed off when she discovered he'd taken over the project. Too bad. This wasn't about charity or generosity. The sooner this car was up and running, the sooner she could sell the thing and churn the profit into a better car. Assuming he could convince her that was her smartest option.

Decided, he set to work before his next maintenance appointment arrived.

Chapter 5

Kenzie left her lawyer's office feeling less than optimistic about the civil suit. The son of a firefighter, Paul Corrigan had been recommended by the PFD. She liked him well enough. He was young and smart and he was willing to roll up his sleeves and get creative. More than all that combined, he wasn't afraid to go up against the notorious Marburg law firm.

Paul had laid out what they had so far and what he expected Murtagh to do during the depositions next week. He was on the verge of explaining his plan to counter those moves when his assistant had interrupted them with the interview disaster. All of it echoed through her mind as she drove toward the pier for her shift at the Escape Club.

"She was too small for the task," Murtagh had said as the studio flashed her academy picture beside a picture of his burned leg. "And I'm not even a big man."

Big baby was more like it, she thought darkly, gripping the steering wheel while she waited for a traffic light to change. When Murtagh had first filed his complaint, she'd told everyone up the PFD chain of command how he'd fought her attempts to get him out safely. He'd argued with her long enough that the fire cut off the first clear escape route, putting them both at more risk.

Still, she'd amended her original plan and managed to get him clear of the blaze before the second floor dropped on top of them. The body-cam footage from a police officer on the scene proved Murtagh had walked to the ambulance on his own power. Of course, as the paramedics tried to treat him, he'd shoved away the oxygen mask so he could complain more loudly about her ineptitude. At the time, she'd chalked up his nonsense to smoke inhalation, and rejoined her crew as they put out the fire.

Both the PFD and her lawyer had statements from the police officer and paramedics and a few bystanders willing to step up in her defense. Those statements had been enough to ward off any disciplinary action against her on the original complaint, but Murtagh had kept on gunning for her.

Though Paul wasn't happy about it, he'd reminded her that Murtagh was getting this outrageous free publicity only because he'd given twenty years to the PFD. He served as his own expert and the media couldn't resist his controversial agenda to limit women in the PFD to desk roles.

Murtagh spouted off as if the women who had fought fires on the front lines as far back as the 1800s had never existed. Good grief, the academy—the same academy they had both attended—had pictures of women who'd stepped up as firefighters while most of the men in the area were serving overseas during World War II. Why wasn't anyone in the media asking his opinion on those women?

By the time she reached the club and parked in the spot near the kitchen at Grant's insistence Kenzie was furious all over again. She sat there trying to breathe through the temper and worry, to push all this to the back of her mind so she could be pleasant for the long hours ahead. Given a few minutes, she'd be able to smile again. Just as soon as she found something better to think about.

The feel of Stephen's lips against hers popped back to the front of her mind and she couldn't help reliving that sweet, tender moment. Not even that kiss was a straightforward happy thought to carry with her tonight. Not when she factored in his reaction. As eager as she'd been to see where something more personal might lead, it had been clear the following morning that Stephen wanted to pretend it hadn't happened.

Which was okay. His reaction was better than okay; it was the smart approach. Angling for a conversation about a kiss would have made her look needier than she felt already. Forgetting that kiss was for the best. She didn't need any more complications in her life right now, especially the sort that came in the form of a handsome, lean mechanic with a sexy scowl.

Getting nowhere, Kenzie left the car and walked in the back door of the club, nearly plowing into Grant, who was on his way outside.

"I was just coming to check on you," he said, with his easygoing smile.

Knowing his history, she wondered if he ever had to

practice the calm, confident expression. Probably not. Grant maintained a pragmatic outlook when it came to adversity, and made a point of always looking ahead and moving forward.

"Here I am," she said. "Who's onstage tonight?"

He ignored her question. "You doing okay?"

"Sure." Though she tried to give him a warm smile, it felt stiff and awkward on her face.

"That's not your best look." Grant exaggerated the move as he leaned back. "Walk with me a minute," he said, turning her around. "If I let you clock in now, you'll scare off everyone inside."

"Your employees are tougher than that," she said, deliberately misinterpreting him.

He held open the door she'd just come through. "My employees need to have something to do and customers to serve, or the club is just another empty warehouse again."

"We don't want that," she said. Though it came out with an edge of sarcasm, she'd meant it sincerely. The Escape Club made a difference for customers, staff and the people who came by seeking "Alexander" to help them through various sticky situations.

She walked alongside Grant toward the river, the breeze teasing a few strands of hair from the twin French braids she'd woven it into this morning for the long day.

"I wanted to say thanks," Grant said.

Kenzie was lost. "For what?"

"Keeping Stephen out of trouble," he told her. "He hasn't been spotted near the community center in almost a week. Whatever you're doing, keep it up."

All she'd done was fill his schedule from open to close and keep him talking about cars. "I haven't done anything special." If Stephen had wanted to go out, he'd certainly had ample opportunity during her shifts here at the club. It made her wonder why he wasn't taking advantage of those hours.

"Well, keep it up anyway," Grant repeated, pulling her attention back to the conversation. "The narcotics unit is having an easier time without him in the way."

"Good to know." She suspected that if they cleaned up the area, he'd give up his dangerous hobby and everyone would be happier.

Grant turned away from the river to face her. "Now, let's go over the television interview this morning."

She didn't bother trying to smile. "I was with my lawyer," she replied. "He said he was heading to the courthouse to ask the judge for a gag order."

"I'm glad to hear that. This civil suit is the definition of frivolous."

"If only the judge agreed with you," she muttered, watching a tour boat chugging upriver. That recurring urge to leave town rose up again and she punted it away. She was sticking it out right here, for Stephen as well as for her case. "Paul keeps telling me these cases usually settle and often turn one way or the other on the smallest detail."

She just wasn't sure it would turn her way.

"Sounds right," Grant agreed. "I was given the option of filing a civil suit against the man who shot me."

She'd never heard that part of his story. "But you didn't, did you?"

"No." Grant sighed. "What was the point?" He shrugged. "Wasn't like a billionaire shot me," he quipped. "My expenses were covered and I wanted to find a new place to fit in. Felt like if I'd had to tell that story one more time I'd lose my mind."

She could sympathize with that. Unless Murtagh dropped the suit she was doomed to relay the events of the rescue a few more times, until the case was settled. "Stephen's bruised ribs are healing," she said, in an obvious change of topic. "He's moving better around the shop."

"Good." Grant's gaze followed the boat, as well. "I saw the Mustang Jason bought. If I have to invest in a car restoration to keep that boy in his garage, I'll do it. Just say the word and I'll convince my wife it's a midlife crisis."

Kenzie laughed, the sound accompanied by a grin that felt completely natural this time. "You're such a soft touch, Sullivan."

"You think so?" He arched his salt-and-pepper eyebrows. "Don't tell anyone."

She raised her hand as if taking an oath. "If news gets out, it didn't come from me."

They returned to the club and she felt remarkably lighter as she tied her apron and headed onto the floor to take care of customers. Although Grant didn't have live music lined up for this time of day, they were doing steady business, which kept her mind away from her troubles.

She was ready for her break when the first of the two bands on the schedule arrived for their setup. Carrying two sandwich platters to the end of the bar, she encouraged Jason to take a break with her and fuel up for what was sure to be a packed house tonight.

"How's the Mustang running for you?" she asked.

"It purrs," he said, a glint of pride in his eye. "Best investment I've made in a long time. I love it."

"Mitch and Stephen do great work."

"And Mitch drives a hard deal," he agreed with a distracted smile.

She was curious what kind of a deal he'd worked with Mitch. She didn't want to snoop into Galway business, but wanted an opening to ask how Jason had come up with the money for such an exclusive car.

The female vocalist did a mic check and Jason watched her, mesmerized.

Kenzie glanced over her shoulder to the stage and then back to him. "You know her?"

"We've met once or twice," he said.

A story there, she thought, though she didn't pry. When Jason dragged his attention back to his food, she pulled up her courage and asked another question she'd been wrestling with recently. "Why did you move to the academy so early?"

"It was a chance to advance," he replied. "Not an easy choice, but the right one at the time."

"What made you decide to give it up to work for Grant full-time?"

"I still teach classes at the academy," Jason answered.

"You do?" Of course, she wouldn't have that sort of career option. If Murtagh won his case the PFD wouldn't risk taking her back in any capacity.

"You're a great firefighter, Kenzie," he said. "And I believe the civil suit will go your way. That said, there are plenty of other career options for you within the department and outside it. It's comes down to whether or not you *want* to look at them."

The only viable option she could see was at Stephen's

garage. Becoming a receptionist/mechanic didn't feel like a new career as much as it felt like hiding. And that was completely discounting Stephen's preference to keep his business limited most days to a one-man operation.

"Right now, I only want to get back to life as it was and forget Murtagh ever existed," she admitted, keeping her voice low.

Jason took a long drink of water, then reached over the bar to refill his glass. "That's understandable." His gaze drifted back to the stage and the petite vocalist with the dark, glossy hair gathered high on her head in a messy knot. "You have a good sense of self, Kenzie. If there comes a time when you need to make a change, you'll recognize it and it will feel right."

His sandwich half-eaten, he picked up his dishes and left the bar.

She finished her meal quickly. Yes, she had options. Firefighting wasn't her only career path, just the one that fitted her best. Despite the support from so many people, she didn't feel entirely whole during these days away from the firehouse. It wasn't all about missing the action of riding out to calls to the shrill music of the sirens. Her team was her family and she missed the camaraderie and unified purpose they shared.

Jason claimed she knew herself, but she wasn't so sure. Did she even have a purpose away from the PFD? The question drifted through her mind as the Escape Club filled with summer concert patrons. Soon she was too busy to think about the myriad what-ifs if the case went against her. The atmosphere was fantastic, with the music flowing over a teeming dance floor. The general lighthearted happiness was a wonderful balm after her stressful morning. And tomorrow, she worked only the night shift, so she'd be able to be at the garage all day.

Her mind on the progress she could make on her own car while enjoying the tantalizing views of Stephen working nearby, she was slow to recognize the middle-aged man standing at a high-top table at the end of her section.

She dutifully stopped to greet him as she would any other customer.

Randall Murtagh's eyes were mean as his gaze raked over her from head to toe. "This is where you belong," he said. He wore a Hawaiian shirt splattered with obnoxious orange flowers, and loose cargo shorts that left the fresh scars from his burn visible on his calf. A complete departure from the understated charcoal suit he'd donned for his interview.

She held her body stiff when she wanted to squirm out of his view. She would not let him see her flinch or cower. "Welcome to the Escape Club," she repeated, determined to maintain her professionalism here as she had in the fire. "Would you like to hear the drink specials?"

Maybe if he had a drink or two, Grant could make sure he got pulled over once he left the club. Although if that happened, Murtagh would probably file harassment charges and pile that on to her civil suit somehow. Well, even the brief fantasy had been a nice respite.

He sneered at her. "I'll have a citywide special. Your treat, right, *honey*?"

"I'm sorry. According to club policy I can't treat you to anything but a glass of water, sir. Would you prefer water?"

"Sir." He gave a humorless chuckle and his beady

eyes lit up in his fleshy face. "That sounds *good* coming out of your pretty mouth."

Kenzie barely suppressed a shiver. The way he'd said that, with his eyes on her mouth, creeped her out. She wanted to kick him and worse. It took every ounce of willpower to assure him she'd return momentarily with his order.

She managed not to break into a panicked run as she arrowed to the service end of the bar, prepared to report the situation to Grant. He was up onstage with the band. No problem. Jason could lend her a bouncer to escort her through her section until Murtagh got bored and left. She didn't want him tossed out; that would give him too much power. No, she just wanted someone to hang close so the man couldn't do anything other than toss insults at her. Although, if she asked for help, wasn't she proving Murtagh's point that she couldn't even handle a tough job as a waitress?

Logically, she knew that was baloney. Teamwork made everything work, from a busy nightclub to a three-alarm fire. He hadn't done anything more obnoxious than be himself, and if he was in here bugging her, he wasn't outside vandalizing someone's car. To cover her bases, she sent her lawyer a text message about the situation while she waited for Jason to give her the beer and shot Murtagh had ordered.

"Slow at the waitressing, too, I see," he said with a sneer when she returned.

Kenzie smiled and gave the man his drinks. "Would you like me to start a tab for you?"

"Not on my dime." He raised the shot of whiskey. "Let's consider this a good-faith marker for what you owe me."

There was no sense repeating the club policy on staff buying drinks for customers. Murtagh probably thought he could get her fired from this job, too. She started a tab, noting that the customer did not give her a credit card. Documentation would give Jason or Grant room to work if he became more belligerent or tried to leave without paying. "I'll need a credit card or permission from my manager, sir, before your second round," she said, with as much sweetness and light as she could squeeze into her voice.

Moving along, she worked through the rest of her section, clearing empties and taking new orders. As she passed him again, Murtagh caught her in a bruising grip, his hand a painful hook at her elbow. "You need to release me right now, Mr. Murtagh."

Kenzie noticed heads turning as customers nearby sensed trouble.

He jerked her back, hard enough to make her wince. "Can't you take the heat, tough girl?"

That he'd made her wince had her temper leaping into high gear. She refused to give him further satisfaction by struggling. "This is the age of cell phones," she said with a tight smile. "If you make a scene, you undermine that woeful victim image you had going on TV this morning. Your legal team won't like that."

His fingertips dug into her skin before he let her go with a little shove. She caught her balance and walked away as quickly as possible. She gave brief reassurances to the few people who asked if she was all right. It wasn't easy to pretend the incident was nothing, but she managed. On her way back to the bar, she gave herself a mental pat on the back for not needing any help to put Murtagh in his place.

Her hands shook as she filled her tray.

Naturally, Jason noticed. "You okay?"

"I'm good." She took a deep breath, smoothing back a few strands of hair that had worked free of her braids. "You know jerks happen occasionally."

"Where?" Jason's gaze roamed through her section. She assumed spotting Murtagh was what made him swear. "How the hell did he get in?"

She shrugged. "Let him have his delusions of importance," she said. "It's not as if he can do anything to me here." Her arm would be bruised by morning, but that would be a problem for later.

"Grant would want him out of here," Jason said.

"Then tell him once he's done. It's not worth interrupting his set." She checked the orders on her tray. "He's claiming I'm buying his drinks. I've only served one round and I'll probably need some help with that issue before he leaves."

"You got it," Jason promised.

"Thanks." Coaching herself to keep calm, she picked up her tray and turned, coming face-to-face with Stephen.

She absorbed the view of him, let it ease the rough edges seeing Murtagh had caused. In dark khaki shorts and a pale blue untucked oxford shirt with the sleeves rolled back to his elbows Stephen was as tempting to her now as he was in his grease-stained work-clothes at the garage. She could tell he'd been running his hands through his hair and she almost reached up to smooth it into place.

"Hi," he said. His mouth tilted up at one side, as if his lips weren't sure about giving her a full smile or not.

"Hi." That half smile was nearly as sexy as the scowl she'd come to expect on his face. What was wrong with her?

His eyebrows dipped as he studied her face. "You're pale."

She rolled her eyes. "It's just bad lighting."

He stepped aside to let her pass. "Something happened."

"Nothing new," she replied. It wasn't exactly a lie. Murtagh had been a persistent problem in her life since the day she'd rescued him. "I wasn't expecting you," she added brightly, in an attempt to shift his focus. "How was your day?"

"Great." That underused, subtle smile made another appearance. "Which section are you in tonight?"

"I'm way out tonight," she answered. "This is a much better spot for you to enjoy the band." From this vantage point she almost couldn't see Murtagh's balding head. If Stephen sat down, he wouldn't see Murtagh, either. "I'll be back in a few minutes."

She didn't wait for a reply, eager to get the drinks delivered and get back to Stephen before this first band of the night finished. During the break there would be a flurry of people settling tabs, leaving, and new customers coming in. With luck, Murtagh would be one of them and she could enjoy the rest of her night in peace.

She purposely went the long way through her section. Deftly avoiding a difficult customer was part of doing the job well, by preventing trouble-causing opportunities. By the time she approached Murtagh, she had only a tray full of empty glassware and bottles. Pausing, she gave him the smile she saved for surly drunks. "Do you need another round, sir?" she asked, pitching her voice so he could hear her over the band.

"As long as you're buying, girl."

"That's against Escape Club policy," she reminded him sweetly. Giving him his total for the special, she waited expectantly, her hand open to accept his cash or a credit card.

He grabbed her hand hard enough to have the bones grinding together. "One way or another, you're paying for what you did to me, little girl."

She barely suppressed the reflex to defend herself. A stomp on his instep, a kick to his knee and this would be over. That kind of negative reaction would likely play right into his hands. If she lost her temper, he would twist it to his advantage in the lawsuit.

"We do reserve the right to refuse service," she said. His grip on her hand tightened and the sharp pain brought tears to her eyes. She blinked them away, determined to hold her own. "You should leave, sir."

"If you're so damned capable of handling anything a man can do, *make* me leave." He upended her tray, smashing glassware against her body and sending the empty beer bottles to the floor.

"Allow me," a rumbling voice said from behind her.

She recognized it was Stephen a split second before his fist connected with Murtagh's jaw. The older man staggered back, releasing her hand. She shook it automatically, more concerned with stopping Stephen as he hauled Murtagh upright by his shirt and reared back to punch him again. Kenzie latched on to Stephen, holding him back as the muscles of his arms bunched and flexed, ready to dish out more punishment.

Cell phones were pointed at the scene from every angle and a few customers had pressed closer, protecting her. The expressions on the nearest faces behind Murtagh ranged from morbid curiosity to disgust. She understood the curiosity and hoped the disgust was aimed at Murtagh rather than her. The Escape Club didn't need any drama or bad publicity, and she knew her lawyer wouldn't want to give the Marburg legal team more ammunition.

A bouncer waded into the fray from his station near the door and Grant was coming from the direction of the stage, slicing through the crowd like a freighter through the water. The music skidded to a rough stop.

"Let him go," Kenzie said to Stephen. "Grant's here. He'll handle it."

Stephen stepped back, his hands raised in surrender as Grant and the bouncer took control of Murtagh.

Grant snapped orders for the mess to be cleared and Kenzie immediately got to work, but her left hand wouldn't cooperate. "Not you," Grant said, with far more gentleness than she'd ever heard. "Jason, take names and numbers of witnesses."

"On it, boss," Jason said.

"Galway, get her to the back. Take pictures first, then help her clean up."

Kenzie knelt down once more, ducking under the threats Murtagh was spewing, to pick up broken bottles and glassware. The pieces kept slipping from her grasp. The vocalist said something, a few patrons laughed and then the music flared to life. It all sounded fuzzy around the edges, as if she had cotton in her ears. What was wrong with her?

"Let the others do that," Stephen said, drawing her to her feet. He tucked her against his side, and she cradled her aching hand close to her stomach.

"But…" She noticed a trickle of blood on her arm as

he guided her away from her section. If he didn't step back it was likely to stain his shirt. "Stephen…" Her voice trailed off. He wouldn't let her move away from him. "You should be careful," she murmured.

"I've got you," he said. "Lean on me."

"I'm fine." She willed it to be true. Every time she twitched a finger, pain lanced up through her arm, burning deep in her shoulder. It couldn't be unbearable pain because she was tough. "Do you know why I'm bleeding?"

Stephen swore as Kenzie swayed. Done playing around, he scooped her up and barked at people to clear a path. Though she protested, it was weak, and he didn't set her down until he reached Grant's office.

"Just sit here a second," he said. "Breathe." He took his own advice, struggling against the urge to go take another swipe at Murtagh.

"I'm fine." She stared at him, her blue eyes glassy.

"I know," he replied. "You're doing great."

Someone from the kitchen hurried in with the first aid kit and clean towels.

"Thanks," he said. "Just put it all on the desk."

Kenzie's hand was already starting to bruise. Stephen was pretty sure the jackass had broken a bone or two. Murtagh had at least a hundred pounds on Kenzie and though she was tough as nails, excessive force amplified by temper could do a great deal of damage. He swore.

"Where's your phone?" he asked her when they were alone.

Without a word, she reached for her back left pocket and winced. Stephen carefully extracted the cell phone for her. He snapped pictures with her phone and his, getting close-ups of her hand, as well as the scratches and splinters of glass piercing her skin from her collar-bone to her elbow.

He did his best to keep his cool as a red haze pressed at the edges of his vision. If he ever saw Murtagh again, he wouldn't stop punching. *Later*, he told himself. Anger from any source wouldn't help Kenzie right now.

"Did he drug me?" she asked.

The idea alarmed him, but he kept his voice calm. "I doubt it."

"Then why am I so woozy?"

The question simultaneously worried and amused him. "Probably shock."

She snorted, then hissed as he started cleaning the first wounds on the delicate skin at the base of her throat.

"I can't be in shock," she said.

He supposed she'd know better than he would. "Pain, maybe?"

"No way. I'm tough."

He wished someone else with more experience was here. Some of these wounds looked deep. Surely some-one on Sullivan's staff had more experience with this kind of thing. "You are tough," he agreed heartily. Would she stay tough when he started pulling out the shards of glass? Her arm looked like she'd gone a few rounds with a shattered window. "Maybe it was the sight of blood."

Her nose wrinkled as she peered at her arm. "I'm a firefighter. Blood happens."

"Uh-huh." Stephen knew some people could tolerate the sight of blood as long as it wasn't their own. Was she one of them? "Guess that leaves us with the logical conclusion that you're just a weakling."

"Am not." She tried to smack at him with her good hand and it bounced listlessly off his arm.

"Almost done," he said. "Then we'll go get an X-ray for that." And maybe stitches for the gash over her elbow, he thought, as he removed a chunk of glass and applied pressure to stem the bleeding. "Grant should call an ambulance."

"No."

He didn't think she was in any condition to decide, but he had his hands full at the moment.

Grant walked in and stopped short, the fierce expression softening as he looked at Kenzie. "How's she doing?"

"I'm fine," Kenzie replied.

"She's dazed," Grant said. "Sounds almost drunk."

"Won't argue with that." Stephen cleaned out the deepest of the wounds on her arm. "I think he might have broken her hand."

"I can hear you." Her nose crinkled again. She shifted a bit, sitting up straight. "He caught me by surprise is all."

The last part sounded a little stronger to Stephen. Pride was a powerful thing and Kenzie had plenty of it. He hoped the improvement he heard was more than just wishful thinking on his part.

"All of us," Grant said. "I'm sorry, Kenzie. He's in police custody right now and won't bother you again. I assume you'll want to press charges. We'll sort out how he got inside later."

"That's the best I can do for her." Stephen followed the trail of scrapes and bandaged cuts from her neck to her wrist. "She needs an X-ray on that hand. I'll take her over to the hospital."

Grant used his phone to take pictures of the glass fragments Stephen had removed. "This is my fault," he muttered. "I should have kept you off the floor," he said to Kenzie.

"Stop." She winced as she pushed herself out of the chair. "I'm here because the PFD benched me. What's the point of having a life if no one will let me live it?"

"Fair enough," Grant allowed.

Stephen was tempted to remind them both that she wasn't going about the general matter of living life out there. She'd been attacked and nearly passed out. Kenzie glared at him as if she knew exactly what he wasn't saying.

"We can't let a jerk like Murtagh think he can get away with that behavior," she said.

"He won't get away with it," Grant assured her. "Let me handle it from the business side. Go on and get X-rays of your hand and take tomorrow night off. The weekend if necessary."

"Tomorrow? But that's Friday night," she protested. "You need all hands on deck."

"Not yours, even if it isn't broken."

She tried to hide her injured hand behind her back, bumped it on her hip and groaned with pain. "Grant, if I don't work—"

"We'll keep you posted," Stephen said to him.

He could see the pain threatening to swamp her again and refused to waste another minute. Although he was nothing short of livid that Murtagh had orchestrated this assault and potentially caused a serious injury, he had to let Grant handle those details.

"Come on, Kenzie. You need to have that examined." He guided her out of the office and down the hall to the break room to pick up her backpack and keys. Outside at the loaner car, he helped her into the passenger side and buckled her seat belt.

"You're treating me like a porcelain doll," she muttered, as he adjusted the driver's seat and then backed out of the parking space.

"Want me to promise it won't last?" he asked.

"Please," she said with great feeling. "If word gets out that Murtagh made me pass out, I'll never live it down at the station."

Stephen appreciated her assumption that she would eventually be back at work with the PFD. Her tenacity was one of her finest features. After this stunt he couldn't imagine a judge bothering with Murtagh's case.

"You didn't really pass out. Not completely," he said. "You could always say I overreacted, too eager to do the hero thing. They'd all believe that."

She snorted. "I won't throw you under the bus unless I have no other choice, deal?"

"Deal."

Fortunately for Kenzie, the wait at the emergency room was remarkably brief. The pain had cast a gray pallor over her skin and she couldn't seem to get comfortable in the chair. When the nurse called her name, Stephen had the irrational urge to go with her. He didn't want to let her out of his sight.

Instead, while Kenzie was back getting treatment, he paced the hallway near the waiting area, trying to make sense of the assault. He couldn't figure out why Murtagh would make such a scene in a public place. It was absolutely illogical, especially since he'd put his hands on her. On the interview this morning the former firefighter had come off as an expert victimized by Kenzie's natural limitations as a woman. It wasn't an accurate opinion, though he'd looked good delivering it. Could Murtagh just be that angry to have been rescued by a woman?

Stephen supposed it was possible. He considered calling his dad to get a better idea of the type of work Murtagh had done during his PFD career. Kenzie's lawyer might not like Stephen asking around, but a conversation with family shouldn't be a problem for her side of the lawsuit. He decided to check with Julia first, in the morning. His reputation as the family grump was bad enough already. He wouldn't make it worse by treating his sister-in-law like a legal expert on call.

What he couldn't resist was reviewing the images of Kenzie on his phone. He still had her cell phone, too, and he knew she'd want to see pictures. He didn't think it was a good idea. Not tonight, anyway. She had enough to process with the attack, pain and potential damage to her hand. As both the brother and son of firefighters, Stephen knew an injury could put her off the job, possibly forever.

Was that what Murtagh meant to accomplish with this stunt? Had he been trying to hurt Kenzie and end her career because he knew his lawsuit was weak? Stephen kicked around the theory and sent Grant a text message for a second opinion.

At last Kenzie emerged from the treatment area, her color a little better and a wan smile on her face when she spotted him. She raised her splinted hand, and he held his breath until he heard what she had to say.

"It's not broken," she said. "They gave me something for the pain and the swelling. The plan is anti-inflammatories, rest and some extra support for a few days and I should be good as new."

He smiled as an enormous weight of worry on her behalf lifted from his shoulders. "That's the best news I've heard all day." He bent his head to kiss her and caught himself just in time. They were a couple of friends, not a *couple*. "I'll, ah, go get the car."

Were they friends? he wondered as he jogged across the parking lot. Had to be, he decided. Although he didn't have many friends left since withdrawing into himself after his fiancée's death, he remembered the general concept. Friends weren't supposed to abuse the trust with inappropriate moves like kisses. Though the woman challenged him and tempted him in turns, he could control himself.

Once he'd pulled into the patient pickup area and the nurse helped Kenzie into the car, she fumbled with the seat belt, eventually managing it on her own this time.

"I'll call Grant in the morning," she said, as he drove away from the hospital. "I'm sure I can work tomorrow night."

His first instinct was to back up Grant and tell her that wasn't an option, but he wasn't her keeper. "Is it the money?" He could spot her some cash if she needed it.

"A little," she admitted. "It's more because I'm on the schedule."

"Technically, Grant said you're not," he pointed out.

To his surprise, she laughed. "You're right. No one argues with Grant. Still, I'm going to try." She raised her splinted hand again. "I have to do something. It's not like I can do much around the garage."

She could keep him company and brighten his day with her stories and laughter, he thought. "You've got another perfectly good hand to answer phone calls," he joked.

"You're lucky they gave me something for pain," she said, chuckling. "Or I'd make you pay for slamming a glass ceiling over my head."

When they reached the garage, he helped her into the trailer and made sure she had what she needed for the night. He left her backpack on the table and hung on to her cell phone. Tomorrow was soon enough to send pictures to her lawyer.

Alone in the garage office, Stephen paced off more restless energy. Although she was safe and as comfortable as modern medicine could make her, he couldn't unwind. Murtagh's mean, glowering expression as he overpowered Kenzie kept flashing through his mind. There was no doubt that Murtagh had had a specific intention when he'd grabbed Kenzie. Stephen just couldn't be sure if it was to embarrass her or hurt her outright. He hoped by morning Grant would have a plan to make certain something like that didn't happen again.

The office was suddenly too small. Stephen needed to get out and do something that mattered. His first instinct was to go to the community center and see if he could make life difficult for another drug dealer. He'd grabbed the keys for the car he'd loaned Kenzie before he remembered he couldn't leave her here alone. He trusted his security system, of course, but that was useless if she needed an extra hand.

He walked into the shop. There wasn't anything to do to keep his hands busy that wouldn't make a racket. Kenzie's car was mechanically sound now, despite still being an eyesore. Would she agree with his suggestion to have the little car repainted and the interior repaired for resale? He'd gone to the club on a whim and a bit of a completed-project high, hoping to ease the stress she hid so well behind that big smile. Of course, he hadn't been able to give her the news on her car or have any kind of discussion, thanks to Murtagh's nasty stunt.

Kenzie had incredible reflexes and fortitude; he'd seen it on the racetrack and around the shop. Though it had surely been the right response, it had to have been a struggle for her to stand there and let him humiliate her and hurt her that way. She was a woman used to holding her own, paving her own way.

Leaning back against the workbench, Stephen looked around his shop. He'd worked hard building this business and his reputation. He couldn't imagine a stranger coming in and forcing him out of it the way Murtagh was attempting to force Kenzie away from her career as a firefighter.

Stephen recognized it was more than a job to her. That kind of service and dedication was a calling. He'd seen the pride and commitment to community on his father's face through the years. That same gleam shone in his brother's eyes, too, as it had from day one. When Mitch had been on administrative leave, he'd been as miserable as Kenzie was now. And that was without the added pressure of a civil suit.

Stephen switched off the lights in the shop and, returning to the office, pulled a bottle of whiskey from the bottom drawer of the filing cabinet. He poured a shot and tossed it back. With luck, it would dull this edgy feeling so he could catch a few hours of decent sleep.

Chapter 6

Kenzie didn't miss her phone until the next day, when she woke up to sunlight streaming through the wide window over the bed. Normally an early riser, she couldn't believe she'd slept so late.

Sitting up, she noticed the brace on her hand. The small tugs of her bandaged cuts and scrapes along her left arm brought the night back in an unpleasant rush. Better not to dwell on it any more than necessary. Once she found her phone, she'd tell her lawyer what had happened and possibly file a police report, depending on how Grant chose to handle the incident. After that, she wouldn't think about it anymore.

She set a cup of coffee to brew as she grabbed a shower and dressed in a loose peasant top that hid most of the marks Murtagh had left behind. Feeling steadier with the jolt of caffeine, she took a couple ibuprofen tablets and searched her backpack and the trailer for her phone, coming up empty.

Following the sounds of Stephen's blaring music and power tools to the garage, she hoped he had her phone. If not, she'd ask if she could use the business line to make a few calls.

The ringing phone in the office caught her attention and she picked it up before it went to voice mail. With luck it would be about the parts she needed for her car. Working on the vehicle would keep her mind off other things while she couldn't go to the club or the firehouse.

Instead the caller was asking about one of the cars Stephen had listed for sale. She handled the questions and checked the calendar she'd set up for him, arranging an appointment for the prospective buyer.

When she went out to tell him about the call, she stopped short in the office doorway, just admiring the way he moved as he worked. He had another rebuild project up on the lift and moved around it with a confident, loose-limbed grace. Her pulse did a tap dance as she enjoyed every lean inch of him packed with that hard, capable strength. And compassion, she thought, recalling the tender way he'd taken care of her last night.

He turned her way, his persistently stern expression softening with concern as his gaze swept over her.

That look had her thinking about kissing him again and doing it right this time. She tightened her abs to give the sudden swirl of butterflies less space for maneuvers.

He used a voice command to lower the volume on the music. "Did I wake you?"

"No." She smiled. "But you should have. All my alarms are on my phone. Do you have it?"

"Yes. Sorry about that." He crossed to the workbench that lined the back wall. "I kept it with me."

"Why?" she asked, joining him.

"Hold it." He held up a hand. "You'll trash your clothes in here."

"I know how to keep myself out of the grease for the span of a conversation," she replied. Though she supposed he wouldn't accept a hug while he was wearing work clothes. She'd have to save that for later. Anticipating that gave her system more of a jolt than the coffee had.

"Grant told me to take pictures," Stephen said, regret weighing down his voice. "I used both your phone and mine."

"Thanks." She was still embarrassed she'd gone woozy over a minor altercation. "Lawsuits aside, I wish I'd fought back," she said. Playing it meek must have messed with her head and her confidence. "Grant tells us we can defend ourselves if necessary until a bouncer arrives."

"Not that simple for you," Stephen replied.

No, it wasn't. Although his understanding helped, she wished she could hit Rewind and handle last night differently.

"You did the right thing," Stephen said. "Grant called this morning to check on you and to make sure you sent the pictures to your lawyer as soon as possible." He wiped his hands clean and pulled her phone from his back pocket. "I almost did it for you. I'm not sure you should look at them."

She should feel annoyed that he'd considered taking over and yet she only appreciated this thoughtfulness more. She peeked up at him, tried to smile. "I'm feeling better, I promise." It was only a small fib. "I'll just select the right pictures and hit Send. I won't obsess over them."

"Okay." The rough pads of fingers brushed gently across her skin, leaving a trail of warmth behind as he returned her phone.

With the brace on her hand it was clumsy work sending the text message and attaching the pictures. Based on the throbbing beating through her palm to her elbow from merely getting showered and dressed, her hand wouldn't be much use for another day or two. As promised, she tucked the phone into her pocket, remembering too late to shift it to her right side rather than her left.

"Did you take a pain pill?" Stephen asked. "I left them on the nightstand for you."

She curled the tips of her fingers over the edge of the brace. "I must have overlooked that," she admitted. "I took ibuprofen instead. It's not unbearable."

He didn't appear to be convinced.

She handed him the message slip with the appointment on it. "You've got some interest in the Charger out there."

His gaze remained locked with hers. "That's great news."

"Have you heard about the progress on the Camaro?" Feeling a blush rising in her face as he studied her, she searched for another topic to distract him.

"It should be moving right along," he said. "They gave Riley the choice of restoring and repairing the original interior or going with all new seats." He rubbed at his cheek, leaving behind a smudge of dirt. "I'm not sure what he'll decide."

She wanted to reach up and wipe it away, and told her

fingers to behave. They were quasi-coworkers and tentative friends. He didn't need her making another platonic move loaded with wishful thinking after being so amazing with her last night.

"Thanks for handling me and, well, all of that chaotic mess last night. Can't believe I passed out on you." The sense of utter security she'd felt in his arms would stay with her forever.

"You didn't really." His gaze drifted back to the vehicle on the lift and his mouth twitched at the corners. "Mitch backed a car over my foot once."

She grinned at his attempt to make her feel better. "Bet you didn't faint over the pain."

"No, I puked. Your way was *much* cleaner."

He was so matter-of-fact that she laughed. "I'll let you get back to…" Her voice trailed off when she saw her little rust-bucket wasn't in pieces anymore. She walked over, circling the reassembled car. This was her project, not his. She'd had it under control. "What did you do?"

"Um, yeah. About that."

Anger, mostly with herself, gaining steam, she spread her arms wide when he didn't complete the explanation. "Yes?"

"Well, that's why I went into the club last night."

And she'd been grateful for his surprise appearance. Who knew what he'd kept Murtagh from doing by charging in to help her? "I'm waiting, Stephen."

He looked to the rafters above and back to her. "I really needed to finish something."

"Was the car in your way?" There were four bays and only two were occupied right now.

"No." It was the only logical reply.

"Let me guess." She tried to fold her arms and the

brace got in the way. "You didn't think I could man-age the job."

"Of course not," he said. "You know what you're doing."

"Then why did you interfere?" She closed the distance between them. "It was *my* responsibility." She couldn't get her emotions under control. This was a ridiculous thing to argue over, but it had been her problem to solve. "I would've been done in a few days." Though the bum hand would have slowed her down.

"I'm sorry. Don't you ever need to see progress on something?"

"Yes." She looked back at the car. "Yes," she repeated with a weary sigh. "I understand that." Unfortunately, the car had apparently represented that tangible prog-ress for both of them. She studied him now, the timing clicking into place. "You finished it before you came to the club."

He rolled his shoulders back, cocked his chin, dar-ing her to react. If only she could decide whether to kiss him or smack him.

"You can take it apart and do it yourself if tightening every bolt means that much to you."

She bit back an oath. "Do I look dumb enough to undo the work of an excellent mechanic?" Two flags of color stained his cheeks at the compliment. She couldn't stay mad, not when he helped her at every turn. "I'll get it out of here and then you can finally sell the loaner car." Stalking over to the control panel, she raised the bay door.

"I was thinking maybe you'd rather sell this one." Stephen handed her the key. "My guy would give you a good rate on the paint and body work. Interiors for this car are easy to come by."

If only it was that easy. "Right idea," she admitted. "Wrong time. I don't have the disposable income to pay any kind of rate right now."

"So use my account. Pay me when you sell it."

Exasperated, she paused, half in and half out of the driver's seat. Why was he being so nice? "I pay my own way." She was already trying to figure out how many hours of office time she owed him for his labor.

"That's clear," he said. "I just thought if you invested a little now, you'd have more money in a week or two. That model and year, in working condition, will be perfect for a kid heading to college."

"Hardly your typical clientele."

"I buy and sell what I want here," he stated.

Unable to come up with any credible response to that, she got into the car and backed it out of the service bay. She couldn't line it up with the other cars that were ready for sale; it looked too pitiful with the rust-and-primer color scheme. Circling around back, she parked it along the fence, where none of his customers would have to look at it while she made up her mind about what to do next.

The car didn't sputter or rattle anymore and that shimmy in the left rear tire was gone.

She cut the engine and sat there a moment, collecting herself. He'd done more than she'd ever planned to do and now he'd given her a fair option. Minimal paint and body work would increase the resale value and make sure he got a decent return on what he'd pumped into it. Selling the car for a decent profit would go a long way to ease the financial stress she was under at the moment. And knowing Stephen, he probably had a buyer in mind already.

Did he have to do everything so well? It was petty for her to be upset with him for being a decent man. No, this was simply her overdeveloped pride rearing its ugly head. She'd been stressed out by the complaint and lawsuit, and feeling small after Murtagh's interview, then harassment at the club. None of that gave her valid cause to be aggravated with Stephen.

Not wanting to accept help was different from not needing the assist in the first place.

Contrite, she walked back to the garage, feeling like a dork, ready to accept his offer to make the most of their invested effort, parts and time. In a rare moment, she found him watching the television, arms folded over his chest. She did a double-take when she realized the images were a cell phone video of last night's debacle at the club.

The angle, taken from over Murtagh's shoulder, showed her clearly, while hiding most of his face. Without an alternate view, Murtagh could almost claim it wasn't him hounding her at all. The audio was terrible and the expression she'd intended as professional came across the television as snarky, while a cultured male voice off-camera explained the situation for the viewers.

"It's quite clear that Miss Hughes does not handle stressful situations well," the man continued. "You'll see she does nothing to diffuse the customer's ire and allows herself to be bullied."

In the video, the tray slammed into her chest. Kenzie gasped, reliving it. "I look pathetic, just standing there like some damsel in distress." The video footage froze at that moment. Even knowing better, she could almost believe the woman on the screen was helpless.

Stephen blocked her view and turned it off. "Sorry." His gaze moved over her, leaving flickers of warmth in its wake as he tracked the resulting nicks and scrapes as if he could see through her top.

She waved off the apology. "At least now we know why he pulled that stunt."

"Your lawyer will have a plan to counter this," Stephen said.

"I hope you're right." She'd promised herself she wouldn't think about it anymore. "I'm sorry I was a twit about you doing the work for me," she said in a bold change of subject. "I like your idea of selling the car." She moved by him and into the office. "I'll go call your paint and body guy. And we'll split whatever profit we make," she said over her shoulder.

"Hang on. That's not fair."

She was done arguing. Dropping into the desk chair, she picked up the phone. When she finished making the arrangements, she found Stephen staring at her. "It is fair," she said. "You did all the labor."

"Not even close. You had a good start on it."

"What about all the parts? Answering your phone hardly evens that score."

"You'd be surprised." He scowled at the phone. "I hate that thing."

"I won't go through with your plan unless we agree to split the profit. And I mean the *profit*, not the gross from the sale," she added, anticipating his next likely maneuver.

He stalked over to the refrigerator under the counter and pulled out a bottle of water. "Fine. Write it up that way."

She swiveled the chair to follow his movements. "Why aren't you a cop or a firefighter?" Watching him, her pulse quickening, she thought he'd be a stunning addition to any fundraising calendar.

"I told you. I was too into cars to think about any other line of work."

"You've got this innate good-guy nature." And he employed it in his own way within his family and community. "Plus you're cool as a cucumber in a crisis."

His cheeks colored again. "You don't know that."

"Do too. You kept your head in the middle of my crisis last night."

He scoffed, started for the door. "I've got work to do."

Her cell phone chimed and the garage phone rang at the same time. "Me, too," she said with a big smile, letting him off the hook now that things felt steadier between them.

There were layers and layers to Stephen Galway and she had the ridiculous urge to peel back every one of them, polishing up all the rough edges along the way. Smitten, her father would have called it.

He would have been right.

Stephen worked through the remainder of the morning and into the afternoon, turning up the music so he wouldn't hear her voice in the office. Alone in the garage had always been his preference, and yet after mere days of Kenzie working alongside him, being alone out here felt wrong.

She had a way about her, smart and strong, with a sweetness under the tough exterior. He told himself to shut up. Thoughts like that led into dangerous territory.

He'd get over this distraction, just like he got over everything else life tossed his way.

In the back of his mind he was assessing the new rebuild project as he dealt with the basic maintenance and repairs on the schedule. He had plenty of standard business to keep his business flush, but once he and Mitch had started with the restoration and rebuilds, Galway Automotive had swiftly earned a reputation in collector circles that had clients seeking them. It helped that they worked well together and had similar, though not identical, taste in cars.

Naturally, as soon as Kenzie drove off to take her car for paint, his concentration shattered. He didn't like her going out there without him, yet there was only so much hovering he could get away with. There had to be a way to kick this need to keep her safely within sight. Kenzie personified independence. While she was gone, he turned down the music and took advantage of her absence to give Grant another update.

"I've sent everything Jason collected from the other customers to her lawyer," Grant was saying. "You're sure she's feeling all right?"

"Seems to be." Stephen checked the clock. "Won't take the heavy painkillers." If she wasn't back in fifteen minutes, he'd call her cell and make sure she was okay.

"She's tough," Grant said. "Try to encourage her to rest."

Stephen gave a snort. "You've met Kenzie, right?"

"*Try*," Grant emphasized. "It's all any of us can do."

True. "I can't believe Murtagh's lawyers found a way to twist his assault on her in his favor." Although when it came to the Marburg firm, Stephen trusted only Julia to play fair.

Grant was equally displeased and baffled by the tactic. "I've reached out to a few reporters I know, making it clear she was following company policy."

"Won't matter much if they like his version better," Stephen pointed out. The unfairness of that had him hefting a socket wrench, wishing he could hold off every possible threat or danger to her.

"I'm not giving in. The man assaulted an employee," Grant said. "By the way, I've texted Kenzie her new schedule. She's off until Tuesday. That gives her recovery time for the hand and her deposition on Monday afternoon."

Stephen rubbed his temples, feeling the headache brewing. "You know, I really didn't need the extra challenge right now," he said.

Grant chuckled. "I believe you're up to it. Keep me in the loop and I'll do the same."

The call ended, Stephen stood in the quiet solitude of the garage, unable to focus. What was taking her so long? Ten more minutes and he'd call her.

Hearing a bigger engine idling nearby, he walked out to see a media van parked at the curb across the street. Apparently they'd discovered she was staying here. No big surprise. The Marburg law firm was familiar with Stephen. He'd made no secret of how he felt when they'd successfully defended Annabeth's killer. They probably recognized him immediately from the altercation at the club. He assumed Murtagh's legal team had given Kenzie's location to the media just to keep tightening the screws on her.

A low-slung, foreign street-racing car with a neon paint scheme and more power than anyone needed in the city rolled to a stop just outside the gate. Joey Garcia, owner of the shop Stephen preferred for the paint and interior details, was behind the wheel. He gave Stephen a wave as Kenzie hopped out of the passenger side, carrying a big brown paper bag. He waved back and pressed the button on the fob in his pocket to close the gate behind her, giving her as much shelter as possible from the media van.

"I brought lunch," she called as she walked up. "Better late than never, right?"

"Right." A good rule when applied to lunch. He opened the office door for her and failed in his gallant effort to ignore the tempting sway of her hips. The woman had legs that commanded attention.

She caught him scowling and raised an eyebrow. "What happened now?"

"You didn't see the news van out there?" he asked.

"I did," she replied. "I'm not sure it's wise to look like I'm hiding out."

"It is," he replied. "What's for lunch?" No point dwelling on what they couldn't change.

"I picked up your favorite." She held up a bag with the logo of a nearby sandwich shop.

How did she know his favorite?

She opened the bag and the rich aroma of a meatball sub filled the room. His stomach rumbled and she grinned. "It was the least I could do after getting mad over nothing."

With that expression on her face, he was suddenly hungry for more than the sandwich. He pulled himself together. She trusted him as a friend. He would not wreck that. "How did you convince Joey to stop for food?" he asked.

"I bought his lunch, too."

"Really? That guy never stops moving long enough to eat."

"Like someone else I know," she said with a grin. "He ordered enough to feed the whole shop," she said, "though he was the only one in sight when I dropped off my car."

Stephen shook his head in disbelief, digging into his sandwich while she pulled out an enormous chopped salad. "Did he give you a good price?"

"He gave me the same rate he gives you for the painting. Said he couldn't be sure about the body work until he had a better look at the rust damage."

"No rust on the frame," Stephen said. "It shouldn't be too bad."

She nodded, picking at her salad, but not really eating. He wondered if the pain was making her queasy. He'd keep an eye on her. There was a quart of his mom's chicken soup in the freezer. She'd brought it over when he'd had a cold around Easter.

"We chose a hot pink color scheme," Kenzie said.

Stephen choked on a bite of his sandwich, washed it away with some water. "Hot pink?"

"I knew it." She aimed her fork at him. "You already have a buyer in mind."

"Not anymore," he muttered.

"Stephen, I've been managing my life for over a decade now. I don't need you to stack the deck for me."

Someone should. She deserved better than what she'd been dealing with on her own lately. Better than the firestorm ahead of her if Marburg continued to work the media in favor of their client.

"Say *something*," she urged. "You know you want to."

That ornery sparkle in her big blue eyes made him

want to say plenty, and not much of it had to do with cars and paint, or the civil suit. He wanted to make her promises to hold her close and keep her safe and happy. Promises he had no business making.

"If it is hot pink, I'll have to check with Mom about some better local prospects."

"I should have expected that unflappable calm to prevail." She rolled her eyes. "There are moments when teasing you is no fun," she said, with a ghost of a smile on her generous lips.

It made him want to smile back. "So what color did you go with?"

"A neutral, medium-gray with enough metallic to keep it shy of boring," she replied.

"Easy-care color."

She agreed with a quick bob of her chin. "A factor I thought would hold great appeal for a college-bound kid."

"How long until it's ready?"

"I believe the direct quote from Joey was 'a week or so'."

"Sounds about right," he said. The conversation had veered back to the Charger and the new rebuild on the lift when someone buzzed the gate for entrance.

"New client?" he asked, pointing to the desk calendar under her salad.

"Not one I scheduled," she said.

Together they studied the luxurious, German-built black sedan through the monitor. Stephen didn't have a good feeling about it, but he opened the gate, anyway. The car rolled inside with little more than a murmur and stopped in front of the office door. A man emerged from the driver's side, his silver hair trimmed perfectly and his tailored, charcoal suit flawless. Despite the heat, he appeared as cool and immovable as an iceberg. Stephen could spot a Marburg attorney from a mile away and this one was carrying a slim leather briefcase.

He was here to offer her some sort of deal. Stephen had watched plenty of legal maneuvering during the trial for Annabeth's killer. Unlike the lawyers working with evidence to convict or clear a defendant, those cutting deals never carried an excess of paperwork.

"Miss Hughes, I'm Lance Webster. May I speak with you a moment?"

"You're with Marburg," Stephen interjected. "Her lawyer should be present at any meeting." Turning to Kenzie, he said, "Call him right now. Use the office phone."

She ignored him, pulling out her cell and entering the number.

"This is a civil case, Mr. Galway. Although you're not *currently* involved, it's my pleasure to inform you Mr. Murtagh is considering filing assault charges against you."

"Oh, I look forward to it," Stephen said.

Kenzie stepped between them, her braced hand on his chest and her cell phone to her ear. "He doesn't mean that."

"Yes, I do." He glared at Webster. "I was protecting her from an assault. I'm confident most witnesses, and a jury if necessary, will see it my way once they have access to accurate footage of the incident." He drew her back just enough to make his point clear to the Marburg puppet. She was under his protection and this was his property. "If you want to talk to Miss Hughes, you'll have to set an appointment when her lawyer can be present," he said. "Please leave."

"We don't enjoy theatrics, Miss Hughes," Webster

said. "Your attorney was informed of when and where we wanted to meet today."

"You invented theatrics," Stephen retorted, unable to contain the outburst.

Kenzie was staring at her phone. "He's not answering." She swiped up and down her call history. "There's no message from him, either."

"Guess you'll have to reschedule," Stephen said to Webster. "I recommend the next appointment take place at an office rather than my place of business."

Just when he thought he'd won this round for her, a car pulled in through the gate, stopping beside the black sedan with a brief squeal of the tires. Also a German sedan, this one was older and a deep red, but had clearly been well maintained.

"That's Paul, my lawyer." Kenzie rushed forward as a younger man scrambled out of his car without his suit jacket. His short dark hair and an elegant circle beard framed his dark complexion. Stephen relaxed when he noticed the temper banked in the man's deep brown eyes.

Stephen was close enough to Webster to catch the man's muttered curse. "Problem?" he challenged.

Webster ignored him.

"This is Paul Corrigan," Kenzie said.

Her lawyer extended a hand to greet Stephen and paid no attention to Webster. Stephen liked him already.

"Could we take this into the office?" Paul tipped his head to the street, where another media van had joined the first.

Though it aggravated him immensely to play host to anyone from Marburg besides Julia, Stephen led everyone into the office. The only benefit would be fewer witnesses if he decided to deck Webster.

"I don't believe you need to be here, Mr. Galway," the Marburg attorney said.

"On the contrary, you threatened me with an assault complaint. I'll stay."

Paul bristled. "For last night? Oh, that is rich."

Webster simply plowed forward with his agenda. "I'm offering your client a settlement. Mr. Murtagh isn't without compassion for her predicament. He is willing to drop the lawsuit if she voluntarily resigns from the PFD."

"No deal," Kenzie snapped.

Stephen nearly gave her a high five for stubbornness.

"The evidence is mounting, Miss Hughes. We can make it clear you are physically and emotionally incapable of doing your job," Webster continued. "You're a liability to the PFD and a risk to the greater community if you remain in your position. It's only a matter of time before someone gets hurt."

"Tossing around threats like confetti." Paul shook his head as if the development disappointed him. "The judge will love this."

"I'm tossing out facts, Mr. Corrigan. You can't argue with the video we have showing your client freezes in a crisis."

"There's more than one angle," Stephen began. "She didn't freeze, you son of a—"

"This case isn't a popularity contest or a publicity exercise," Paul interrupted. "I don't believe this is an offer you make unless you see the writing on the wall as well as I do. Your client's bizarre attempt to intimidate my client has put your case in jeopardy."

Stephen liked Kenzie's lawyer more with every minute.

Webster shifted his snooty gaze to Kenzie. "This settlement gives you a gracious exit from a difficult situation. Our client is only asking you to pay his legal fees. If our case moves forward the judgment against you will be financially devastating with legal fees, medical expenses, and pain and suffering factored in. And you'll still be out of work."

"He's bluffing," Paul said to Kenzie. "Don't give this a single thought."

Stephen agreed, though he managed to keep the opinion to himself.

The Marburg attorney handed over the documentation to Paul. "Our offer in full detail," he said. "It will remain open until the depositions begin."

He turned on his heel and left.

Stephen, Kenzie and Paul waited in a tense silence until the sleek black car backed out of the yard and drove out of sight.

"I'll let you two talk," Stephen said. He wanted to go pound something into dust. Dismantling the new rebuild would have to suffice.

"Wait." Kenzie caught his hand as he stalked by. "Stay, please?"

He jerked his chin in a quick affirmative, letting her lace her slender fingers through his.

Paul read through the settlement for them. It was remarkably brief, considering who had delivered it.

Kenzie groaned at the stated legal fees. "It would take me years to pay that off at my firefighter pay. As a waitress? Not a chance." She rolled her eyes. "And that doesn't even count what I'd owe you."

"Everything is negotiable," Paul reminded her.

"Not her career," Stephen stated. She squeezed his hand. "You both know she didn't do anything wrong. The PFD investigation cleared her when the initial complaint came in. You need to focus on why Marburg is trying to force a settlement now."

"My office has been fielding calls all day," Paul said. "Marburg controls the story in the public right now. If you'd give an interview we could—"

"What about the gag order?" she asked.

"No luck there," he admitted.

"I still won't do it," Kenzie said. "You said yourself it's not a popularity contest. The PFD cleared me. Pandering to the public isn't the answer to his harassment. I won't sink to Murtagh's level like we're trapped in some twisted reality television show. If I shared all the details of his rescue now, it would sound like I'm shaming the victim."

Knowing she was right didn't make hearing it any easier. "Let Grant work the media and counter Marburg's account of last night," Stephen suggested.

"What's that?" Paul asked.

"Grant Sullivan owns the Escape Club," Kenzie explained. "He told me he sent the other eyewitness videos of the altercation to you. He has friends in the media."

"My assistant is working through it," Paul said.

Kenzie narrowed her gaze at Stephen. "When did you talk to Grant?"

"You were picking up lunch," he replied. To Paul he added, "As the club owner he can explain her response and lack of reaction better than she can."

"Good, good. So unless you're interested in this sorry excuse for a settlement, I'll move forward with deposition prep."

Although that should have reassured her, Kenzie continued to cling to Stephen's hand and he felt the subtle tremble in her grasp. He stroked her finger with his thumb, trying to reassure her. "It will work out," he said.

"He lied in his initial complaint to the PFD," she said absently, as if that detail was the only thing in her favor. "They discovered it, of course, but they didn't pursue it according to the law, as a courtesy."

He knew she had plenty of valid reasons to be concerned, yet she was in the right and Murtagh was being a complete jerk with the civil case. "Marburg attorneys will sink as low as they need to in order to win a case," Stephen grumbled. At her long look, he added, "With a singular exception."

Her lips twitched, tempting him to steal another kiss.

Her lawyer rolled up the offer and tapped it against the desk. "Despite the lousy press and the blustering Webster, your case is solid, Kenzie. We'll get through this."

"Thanks, Paul."

She escorted the lawyer to his car and Stephen returned to the work waiting for him in the shop. He watched Kenzie reenter the office, thinking she looked as if the weight of the world rested on her shoulders. Her dejected expression was all wrong, muting her normally friendly sparkle and tugging at her lovely mouth. It was outrageous that such a good person had to go through this kind of crap. Quips and platitudes about life and lemons, hardship and strength were useless to someone in the middle of the storm.

He stalked into the office. "You have this under control."

"Thank you." She curled forward, resting her head on her folded arms on the desktop. "I don't think my life has ever been this out of control."

He thought about the inventory in the yard and the two open bays in the shop. "Come with me."

"Where?"

He motioned for her to get up and follow him as he went out to the yard. "Choose one," he said, when she came to a stop beside him, surveying the worn and shabby cars he and Mitch had picked up at the last auction.

"What?"

"You heard me." He tucked his thumbs into his back pockets and waited.

"I heard you, but you're not making any sense," she replied. "Choose a car for what?"

"When we buy cars, Mitch and I do an initial inspection and create a basic plan and parts list. It's tucked in the driver's side visor. Go through the inventory here and choose the one you want to work on." He started back to the shop.

"Seriously?"

He turned at the sharp tone and found himself on the business end of her annoyed gaze. "What did I say? You know this is what we do."

She waved the hand with the brace. "I'm not much use here."

"That's temporary." He stared her down. This was supposed to make her happy, and if happy was too much at the moment, he'd thought it would provide a good distraction. "Once you choose, you can move the car inside, take a closer look at it and get the parts ordered so we're ready to go when that brace comes off."

She made a noise in her the back of her throat. "Stephen, come on."

"Would you rather I started some fires so you can put them out?"

She sucked in a breath, her eyes blazing, and then she laughed, the sound rolling over him in waves that drained away all the tension of the past hour.

"I'm sorry." She walked up to him and wrapped her arms around his waist. "I'm being an idiot."

He didn't know what to do with his hands. He knew what he wanted to do. Stroking a palm over her braided hair and following her subtle curves from shoulder to hip probably wasn't the right move between friends. He settled for awkwardly patting her shoulder.

"Thank you." She gave him a little squeeze and stepped back. "For last night and for today. And for re-building my car."

"You had that under control," he said. A little grime from his shirt had transferred to hers. Hopefully, when she saw it, she'd remember she'd hugged him. "I just…" Just what? Trying to find a better explanation would only raise more questions about his feelings and intentions. He wasn't ready to face those answers.

"I'll let you get back to work," she said, moving toward the row of cars.

"Would it help to get out of here?" The fence blocked the nosy media, but as she'd said, she wasn't the type to hide from anything. "Later tonight."

She turned back, curiosity dancing in her vivid blue eyes. "What do you have in mind?"

"There's a drive-in theater. If you're up for a short road trip."

"What's showing?" she asked.

He had no idea. "Does it matter?" It would be a complete change of pace for both of them, with a pleasant, relaxing drive on either end of it.

"Not at all." The grin on her face lit her up from head to toe. There, that was the energetic, conquer-the-world Kenzie he'd met last week.

Telling himself he hadn't just asked her out on a date, he went back to the shop to wrap up the one brake job he had left on the day's schedule.

Chapter 7

The rest of the afternoon flew by and Kenzie knew it was all because Stephen had put her back on even footing and given her a much-needed distraction. He really was a good guy under the gruff attitude. Of course, he was a Galway, and she suspected it might be in the DNA Mr. and Mrs. Galway had passed down to their kids.

She found herself able to concentrate on the details of supporting the garage and feeling useful in the process. After a long debate of the choices, she'd chosen to work on the 1966 Chevy Nova. Not her favorite of the classic muscle cars, but according to the paperwork, it was a relatively straightforward build. Though she'd been tempted by a Mustang fastback out there, knowing those were a favorite of Mitch's she'd steered clear of it.

When she'd pulled the Nova into the bay, Stephen had arched an eyebrow, then resumed his own work, making her wonder what he thought of her choice. Between calls for service appointments next week, she started searching for parts and pricing out what she thought it would take to restore the Nova. The time line could drag out and she wondered if Stephen would let her come by and stay involved on the project even after she returned to the PFD.

She *would* return to the PFD.

The scents and sounds of a working garage soothed her more than she expected, even though she wasn't out in the middle of it. There was comfort in this environment as memories of time with her father rolled through her mind.

She hadn't anticipated staying here on Stephen's property or leaning on him this way. She was so grateful for how he made her feel included and valued during this ordeal. The idea of going through the ups and downs of the civil suit, of dealing with Murtagh's antics while crashing in some anonymous motel room alone would have been overwhelming. Every time her lawyer mentioned working through the systems and processes she wanted to scream.

If she'd faced the Marburg attorney's intimidation on her own, she might have caved to the pressure, or said something that would have made her lawyer's job more difficult. Stephen had been a real friend, a steady, unflappable support when she'd most needed it.

She booked a few more appointments for the next week, all basic maintenance she could help with as her hand healed. Anything to keep herself busy next week as Paul dealt with the depositions.

Thinking about the evening ahead at the drive-in sent her mind back down memory lane. When she and her sister were little, their mother would pack sandwiches and their favorite junk food and cookies. To re-create that, Kenzie would need to make a grocery run. She glanced at the monitor that gave a view of the two media teams outside the gate. The idea of venturing out there beyond the privacy and security of Galway Automotive made her heart stutter. Who would have guessed reporters would mark the limit of her courage? She just couldn't bring herself to do it. Not today.

Though she was well aware tonight's outing wasn't a real date, she wanted to do something nice for him, as well. When he'd offered to help her last week, he couldn't have known she'd be this much trouble. Right now, all she could give back were little gestures. Calling one of Stephen's favorite delis, she placed an order for delivery and hid the food that arrived in the camper until they were ready to leave. Once she was back in her apartment, or back on shift where she had access to the firehouse kitchen, she would whip up something homemade.

He delivered the last car and closed the gate behind another happy customer. She vacated the office so he could clean up, and when he knocked on the camper door, she had to stomp out all the tingles of desire that went rushing through her system. The casual cargo shorts and graphic T-shirt emblazoned with a vintage Camaro emphasized the lean build honed by long hours of work.

"You ready?"

She nodded, not trusting her voice. Grabbing the cooler and tote she'd packed, she followed him outside and stopped short.

He was standing in front of a gorgeous convertible

roadster in a gleaming midnight blue with a stunning white interior.

"Holy cow," she murmured. She was almost scared to put the cooler anywhere near it.

"I took my time with it," he said.

There was a story behind this restoration. She could see it in the wary, defensive glint in his eyes. "I can tell. It's beautiful." She wished he felt as safe with her as she did with him, just so she could hear the full story.

He took the cooler and tote from her, securing both behind the driver's seat. "I'd planned to pick up dinner for us on the way," he said.

"I was feeling nostalgic." She shrugged. "My mom always did this when we were kids."

He nodded in understanding as a faint smile toyed with his lips. "Mine, too."

"Think they'll follow us?" She tipped her head toward the media gathered outside the gate.

"Only until we lose them," he replied. "I made a dinner reservation for us down on Market Street. It will be easy to sneak away unseen."

His plan worked like a charm and the weather was beautiful as they left the city, the wind cool and swift, preventing conversation. The silence was fine with her. Her mind blanked as Stephen drove, and the tightness that had locked up her shoulders since the Marburg attorney's visit finally eased.

The drive-in was at about half capacity when they arrived. The marquis showed a double feature of two high-action blockbusters of summers past. Stephen found a great spot for them, middle of the row toward the front. He popped the trunk and pulled out a blanket to protect the pristine upholstery.

"I have a philosophical question for you," she said, unpacking the picnic of slider sandwiches, juicy peaches and junk food. "Can you watch a movie without popcorn?"

"Not at a theater," he said.

She blotted the corner of her mouth with a napkin, swallowing quickly. "Me, neither. I've never figured out how they make movie popcorn so addictive."

His lips twitched. "We'll get stocked up before the first movie."

"You're a good man, Mr. Galway."

His eyebrows dipped low, but didn't linger in a frown. She counted it progress, though why she felt it was her job to help him lighten up was beyond her.

They chatted about their favorite movie genres until the previews started and Stephen made a run for soft drinks and popcorn.

"Thanks for this," she said at the end of the first feature. "You were right about getting away from everything. It helps."

"I'm glad," he replied cautiously. "I try to get out here at least once a summer."

"Really?"

"Drive-in movies and summer go together."

She agreed, thinking back to long summer days of watching her dad race and late nights watching movies from the family car, giggling with her sister as they kept each other awake. As people milled about between features, she caught plenty of appreciative looks and murmurs as they passed the car.

"If you wanted to sell this one, you could probably manage it tonight."

"People make offers every time I take it out," he said. "This one will stay with me."

He didn't have to spell out his reasons for her to understand the sentiment. "Some cars are special," she said, twisting around to pull another bottle of water from the cooler.

"You get it." He sounded startled.

"Have you forgotten I was raised by a car-crazed man masquerading as a firefighter?" Perched as she was between the seats, she was close enough to catch him eyeing her legs. The pure male interest made her grateful for the great bone structure from her mom's side and the perfect fit of her favorite cutoffs.

"Not a chance. I've seen you work."

The compliment made her blush as she dropped back into the seat. "Why don't you hire full-time help?"

"I prefer the quiet."

She laughed at that, could hardly catch her breath long enough to explain, "Your heavy metal work music is a noise violation."

His mouth broke free of the habitual, stoic mold and the resulting grin was spectacular. She wanted to see more of that open, happy expression.

"Thanks for making me laugh during the worst week of my life," she said, a little breathless. "I truly appreciate everything."

"You're welcome." That sexy grin faded back to serious determination. "Marburg is known to use some nasty tactics to blur the facts, but I can't see them winning this case. Don't let their antics get to you."

She was moved, and inordinately pleased, by his support and belief in a positive outcome. He'd seen Marburg in action, when justice for his fiancée was on the line. "I hope you're right," she said with feeling. "I have other skills, but I already miss the firehouse and everyone there."

He reached over and opened the water bottle, his hand covering hers in the process. It seemed her entire body zeroed in on the sensations of the cool plastic under her palm and the heat of his hand on hers.

Suddenly, he sat back, taking that tender heat with him. "I bought this car for Annabeth a week before she died," he said. "Restoring it for her was supposed to be a wedding present. I finished it before what should have been our first anniversary."

The sorrow in his revelation gripped her heart like a vise. "She would've loved this," Kenzie said.

"I want to believe that." Stephen dropped his head back against the seat, gazing up at the sky. "Believe it. She loved you." Kenzie ran a hand over the beautiful finish on the dash, a safer move than touching him. "This is clearly the work of a man who put his heart into every inch of the restoration."

"I couldn't let it go." He raked his fingers through his hair and swallowed hard.

The previews for the second feature started, ending the conversation too soon for Kenzie. It seemed to her he wanted to talk about Annabeth, that he needed to do so. She vaguely recalled the general news reports about Annabeth's murder. Through Mitch she knew how deep the family concern for Stephen went.

It dawned on her as they watched the action on the screen that once more, inadvertently, she was doing as Grant requested and keeping Stephen away from the community center he typically haunted. Well, if some good came from the stupid civil suit and her interruption of Stephen's routine, then she'd call it a silver lining and be thankful.

When the second feature ended and they were on the road again, Kenzie contentedly watched the stars wheeling overhead. The roadster hugged the pavement and she wished they could keep going. It would be delightful to drive all night and wake up in a place without Stephen's traumatic past and her frustrating present. She wondered who they might be together without the baggage.

She braced herself as they neared the neighborhood, immensely pleased to find the media crews hadn't returned to their posts in front of the garage. "Thanks for a great night," she said, coming around the convertible for the tote and cooler moments later.

Stephen already had both in hand. "You get the door," he said.

She did, holding it for him as he walked in ahead of her and set the items on the table.

"This was fun," he said, tucking his hands into his pockets.

It seemed as if the admission made him uncomfortable. "It was precisely the distraction I needed," she said. "I owe you one."

"Not at all." He waved it off. "You need anything before I go?" he asked, with a pointed glance at the brace on her hand.

"No, thank you." She had to get a handle on this weird blend of affection and lust surging through her. It was probably a combination of proximity and loneliness. Everything about him turned her on, from the way he drove to the rare grins to the reluctant, rusty laughter. He had integrity, and he was a great guy whether or not he was scowling. She admired his clear view of what he wanted out of life and the way he worked to make it happen.

His chest swelled on a deep breath. "You really think Annabeth would've liked the car?"

The hope in his eyes made hers sting with tears she couldn't let him see. "I'm sure of it," she said with a smile.

"I felt cheated when she was killed." His voice was barely more than a whisper, but the grief in those words was an agonized shout. "Life just…stopped."

She'd experienced that same timeless pain. "It was like that when my dad died. There's life before and a yawning emptiness after." One day he was fine, the next the doctors gave him six months to live. As a family, they'd followed his courageous lead and made the most of every minute he had left. It had never felt like enough.

"How?"

"Cancer," she said. "He died five months after the diagnosis. No matter how it happens, I don't think we ever have enough time with the people we love most."

"But your laugh…" His voice trailed off, the corners of his mouth tightening around the emotion he held in check.

"I feel my dad with me when I laugh," she admitted. "Humor was his way of coping with everything." She wanted to give Stephen hope that he'd start living again when he was ready. "We all get through grief in our own way and at our own pace."

Stephen reached out and tucked a loose strand of hair behind her ear, his hand curling around the nape of her neck. Slowly, he drew her close, his hazel eyes warm and golden as he bent his head to touch his lips to hers.

Firm, warm, knowing, the arousing sensations of the

kiss flowed all the way through her body. The rough texture of calluses on his palms, the summer-night scent of his skin, the hot, rich taste of his tongue stroking across hers. Her brace bumped clumsily into his shoulder and he tucked it close to his side. The fingers of her good hand found the thick softness of his hair as his strong arms circled her and brought her body flush to his. They kissed and explored until simply breathing became an erotic maneuver as her breasts rubbed along the hard planes of his chest.

"Kenzie." He whispered her name against her throat, his big hands flexing into her hips. His breathing ragged, he rested his forehead to hers. "I need to go."

"Okay." Indulging the urge, she traced the carved outline of his forearms as she pulled away from him.

He lifted his head and stepped back. "Mom will be expecting both of us again for dinner tomorrow." The familiar scowl shaded his gorgeous eyes. "I don't have a believable excuse for either of us to get out of it."

"It's fine," she said with a smile. He looked miserable. Once more she imagined the joy of driving away into the night, with him, toward a fresh start. "I'll be ready on time."

"That's not all."

She waited.

He shifted restlessly. "Can we make sure they don't think there's something here?" he asked, wagging a finger between them.

After that kiss? "Of course." She'd pulled panicked victims from fires and accident scenes. Surely she could project calm, platonic vibes for the duration of a family meal.

"I don't mean to offend y—"

"We're friends, Stephen," she said, cutting off whatever he was trying to say. In her experience friends didn't kiss with that much pent-up passion and she refused to beg him for something he clearly wasn't ready to give. "Don't worry about it."

His scowl deepened, though he seemed satisfied with her reply as he said good-night and walked out.

In bed, Kenzie tossed and turned. His mother and sisters would pounce on the smallest flicker of a personal attachment between her and Stephen. The real worry was making sure his family didn't pick up on her receptiveness to the idea. She was crushing on a man who wasn't ready for anything more than friendship.

Making matters worse, she couldn't get clear on her motives. Was she just vulnerable and he was convenient or had she stumbled over the right guy at the wrong time? Stephen seemed rooted to the idea that his one chance at a long-term relationship had come and gone.

She pressed her face into the pillow, muffling a howl of frustration. Unfortunately, that hot, unforgettable embrace had to be the end of it, despite the alluring potential of trying to change his mind.

The next afternoon, Kenzie stepped out of the trailer with that generous, friendly smile and Stephen discovered he'd worried all night for no reason. She didn't seem the least bit aggravated or awkward with him, and there was no hint of that exquisite heat he'd felt pulsing between them last night. He told himself he was grateful for her understanding. Getting in too deep would only hurt them both when he couldn't live up to her expectations.

He ignored the niggling voice in his head that pointed

out he didn't *know* her expectations. What he knew was that he wasn't cut out for another relationship. He was too hung up on Annabeth.

Dinner with his family was only a slightly smaller affair than last week, since his brother Andrew and his family were out of town on vacation. Like last week and most Sunday dinners, the conversation had meandered around and through a variety of topics, and Stephen had listened, letting the familiar patterns soothe him.

"Did you see the news last night?" Samuel asked Stephen after dessert had been cleared away. Only Stephen, Mitch and their father remained at the table. Everyone else had wandered off to other interests, ranging from cleanup to the swing set out in the backyard. Stephen could just catch a glimpse of Kenzie's bright hair in the kitchen as she dried dishes for his mom. Not that he was keeping track of her.

"Trying to avoid it," he replied, thinking of yesterday's media crews. He and Kenzie had tacitly agreed to let others keep tabs on the media coverage and opinions. It just wasn't worth the frustration. Neither her lawyer nor Grant would let her walk into anything unprepared. Catching the meaningful glance between his brother and father, he had to ask. "What did I miss?"

"There was another shooting at the community center," Mitch supplied.

Stephen swallowed the colorful oath on the tip of his tongue. "What happened?" If he hadn't been out with Kenzie could he have been there to stop it? His heart hammered against his rib cage. "Did anyone from the community center get hurt?"

"No," Samuel assured him quickly. "The police said a drug deal went awry between dealer and customer.

Shots were fired," he continued. "Only one dead, the suspected dealer was wounded, and the cops scooped up everyone in the area."

"The street's clean?" Stephen hoped his interest wasn't too obvious.

"For the moment it seems to be," Mitch said. "I heard through the grapevine that they've had a slew of anonymous tips in recent months that helped them identify the key players." He gave Stephen a long look.

If his brother expected him to admit that he'd been sending in those tips, he was out of his mind. "Good news all around." Stephen relaxed, inwardly pleased that something he'd done out there had gone right. It wouldn't bring back Annabeth, but it eased the guilt plaguing him.

From the kitchen, he heard Kenzie's laughter and then one of his nephews squealed. The back door creaked open and slapped shut again.

"How is she doing?" Mitch asked.

"The hand is improving rapidly," Stephen replied. Over dinner Kenzie didn't share the news about the visit from Murtagh's snooty attorney, so he didn't share that information, either. "She probably won't need the brace for more than another day or two."

"That wasn't what I meant," Mitch said. "Depositions start tomorrow."

Of course Mitch would know that through Julia, if not the PFD pipeline. "She'll get through it," Stephen said with confidence. "Her lawyer impressed me."

"When did you meet him?" Mitch asked.

"He stopped by yesterday," Stephen replied. "After that bad-angle footage from the club hit the news."

"The story Murtagh is trying to peddle is ridiculous,"

Samuel said. "I'd love to have about fifteen minutes alone with him."

"You think that would help?" Stephen asked.

Samuel muttered an oath. "No, he's too bitter and too willing to blame his problems on others."

"I know you hate having Kenzie underfoot," Mitch said. "You're doing a good thing for her. Staying alone at a hotel or something would've been too risky in my opinion. She doesn't like to admit it, but she needs the support of good friends right now."

Stephen didn't bother replying. If he claimed it was no trouble lending his trailer home to Kenzie, his dad and brother wouldn't believe him. If he grumbled about it that would open a door for one or both of them to lecture him about being too much of a loner. He suspected one of the reasons Mitch hadn't been around the shop as much lately was because he hoped some attraction or romance would develop.

The attraction was there, all right. Just the memory of that kiss sent a hot zing along Stephen's skin. Flirting and romance had never been his strong suit. Kenzie might be open to a lighthearted fling, if he could find a way to fight off the persistent guilt of the idea.

Switching the subject to cars, he gave them an update on the Riley project and told them he had an appointment with a potential buyer for the Charger. It was enough to keep the conversation on safe ground until Kenzie was ready to leave.

"Annabeth would want you to be happy," Samuel murmured, when he pulled Stephen in for a goodbye hug at the door.

"Dad." Stephen shook his head. This wasn't what he needed at all. Annabeth had been everything to him and their plans had been his whole world. Without her he couldn't seem to find his way in anything other than business.

He knew his parents and siblings were frustrated with his unwillingness to move on. Stephen didn't know how he could love one woman with every fiber of his being and then be fair to either her memory or another woman in a new relationship. Losing Annabeth had extinguished something inside him and he wasn't interested in setting himself up for that kind of sorrow again. It would break him.

"If we can do anything to help after the depositions, say the word." His mother pushed a basket of leftovers into his hands.

"This is too much, Mom."

"Not for two and not with stressful days ahead," she countered with a serene smile.

No point in arguing. His family was determined to read more into his hospitality toward Kenzie than necessary. "Got it." When Kenzie went back to her life, they'd understand that alone was how he intended to remain.

Back at the garage, he changed clothes and went into the shop to work, in an effort to keep his mind and hands off the woman living in his trailer. He didn't see her until he walked into the office after his appointment with the potential buyer.

She sent him that gorgeous smile. "Any luck?"

"We might have a deal," Stephen said. "He's thinking it over."

"Is it a money issue or a wife issue?"

Neither concern had crossed his mind. "Does it matter?"

"Only if you want to close the deal," she said, her gaze returning to the computer monitor.

He shrugged. "Everything okay?"

"Yes," she replied absently. "Just tracking down parts for the Nova."

He went to the refrigerator, inexplicably reluctant to leave. "How is the hand feeling?"

"Better." She wiggled the tips of her fingers. "I haven't decided if I should wear the brace for tomorrow's depositions."

Stephen couldn't think of a good reason to leave it off and waited for her to elaborate.

"Is it a sign of my 'frailty' if I wear it or is it a reminder that Murtagh's a jerk?"

"Reminder," he answered immediately. "The man attacked you in a place of business. Wear it and make sure everyone knows why you're wearing it."

She frowned. "You're probably right," she said, twining the end of her braid around her finger.

He had a sudden urge to see how her hair would look if she left it down. "How do you braid your hair with only one hand?"

She did a double take and then laughed, the sound instantly brightening her face and the entire office. "Practice," she teased. "Seriously, they told me I could leave the brace off to shower and all that."

An image of her in the shower filled his mind, pushing out all other coherent thoughts about cars or parts. Crap. He wasn't as immune to her as he wanted to be. *Needed* to be. His hormones had picked the wrong time to come back online. He couldn't let himself abuse her generous spirit just because she was nearby.

"I'll, ah, just get back out there. Let me know if the guy calls back about the Charger."

"Sure thing," she replied.

Somehow Stephen made it through the rest of evening without going into the office and pulling Kenzie into his arms.

Chapter 8

Kenzie was up and out of bed well before her six o'clock alarm on Monday morning. If she'd gotten any sleep at all overnight it was purely by accident. She'd tried reading, meditation and yoga, even a white-noise app on her phone, and still she hadn't been able to quiet the worries that gained strength with every hour closer to deposition day.

She wasn't due at Paul's law office until nine. If Murtagh hadn't messed up her hand, she would be out in the garage burning off this extra energy and indulging in the eye candy that was Stephen elbow-deep in an engine.

Showered, she tied her hair back loosely to give it time to dry. It was too early for her dress uniform, so she chose a camisole top and yoga shorts while she sliced a banana over her breakfast cereal. At the table, she poked at her food while she attempted to review the notes Paul had assembled since taking her case.

Her gaze kept sliding to the class A uniform hanging on the front of the closet door. According to regulations, she could wear the skirt, but she could already picture Murtagh's sneer if she walked in to the deposition with her legs showing. She and Paul had gone back and forth over the wardrobe options and decided the formal uniform sent the most professional and competent message. If Murtagh had his day in court, she'd be wearing the thing far too often during the trial.

She shifted, putting her back to the uniform, and forced down a few more bites of breakfast. When her stomach protested, she dumped the remainder into the trash and took care of her dishes. Her mood lifted a little when she heard the music pumping out from the shop.

Though she had no idea if the desire simmering between her and Stephen would amount to anything, it was comforting to know he would be here when she was done with the legal processes today.

She could get lost in his kisses every day for the rest of her life and still want more. Friendship was a good thing. Loyal, genuine and candid, Stephen was the best kind of friend to have in her corner. If that's all he could give her, she wouldn't be greedy.

Taking care with every aspect of her appearance, she dried her hair and brushed it back into a bun at the nape of her neck. She deftly applied subtle makeup and dressed, thinking about each layer as more armor against Murtagh. Sliding into her patent leather pumps, she patted gloss onto her lips and put the brace on her wrist. With her hat under her arm and a purse that matched her shoes in hand, she left the camper. Whatever happened next, she would handle it with professionalism and dignity.

Stephen stepped outside and she fought the urge to walk right into the shop, lower the door and never come out again. Other than the firehouse, this was the safest place she'd known since her dad died.

"Looking sharp," he said in his quiet way.

He might as well have recited a sonnet, she thought as she felt the heat rising in her cheeks under his serious gaze. "Thank you." She rolled her shoulders back. So many thoughts rattled through her head all at once. Stephen. The case. That kiss. The talking points Paul had given her. Stephen.

"You've got the brace on?"

She lifted it so he could see it better, wishing she could have a hug—or kiss—for luck.

He nodded once. "Go get him."

Oddly enough, those three words were exactly what she needed. She climbed into the loaner and left the yard, heading downtown to her lawyer's office. She'd just found a parking space in the garage two blocks away when her cell phone sounded with the tone she'd assigned to Paul.

She answered on the next ring. "Hello?"

"Where are you?" Paul asked in a low voice, as if he didn't want to be overheard.

"I just parked." She looked at the dash clock. She was on schedule to arrive fifteen minutes early. "What's wrong?"

"Go home."

"Pardon me?" Technically, she didn't have a home until the landlord finished the repair work.

"Do *not* come into this office."

"But—"

"Go straight home. Don't stop anywhere. Keep your phone close."

She tried to ask another question and realized he'd disconnected. What had Marburg and Murtagh done now? It took her only a few seconds to discard the idea of walking into the office and demanding answers. She'd hired him to handle this case and he hadn't let her down yet.

Following directions, she drove straight back to the garage.

Stephen came out, a shop towel over his shoulder, a worried frown pleating his brow. "What's wrong?"

"Paul sent me away," she replied, fuming.

"Why?"

Great question. Too bad she didn't have any answers. "I don't *know*." She had to pause and gather her composure before she could relay what had happened in the parking garage. "I guess I'll be your receptionist today. Give me a few minutes to change."

"You know I don't need a receptionist," he said, trailing her.

She was amped up just enough that if he stepped a toe inside the camper she'd throw herself at him. Those hot kisses of his would go a long way to vaporizing the crazy scenarios running through her mind. What was going on?

"Then you'd better find something else for me to do," she said. She stomped up the steps and slammed the door.

With her hands trembling and her constant check of her phone display, it took her twice as long to get out of her dress uniform and hang it up neatly. She was angry, with no clear target. For all she knew Murtagh was dropping the case. Or the judge had changed his mind about the frivolous nature of the case. Whatever it was, she wanted to *know*.

She found her favorite cutoffs and a T-shirt she'd picked up for free from one of the bands passing through the Escape Club. Dressed, she double-checked that her phone was set to the loudest alert, with the vibration on. Tucking it into her back pocket, she grabbed a pair of socks. She shoved her bare feet into flip-flops and crossed to the office, where her work boots waited under the desk.

Proving his vast wisdom, Stephen had taken shelter in the shop.

Proving she had a measure of common sense left, she traded the flip-flops for the boots and sat down to work. Whether he needed her or not, she could manage the phones and handle some invoicing with the bum hand. More importantly, those tasks had clear results. She needed that illusion of control while she waited for news from her lawyer.

The day ticked on and the only positive she could see was the lack of media outside. It seemed only fair that she might learn what was happening before the reporters caught wind of it.

At lunchtime, her stomach was too jittery to be of any guidance. She wandered into the shop to ask Stephen what he wanted her to order. Ignoring the Nova waiting for attention she couldn't provide, she let her gaze rest on Stephen. As she breathed in the pungent air of a working garage, a lovely calm unfurled inside her.

"You should have coveralls on," he said, without looking her way.

Just to prove she didn't care about stains, she boosted herself up to sit on the edge of a workbench.

"Feeling better?" he asked.

"A little," she admitted. "You need lunch."

From under the hood of a sedan, he turned, one eyebrow lifting. "You don't?"

She looked away. "Subs or pizza?" Either choice gave her a meal for later, assuming her stomach would settle down once Paul explained things.

"Pizza," he replied. "Add one of those chopped salads to our usual order."

Her gaze snapped back to him, though his attention was on the engine. Was he trying to take care of her or was he expecting someone? "Why?"

"My mother taught me to eat my veggies."

She twisted around and used the phone to place the order for delivery. When she was done, it slowly dawned on her that they did have a usual order. After little more than a week of bumping along, they had a routine that he seemed comfortable with. Did he realize it?

Not that her assessment signified anything between them on a personal level, but he seemed to be relaxing about having someone other than Mitch in the shop with him regularly. Growth was a good thing, especially for Stephen, who showed signs of being stuck too long in his own head.

They didn't talk much over lunch, which was probably for the best. With Stephen hovering, she managed to eat an entire slice of pizza in an effort to avoid a lecture. As she was storing the leftovers in the refrigerator, his cell phone sounded.

He scowled at the display and, in the process of sending a text message reply, walked out of the office. Telling herself it was absurd to be jealous that he was getting text messages, she returned to the desk and willed the business phone to ring.

Desperate to stay busy, she started cleaning every visible surface in the office. She'd just finished mopping the floor when her cell phone shivered and screeched from her back pocket. The display showed it was Paul. "Finally," she said as she answered.

"You're at Galway Automotive?" he asked without any greeting.

"Yes."

"I'm on my way," he said. "Just sit tight."

Her hand gripped the mop handle hard. "What happened?"

"The short version is it's over," he said. "Murtagh dropped his suit. I'll explain everything, but I don't want to do it over the phone."

The call ended and she stood there, utterly stunned, leaning on the mop for support.

"You all right?"

She gave a start at the sound of Stephen's voice. He was watching her from the office doorway, and he looked as if he wanted to smile. Or give her a high five. Or something.

"What do you know?"

"It looks great in here. Thanks."

"Stephen, stop messing with me."

His rare grin broke free and he gave the floor a long perusal before walking in. "Julia said she was on her way over with good news about your case."

If he'd known since lunch and hadn't shared, Kenzie wouldn't be responsible for her reaction. "When did she say that?"

"About three minutes ago."

She was tempted to ask him to show her his phone and prove it. That was too much of a jealous, insecure girlfriend move. "Well, it's a good thing I cleaned up if we're entertaining pricey lawyers again," she quipped.

Stephen made a sound that might have been a laugh. She was too antsy about what Paul had to say to trust her interpretation.

Fortunately, she didn't have long to wait. Julia arrived moments before Paul, but refused to spoil what she referred to as Paul's victory speech. When the four of them were gathered in the office, Paul explained that he was able to catch Murtagh lying about Kenzie's rescue efforts in the deposition. Faced with the perjury, the judge questioned Murtagh further and then tossed out the case.

"Murtagh is supposed to cover your legal fees, too," Paul added.

She felt as if a thousand-pound anvil had been lifted from her shoulders.

"And Marburg has issued a press release distancing the firm from Murtagh," Julia said. "I expect it to break on the early evening news. Though I wasn't on his legal team, I did make sure it was okay if I was here to share the news. As a friend."

Kenzie wrapped Julia in a big hug, swaying from side to side. Next, she embraced Paul. "I can't tell you how happy I am." She looked across the room to Stephen and decided to save his hug for later.

"There's more," Paul said. "Assuming your hand is examined and cleared for duty by a PFD doctor, you can go back on shift as early as tomorrow."

"What?" She was sure she hadn't heard him correctly.

Her life was snapping back into place almost as quickly as it had shattered.

"That was the last piece of the puzzle," Paul said. "I've spoken with Chief Anderson and he asked you to come by the firehouse tomorrow regardless of what the doctor says."

She checked the wall clock, wondering if she could wedge herself into a doctor's schedule yet this afternoon.

"Tonight, though," Julia said, "you're expected at the Escape Club for a celebration." She waved her phone. "Grant's orders." She looked to Stephen and Paul. "He's expecting all of us."

"We'll be there," Kenzie answered, before Stephen could make some excuse.

When they were alone, it seemed the moment for hugging him had passed. Shame on her for missing a prime opportunity. "You could take the Charger tonight," she suggested. "Might get some new interest."

"We'll see. You should get over to the doctor's office." With only a hint of a frown on his face, he turned toward the shop.

With a happy gasp, she lunged for the smaller suitcase that had been shoved against the storeroom wall with her other boxed-up belongings.

"What are you looking for?" Stephen had followed her and braced a shoulder against the door jamb.

"My station gear…" She put a little song into the words as she repeated them while she searched. She could proudly wear her uniform again. "I can't go to the doctor for a PFD exam in cutoffs." Hearing him chuckle, she turned around. "Are you laughing at me?"

"Hard not to," he said. "You're as excited as a kid on Christmas morning."

She wrestled out the clothing and shoes she needed, the smile on her face making her cheeks ache in the best way. She did a little happy dance and earned a real laugh from him. Though unpracticed, it was still a great sound. "I'm a firefighter again."

Kenzie wanted to get moving, but Stephen filled the doorway. She wasn't sure she could get by without burrowing into that quiet strength and lingering in an embrace she could easily crave.

"You never stopped being who you are," he said.

There was an odd note of curiosity in his voice and a distance in his hazel eyes that drew her full attention. "What do you mean?"

He stepped back, letting her out of the storeroom. "It takes guts to keep living and believing when your life is torn up. You're an inspiration, Kenzie." He raised her braced hand and kissed her fingertips. Then he walked out of the office and into the shop.

Astonished, her fingertips tingling, Kenzie soaked in the moment.

His laughter and words and the feelings coursing through her and the potential meaning behind all of it… If she didn't have to get her hand checked for work, she would be pursuing this conversation right now. As it was, she made a mental note to discuss it further tonight.

Changed and ready to go, she waved goodbye to Stephen as she climbed into the loaner. She needed some distance to stay on task. She carried the ER report with her to the doctor's office, practically floating while she waited to be seen. Stephen might be right that she'd never stopped being a firefighter, but wearing the uniform made it so wonderfully official.

The doctor cleared her for duty and she sent Stephen a

happy-dance text message. Adding the report to the paperwork she would take to the chief in the morning, she headed back to the garage. Stephen was still working, so she scanned the reports into the computer and sent them on through official channels before she went to the camper to dress for the celebration at the Escape Club.

She stepped into a floral-scented camper. Pale pink tulips, vibrant blue irises and bright sunflowers filled a big vase in the center of the table. The card was a simple congratulations written by Stephen personally, if the grease smudge in the corner was any indication.

He surprised her further when she walked outside to see him pull up in the convertible roadster. Combined with the sweet gesture of the flowers, she wasn't sure how much affection she should read into that decision. Refusing to put it off any longer, she wrapped her arms around him, making the hug as platonic as possible.

"Thank you." She stepped back, suddenly unsure what to do next.

"Guess the flowers were the right touch," he said.

"Yes, thank you for those, too."

His warm gaze swept over her. "You look great."

She'd chosen the dress and sandals she'd worn to her first Sunday dinner at his parents' place. He'd opted for dark jeans, a red polo shirt and deck shoes. "You, too. Red is your color."

He arched an eyebrow. "I'll make a note."

She laughed, feeling balanced by the quip. He had a way of steadying her that she would miss once she was back in her apartment. Stubbornly resisting the subtle melancholy that tried to creep into the moment, she moved toward the car and the party that awaited them.

* * *

Stephen thought he'd seen every facet of Kenzie in the highs and lows of today alone. She'd worn her class A uniform this morning with stern pride and professional resolve. Seeing her in the cutoff shorts and graphic T with those work boots put a pulse of need into his blood-stream like it did every other day. It didn't seem to matter that her mood had been razor-wire sharp instead of her standard happy one. She'd positively glowed when she was back in her station gear and he'd found that sexy as hell, too.

Not as sexy as the dress, he thought when her arm brushed his as she sipped her champagne. The way that hem flirted with her long legs made his palms itch to touch and slide and tease her until she was as needy as he felt. He took a long drink of ice-cold water and tried to convince himself to let her catch a ride back to the garage with someone else.

Grant had spared no expense on the celebration; champagne flowed as toasts were raised to Kenzie. Everyone she worked with at the club came up to congratulate her on the dismissal of the civil suit, praising her fortitude. Mitch and plenty of other firefighters had been invited, as well, and all of them told Kenzie how happy they were to have her back.

He should go, Stephen mused. Parties weren't his thing. He didn't move, however, wanting to soak up every last ounce of her happiness. Was that even fair of him, to bank a little of her joy so he would have some later? He toyed with the car key in his pocket. Mitch and Julia should drive her back. If only the idea of letting Kenzie out of his sight didn't make him want to growl.

"You're scowling," she murmured, leaning close.

She made him smile and laugh, two things he'd thought were gone from his life forever. Her hair, woven into a single braid again, carried the scent of flowers. Flowers he'd given her. A sudden rush of possessiveness startled him. He fought an inner battle for perspective and lost.

"How long is your hair?" He touched the end of the braid where it rested between her shoulder blades.

She trembled under his touch. "Pardon me?"

He met her gaze and those lovely blue eyes burned hot with a desire and heat that mirrored his. "You heard me."

The tip of her tongue moistened her lips and he almost kissed her there in front of everyone. "I'm not sure."

He stared at her, waiting.

Her gaze dropped to his lips. "You'd have to take it down to know for sure," she said.

"Is that an invitation?"

"It is." A slow smile lifted her lips. "Do you plan to accept it?"

He couldn't get her out of the club fast enough. It only complicated matters that he was trying not to reveal his desperate intentions to anyone present. Without traffic, he might have broken land speed records on the way back to the garage.

At last they were safe behind the shelter of his security system. He parked the convertible in front of the trailer and pulled her close, indulging the urgent need to kiss her, reveling in the champagne-spiked heat of her lush mouth.

He broke the kiss only long enough to hurry her into the trailer. She laughed, the sound fizzing through his system as he turned her into his arms and picked up where they'd left off in the car.

She was so responsive, matching his ardor and pressing into his touch, his body, drawing out passionate needs he'd never thought he'd experience again. He tugged at the elastic holding her braid and eased her hair loose inch by inch, until it fell in waves around her face, spilling over her shoulders and down over her breasts.

He nuzzled into the pale, silky warmth of her glorious hair, scattering kisses up and down her throat. She'd left off the brace tonight, and when her hands slipped under his shirt to caress his chest and abs, he was lost.

He picked her up and carried her back to the bed. Peeling away her clothing and his, he marveled with every discovery of what made her sigh and gasp and cling. She gave and gave, bringing his body to life with every kiss and touch, every sweet moan and plea for more.

At last he sank deep into the embrace of her body and they were joined intimately. He looked down into her face and her smile held a tenderness he'd never seen. Yet another facet of this incomparable woman.

Something shifted deep in his chest at the gift so freely given, a sweet loosening that flowed through every fiber of his body. Her hands ran up and down his arms, her fingertips flexing into his back as he moved within her and found the sensual rhythm that carried them both to a shattering climax. When he collapsed beside her, pleasantly exhausted, she curled into him without a word, her hand resting gently over his thundering heart.

A few hours later, Stephen disentangled himself from Kenzie's long limbs and scooted out of the bed, immediately regretting leaving her warm, supple body. Her long, silky hair fanned out across the pillows and her eyelashes were dark crescents against her cheeks. Asleep she looked as happy and content as she did awake, as if any minute a figment of her dreams would crack a joke and make her laugh. He would never figure out how she managed it.

God, she was beautiful, inside and out.

He gathered his clothing, pausing just long enough to make sure she slept on. Tiptoeing to the front of the trailer, he tugged on his jeans, tossed his shirt over his shoulder and picked up his shoes. Sneaking away like this was cowardly, but he convinced himself she wouldn't want him underfoot while she readied for her first morning back on shift.

Stretched out on the couch in the office, he decided there would be plenty of time to talk about what last night meant—if it could mean anything—once she came home from the firehouse.

Home. The word tripped him up. Although she was staying in his place this wasn't home for her. It couldn't be. That loose and free sensation in his chest felt wobbly and lost now that he was alone. Clearly, he didn't have the mettle to leave himself open to the inevitable heartache of really sharing his life once more. She deserved a man who could do that.

Her career was fraught with danger. Though he knew the risks were carefully managed through training and teamwork, she voluntarily put herself in harm's way to save others.

Afraid of being broken beyond repair, he wasn't the kind of man she needed at all. Stephen was more than a little shocked by the sting of that realization.

Chapter 9

Kenzie was on such a high being back at the firehouse that she didn't have time to dwell on the awkwardness of sleeping with Stephen last night. She'd told herself repeatedly it was good that he hadn't been there this morning. Trying to come up with breakfast and conversation would've been so much worse. This way last night could stay in its own miraculous little time capsule. Two people capitalizing on a special moment to enjoy a physical outlet for stress.

And what an outlet, she thought, remembering his hands in her hair, on her skin. *Mind on the job*, she coached herself. Though she didn't wish anyone harm, she hoped for a busy shift. It would help her get back into the routine.

Lieutenant Daniel Jennings waited for her to finish pouring her coffee. "Glad to have you back, Hughes."

"Thanks. It feels good to be home." She sipped the dark brew. "Is everything set for the wedding?"

His smile oozed happiness. "I'll say yes, but only because my bride-to-be isn't here to disagree."

She caught up with the rest of the men and women on her shift, pleased no one seemed inclined to discuss Murtagh or why he'd dropped the suit. She suspected they'd heard about his perjury through the grapevine, anyway. Time flew by between answering calls and handling the maintenance details that kept the personnel, equipment and firehouse in peak condition.

Throughout the afternoon she saw the occasional media van roll by, but didn't think anything of it. Since Murtagh's fifteen minutes of fame had expired when the judge tossed out his case, Paul had warned her the media might come looking for a comment from her. She had no intention of providing any sound bites. Even though today was a joyful one, she would continue to direct reporters to her lawyer. She intended to keep all the legal nonsense firmly behind her.

With energy to burn, Kenzie kept so busy that she didn't realize she was at the center of another firestorm until Chief Anderson called her into his office after their latest emergency response.

"What's up?" she asked. There was nothing as awesome as being back at the firehouse with a crew that felt like family. Here, everyone had her back and she had theirs. She didn't have to convince anyone of her ability to act or make the right decisions. Everyone here knew Murtagh had gone out of his way trying to make her look bad. Feeling alone against the world's judgment had been the worst part of being on administrative leave.

"Have a seat," Anderson said, his face serious. "We've been dealing with circling media sharks all day."

"Is Murtagh doing interviews again?" She wouldn't put it past him to keep right on complaining about her, despite the dismissal of his civil suit. Surely she was entitled to more than a twenty-four-hour break from his antics.

"Not exactly." The chief handed her a folder. "This seems to be new trouble and it's too early to tell if Murtagh is connected." He cleared his throat. "These hit the noon news cycle, with more details promised at the evening hours."

"What kind of details?" She opened the folder and gasped. Nude pictures of her in the firehouse showers, her body barely concealed by billowing steam, were accompanied by the vulgar insinuations that her primary role at the PFD was to satisfy her male colleagues.

For a moment the horrible violation stole her breath. This couldn't be happening. Had someone really put cameras in the bathrooms? Gross. She wanted to shred the pictures and then go hide under a blanket or turnout gear. As long as there were layers and layers between her skin and the rest of the world.

Then she looked closer. That wasn't her body in the pictures, just a woman with blond, braided hair posing in a steamy shower. The tilework in the background wasn't the same as the firehouse. "These are faked."

"I know." Chief Anderson cleared his throat. "Still damned awkward to have this conversation. I've sent that information up the line. The media isn't going to know the difference, might not even care as long as they're getting a story. Reporters and photographers from all sorts of outlets are likely to hound you for a comment or reaction.

"Better keep going," he said, his voice grim.

"Pardon me?"

"The file," he said. "Keep going, so you have an idea what to expect."

There were several pages of screen shots where the faked nude images had been tagged with her name and plastered all over social media. The comments were riddled with lewd suggestions.

Outraged, she forced herself to continue. There were more screen captures of Kenzie out with friends at a bridal shower, a bachelor party for Daniel Jennings, and other recent social events with girlfriends or off-shift gatherings with her crew. The captions were crass, implying she was forever in pursuit of a good time or a convenient man.

"Several of these were pulled from my social media accounts."

"Yes," Chief Anderson replied.

She paused at a great shot of her and the chief at one of the PFD family picnics last summer. "I love this picture."

"Me, too," he said.

Now that moment was tainted by whoever was trying to drum up a scandal.

Seeing a picture of her interacting with Jason at the Escape Club, she groaned. "Murtagh must be behind this," she said, handing the folder back. "That photo was from the night he attacked me at the club. He's certainly painting me in the worst light possible."

"On my word that this is another attack against you,

the department has launched an investigation. They've warned me it could take some time to sort out the source."

"The PFD can clear up the most offensive part of this by simply posting pictures proving that isn't one of our bathrooms."

"That still leaves people to jump to the conclusion that you posed for the pictures elsewhere."

She hadn't thought of that. "It isn't me." How could she prove the woman blurred by the steam wasn't her?

The chief stacked his palms over the folder. "I know you don't want to hear this, but the department is recommending administrative leave."

"No." She surged to her feet and planted her hands on her hips. "I didn't *do* any of this. It's outright slander." This was becoming the worst summer of her life. "I'm a victim!" She snapped her mouth shut, the words leaving a bitter aftertaste on her tongue.

"I understand you're caught in the middle. The department is following a set protocol. It's a publicity nightmare."

"No kidding?" She turned in a tight circle, trying to keep her temper in check. "Chief, please. I just got back on the job." She struggled to breathe through the sudden panic clawing at her chest. "The civil suit was dropped because Murtagh got caught up in his lies. You and I and the rest of the PFD knew I wasn't at fault to start with."

"This is different. To the department, this looks like conduct unbecoming," he said. "Right now we don't know who set this in motion, only that your name is on the pictures. The fact is, there are enough legitimate postings misrepresented to give credit to the faked photos."

Her stomach pitched. "That's absurd."

"Call your lawyer, and the union rep, too."

Just when she'd thought the days of saving for legal fees were over. "It isn't me!" She reached for the folder and shuffled until she found one of the pictures that had been pulled from her social media accounts. "Your wife was there, along with other wives and kids, too. There isn't a man in these pictures I've ever been with romantically."

"I've told them all of that. I'll make your side of this crystal clear in my written report, as well. We still need to work within the established system."

She bit back an oath as red hazed her vision. "This is the worst form of bullying. The PFD should want to avoid the appearance of giving in to this kind of stunt."

"Public relations are a serious matter, Kenzie. Going through the steps doesn't feel fair to you, but it's necessary for the greater good of the department."

"Right." She closed her eyes, counted to ten, but still couldn't calm down. "I do what's necessary while this miserable bully gets to do whatever he damn well pleases to trash my name and reputation? If you suspend me again you play right into his agenda."

"Lower your voice," Chief Anderson snapped. "I understand your point of view. I know your integrity and work ethic. You're a valued member of this house."

"Not for long, at this rate." She folded her arms over her chest. What would she do if this ended her career? Last week Stephen had joked about hiring her full-time at the garage, though he really didn't want anyone else around. She loved it there. Part of the reason the situation worked was because they both accepted that her invasion of his sanctuary was temporary.

"I'm doing all I can to prevent that," Anderson said.

He sighed heavily. "Let me make a call. While I do that, go speak with your lawyer."

"And my union rep," she said. "Yes, sir." Dismissed, she went to her bunk and called Paul. That conversation didn't go much better than her conversation with Chief Anderson. Who knew how hard it was to prove the source of cyberbullying and fake pictures? Oh yeah, everyone.

They might never prove Murtagh was behind this slanderous attack on her entire life. She had to hope they could track down the original source of the nude photos and prove it wasn't her.

Kenzie was sitting on her bunk, wondering what to do next, half wishing for the distraction of another emergency call, when her cell phone hummed in her hand. When the display showed Galway Automotive, she tapped the icon to answer. "Hi."

"Any idea why news vans are circling my place like sharks?" Stephen asked without preamble.

"Yes," she replied, utterly dejected. She could hear his favorite heavy metal group on the stereo in the background. "I know I shouldn't ask you for any more favors. If you could pack up my stuff in the camper, that would be a big help. I'll text you an address to drop it off."

"What?" The background music died. "What are you talking about?"

"Moving out." It had been fun while it lasted and last night had been amazing, but Stephen had no patience for this kind of chaos. She didn't have any illusions that sex meant relationship in his mind. When he did make that decision, he deserved a woman who wouldn't bring media vans along for the ride. "I'm giving you some much-deserved peace."

"Your apartment's ready?" he asked.

The confusion in his voice made her pause. "Well, no."

"Then why would you move out?"

She'd just told him. "Because of the circling sharks," she replied, exasperated.

"You sound tired," he stated.

"I am." Tired of being hounded and hassled by a man who kept getting away with it.

"What's wrong, Kenzie?"

The tenderness in Stephen's voice undid her. She supposed it was better if he didn't hear it from the reporters. "Someone has been on a mission spreading lies and nasty pictures online, demeaning my work and my character. The media is circling your place hoping to get a comment."

"Great."

"They'd be happier if they caught me in the act of performing some sexual service, too."

He swore.

"I agree completely," she said. "The PFD may take disciplinary action."

"Against you?" He slammed something that clanged loudly. "You didn't do anything wrong."

His outraged confidence in her innocence made her feel warm all over. She appreciated that his first reaction was belief in her. "I'm told appearances matter in public and community relations. More process and systems to work through. I haven't been dumped back on admin leave yet. Given enough time, they should figure out I'm not the problem, and any investigation or disciplinary hearing will end in my favor." She wished she believed that.

The silence on his end made her think the call had

been dropped. More likely he'd hung up, except her screen showed he was still there. "Stephen?"

"Mitch is on shift with you?"

"Yes."

"Have him take you to his place after work."

She supposed it made sense, although she didn't want to crash with newlyweds. Especially not after she'd slept with her friend's brother. "What about the loaner car?"

"I'll pick it up from the firehouse later."

"Hang on," she said. "I can't do that. If the media catches me riding home with Mitch it will only add fuel and credibility to the nasty rumors." She understood Stephen didn't want her at the garage, yet staying with Mitch wasn't the answer.

"I don't want you dealing with this alone," he said.

"Thanks. At the moment I don't see an alternative." The alert rang through the firehouse as another call came in. "Gotta go. I'll check in later."

She pushed the conversation and the soft feelings Stephen's concern left behind to the back of her mind. If they wanted to sideline her again, they'd have to catch her first.

Stephen sent a text to Mitch, knowing it would be a while before his brother could reply if they were headed out on a call. It couldn't be as bad as she thought, although… His gaze drifted to the monitors showing media vans completely circling his block. Maybe it was.

At the computer, he typed Kenzie's name into the search box and sat back as the results flooded his screen. The articles and pictures left him shell-shocked. The outrageous claims and ugly insinuations made him want to toss his monitor through the window. This was a blatant attack by a coward hiding behind a keyboard. He closed the various windows and cleared the search from the computer history.

It had to be Murtagh. Stephen fisted his hands on the desktop, wishing he had a direct target.

He agreed with her that *processes* and *systems* were lousy words when she was under the pressure of this obnoxious, damaging bullying. He might not like the media attention personally, but he could ride it out for her sake.

She sure as hell couldn't go anywhere else in town and have the protection his fence and security offered her. He had to come up with a better solution than letting her cope with the chaos alone.

Picking up the phone, he called Grant for an assist. With luck, the former cop knew someone capable of unraveling the cyber side of this mess. A few minutes later, Stephen was relieved to hear Grant had already set things in motion.

Next, he dialed Joey Garcia at the paint and body shop and called in a favor. If he could get Kenzie back home without being harassed by any reporters, maybe she'd understand she really did have someone in her corner.

Although he might not be in the market for a real relationship, he sure as hell knew how to be a good friend.

Kenzie was overwhelmed by the warm fuzzy feelings of being cared for. She was used to doing more than pulling her own weight in any circumstance, and made a habit of handling her life on her terms. Stephen had stepped up in a big way. She still wasn't sure how he'd done it, leaving her one of Joey Garcia's showy street racer mods for the end of her shift, and instructions to drive to Joey's shop rather than Galway Automotive.

At Garcia's warehouse, behind the shelter of a closed bay door, Stephen had been waiting for her. He took her backpack out of her hands and led her to another of Joey's cars, this one with tinted windows. Once he was sure no one from the media had caught on, he drove her over to Mitch and Julia's house.

The four of them had enjoyed a pasta dinner with all the trimmings, complete with gelato for dessert. They played a couple card games, and the only hard-and-fast rule of the night was no one could mention anything about Murtagh or work in general. It had been pure bliss.

After reversing the cars on the way back, he got her safely behind the fence surrounding the garage. When she'd tried to thank him, to let him know how much the evening meant to her, he only gave her a slow, bone-melting kiss at the camper door and told her to get some rest.

What was she supposed to think when he did things like that? She'd known he was one of those rare men in the world who knew when and how to do just the right thing, but this was an unexpected, charming side of him.

As she undressed, she'd found it easier to follow his instructions to rest, after such a relaxing evening. She'd crawled into bed and fallen asleep thinking of Stephen. He was her first thought in the morning, too, even before she checked her phone to see if the PFD had put her back on admin leave.

Not yet.

She hustled through her morning routine, eager to get to the firehouse as early as possible. The Charger was waiting in front of the camper with a big Galway Automotive For Sale sign in the rear window. She'd laughed, happy for him to get some free publicity if the media followed her today. Advertising potential aside, she was relieved to find the streets in front of the garage and the firehouse media-free.

The station wasn't as busy today as they'd been yesterday, and she found she didn't need the busyness with this lingering, overall good feeling. Every hour she was on duty gave her hope that the PFD would see through the obnoxious cyberbullying tactics and let her stay on the job.

Late in the afternoon they were all worn-out from clearing a faulty smoke detector system in a nearby apartment building. As the driver slowed to make the turn to the firehouse, he brought the truck to a stop. Hearing Lieutenant Jennings curse from his seat up front, Kenzie twisted around to see what had upset them.

Hate messages aimed at her had been scrawled across the white garage door in red spray paint. Murtagh, or some knucklehead sharing his views, had made his displeasure with female firefighters quite plain. Her stomach churned at this direct assault on all of them as a house.

Naturally, the graffiti meant the vultures, in the form of news crews, had returned. Vans were stationed across the street, and cameramen and reporters were jockeying for the best angle, no doubt getting prime footage to go along with their endless opinions of her PFD career. Thankfully, none of the reporters seemed to be interviewing Murtagh.

There was no question in Kenzie's mind who had done this. Her first hope was that Murtagh had finally been caught in the act of causing trouble. That would be a far better spin on this bizarre story than the hateful messages against women who served the city with skill and commitment. Secondary to that, she hoped the men and women she worked with and for wouldn't hold this against her.

For the first time, she gave serious thought to moving away. Not wishful thinking because she was discouraged this time. No, as the idea rolled through her mind it gained momentum and substance. She could relocate and find work in another state. Maybe down in Maryland, closer to her mom and sister. She liked that area, although joining another fire department would depend on how well she could clean up the cyberbullying trash.

As the door rolled up and the truck parked in the bay, she joined the rest of her crew resetting everything for the next call.

Mitch rapped her gently on the shoulder. "It'll pass," he said. "We've got your back."

"Thanks." She wasn't sure she believed that it would pass. It seemed like every time things went her way Murtagh did something worse to impede her forward progress. Why was he so damn fixated on her?

"I'll get started on the cleanup right away," she said. Erasing Murtagh's hate would give her time to think through the potentially tough choices right in front of her. She felt like she was at a crossroads and she couldn't see enough to know which direction was best.

Chief Anderson found her in the supply room. "I need a word with you."

"Yes, sir." Misery dogging her, she followed him to his office and closed the door.

"You know you're important to this house, to everyone in it?"

She swallowed. He'd said that yesterday. "Yes." Attempting to say anything more than that single syllable put her emotions too close to the surface.

"We have security cameras, as you know, but the footage isn't clear." Anderson clutched the arms of his chair. "The one camera with the best angle was found broken this morning. We haven't had time to get it fixed. I've spoken with the police and they will canvas the area for any witnesses or leads."

She bit back the urge to toss accusations at Murtagh. The chief knew every lousy thing that had been said about her no matter if it was graffiti on a door, online, or in a formal complaint.

"Those are the facts," the chief said.

"Okay." She pressed her lips together, willing the trembling to stop.

"You're an excellent firefighter, Kenzie."

"Thank you, sir." Using her first name meant he was attempting to soften tough news. Again. She shifted toward the door. "I'll get on that cleanup," she interjected.

"I've already called a professional. You can help if they let you."

She focused on the option to help, clinging to every ounce of positive. That meant he expected her to be here when the professionals arrived.

"I've been asked to put you on administrative leave again."

That last bit of hope burst like a balloon. Kenzie stifled the automatic protest. Chief Anderson spoke plainly. He reminded her of Grant in that habit.

"I negotiated a compromise. You can be here on shift. You just won't go on calls."

What good would that do her, the house or the PFD? "I'll brush up on my cooking skills," she said.

"Everyone up the line believes Murtagh is behind this. This is *not* a disciplinary action," he said. "We're taking these measures to protect you."

"Of course. I appreciate it, sir."

"If I could haul Murtagh in here and make him scrub those obscenities away with a toothbrush, I would."

She nodded, the image lightening the burden just a little. She wasn't in this alone. With this stunt, Murtagh had attacked everyone at this house and earned the enduring displeasure of the PFD as a whole. Whatever he thought he could gain by forcing her out of her career, this wasn't the way to get it.

She steeled herself to ask her only remaining question. "Chief, if I were to relocate, would the PFD provide a good reference?"

He sat back in his chair, studying her. "You want to leave Philly?"

"Not at all." She straightened her shoulders. "I just feel it's smart to consider the option for the sake of the PFD as well as myself."

The chief pinched the bridge of his nose. "I sure as hell hope it doesn't come to that," he said. "Your exemplary record of service stands on its own and I believe any reference would reflect that."

"Thank you, sir."

She left the office on unsteady knees, inordinately relieved and wondering what Murtagh would try next. In the kitchen she took an inventory, making a shopping list. When the professional cleaning crew arrived she went out and insisted on helping.

By end of shift, Mitch followed her home, and she returned to Stephen's garage too tired to be angry about any of it.

Stephen stepped out of the office as soon as she parked in front of the camper. Did he have to look so sexy leaning against that door? She knew they should talk about what was brewing between them, specifically where they stood after that amazing bout of sex. Surely a conversation like that could wait until tomorrow.

"You okay?"

She paused at the camper steps. "Mitch called you."

Stephen nodded. "Sent a picture, too."

"I don't want to talk about it." Kenzie wanted to scream. She wanted to go inside and indulge in a private, ugly cry to clean the emotional slate so she could go back to being strong and stoic tomorrow.

"There's smothered chicken casserole in the oven," Stephen said. "Salad in the fridge." He gave her another long look and then stepped back into the office.

She gaped at him. "Thanks," she called out belatedly.

"Welcome."

She stared at the closed door, knowing it wasn't locked. He kept it open, as promised, in case she ever needed anything in the night.

She suspected that what she really needed—communication, intimacy, connection—he wasn't ready or able to give. With an effort, she marched into the camper, intending to take a shower before she bothered with food.

The space smelled heavenly with the comforting aromas of garlic, paprika and bacon. She opened the refrigerator and found a bottle of white wine beside the salad. Mitch might have given him a warning, but just like last night, Stephen had stepped up on his own. It scared her to realize she could get used to this…this care and affection. He was inherently kind and thoughtful, and just kept those aspects buried under the scowl and brusque conversations to keep people at arm's length. She loved all those variations of him.

If—when—she moved away, she'd miss this almost-friends-with-benefits thing they were dancing around. Given time and less baggage, they might have a chance at something more. Unfortunately, this was where they were, who they were, and she'd be better off accepting reality.

Shaking off the melancholy, she pulled the plastic container she'd brought from work out of her backpack. She'd had plenty of time in the kitchen after the graffiti cleanup was done, and used the time to bake several batches of chocolate chip cookies, using her new favorite recipe from Shannon, the soon-to-be Mrs. Daniel Jennings.

Kenzie sank into the bench seat at the table. How was she ever going to leave the PFD family she loved so much? This city was her birthright, and she'd earned her place as a firefighter. Contrary to Murtagh's poisonous claims, no one had handed her a spot simply because she was Ken Hughes's daughter. The opposite, really. It hadn't been easy to walk in the wake of a man so well-respected.

Wrapping two cookies in a paper towel for herself, she took the remaining four in the container over to the office and knocked on the door. It opened quickly, as if Stephen had been standing right there waiting for her. It was a nice fantasy.

"I thought you'd like these," she said. "Chocolate chip cookies," she added unnecessarily, as he popped the top and the sweet aroma of dark chocolate goodness wafted up between them. "Thanks for making sure I had dinner."

"You made these?"

"Slow shift," she replied with a shrug.

He braced a shoulder against the doorjamb and his lips gave a subtle kick at one corner. "My sisters call it stress baking."

"They might be right," she allowed. "Good night, Stephen."

Those hazel eyes heated as he studied her. "Thanks for delivering dessert."

"Sure. Enjoy." She took a step backward toward the safety of the camper. That hungry look in his eyes made her want to grab him and kiss him and enjoy an altogether different type of dessert. One mistake of that variety was probably more than enough for both of them, no matter what her hormones and heart were saying about it right now.

Working light duty within the safety of the firehouse was almost worse than being forced to stay away completely. Almost. She made it through her overnight shift without any additional Murtagh-related antics. Unfortunately, according to her lawyer and Grant, progress was slow on the cyberbullying investigation. Although the nude photo had been found posted on several stock image websites, obviously the source, it was only one piece of that puzzle.

On Thursday, her first day off from the PFD, she hit the garage early because some of the parts for the Nova had come in. Between standard maintenance jobs, she was working through the initial assessment of the classic car.

In the garage, she set an alarm so she would stop work in time to clean up and change for her scheduled shift at the Escape Club. When the clanging bell sound interrupted the heavy metal music Stephen had cranked up, she turned it off and finished up an oil change for one of Stephen's regular customers. "All set here for Mrs. Giaconne," she called. "Want me to make the call for her to pick it up?"

"I'll take care of it," Stephen replied.

"Great." Kenzie stripped out of the protective coveralls, feeling Stephen's gaze tracking her movements. It gave her a charge to know he appreciated the view. And it was a pleasant diversion from the reason she was suddenly underfoot, invading his space again. No one wanted her going anywhere alone right now.

Though the police had questioned Murtagh about the nasty messages spray painted across the firehouse, he hadn't been arrested. Grant had learned Murtagh had an alibi. Kenzie appreciated having such great support, but she wanted her life back.

She wouldn't put it past the craggy old man to have paid a couple kids to tag the firehouse for him. The one person caught on camera moved better than she'd ever seen Murtagh move. Then again, he'd shown some strength and quick reflexes that night at the club when he'd been proving his point that she was too weak to handle trouble.

Which was the act and which was real?

"Are you coming by the club tonight?" she asked, as she traded her boots for her flip-flops.

Stephen stepped back from the brake job in front of him, scowling at the rotor. "We'll see."

She knew that look by now. He'd found something that insulted his mechanic's heart.

"Want me to check for parts?" she offered. "I have some time."

He made a noise she didn't worry about interpreting. "I'll do it," he said.

Working beside him for these two weeks, she'd come to understand how his brain sifted information. He was a genius with engines, with everything a car could throw at him, really, and he did superb, thorough work. Her father would have happily spent hours in this garage beside Stephen, sorting out problems and solutions.

Strange that it took her this long to get interested in a man she believed her father would have approved of. More than that, he would have found a kindred spirit in Stephen. Too bad she couldn't figure out if she had a chance of actually dating him.

She walked out to the camper before she said something she might regret, something that might put him on the defensive. They weren't exactly walking on eggshells around each other since the night the civil suit had been dismissed, but neither of them seemed to know what to do with the other.

Well, she had some ideas she would happily have employed if she could figure out if Stephen wanted to go down that path.

Maybe she had crossed a line, though he'd started it, asking about her braid. And she hadn't been alone as they'd steamrolled right through that friendship boundary. Stephen had been right there with her, through every kiss and touch. Until the morning after, when she'd woken up alone. Other than that one tender kiss and countless thoughtful gestures, he seemed to prefer ignoring the event altogether.

Since she'd gone back to the PFD, they'd settled into this weird routine of friendly camaraderie with an undercurrent of sexual tension that kept her on edge. Stephen was too stoic to give her any idea what he was feeling. Other than distant.

The situation was something she should sort out with a sister or girlfriend, except she didn't have one of those handy at the moment. It wasn't a discussion she wanted to have over the phone with her mom, who was worried enough about her already. And it wasn't a discussion she felt comfortable having with Julia, his sister-in-law.

In the camper, she pulled all the shades down. It was a paranoid move, yet she couldn't stop herself. The media was still seeking a comment from her about the cyber-bully who'd targeted her. Despite the security around Stephen's garage, she struggled against a persistent sense of dread.

"Anyone would," she told her reflection as she tied the end of her braid. "The jerk only wins if you let him."

Once Murtagh had perjured himself in the civil case, public opinion had turned on him. Even without solid proof, she got the feeling the man had no intention of letting up. He'd been cagey about it, but she knew deep down in her gut he was responsible for every attempt to embarrass her and the department.

As much as she wanted to ignore Murtagh, her mind kept trying to figure out what he hoped to gain. It was like trying to find the source of an errant rattle in a car frame.

She glanced at the wedding invitation she'd tucked into her makeup case. On July 4 Daniel Jennings would marry Shannon Nolan and have an instant family with her young son, Aiden.

Kenzie remembered how fast and hard he'd fallen for both the woman and her little boy. Actually, Aiden had won over everyone on his very first visit to the firehouse.

The wedding would be amazing and she wanted to go celebrate such a wonderful milestone with friends who were as close as family.

Weeks ago, she'd responded that she'd be attending the ceremony and reception alone. Daniel had made it clear on her first shift back that she could bring a date. Everyone in their circles knew she'd been staying with Stephen since her apartment closed. Clearly, speculation about them was gaining traction.

It wasn't a surprise. In her community people cared about each other. People knew Stephen as the son of a firefighter and older brother of another. They also knew Stephen had become morose and withdrawn since his fiancée's murder. Him letting Kenzie live with him and helping her at every opportunity was raising all kinds of eyebrows.

If she asked him to go with her to the wedding, would that hurt him more than it helped her?

Silly to get too wound up about it before she'd even asked him. Tying her sneakers, she grabbed her backpack and keys. If she didn't get moving she'd be late and that wasn't who she was. Dressed in her Escape Club uniform, she headed back to the garage to tell Stephen she was leaving.

And ask him to go with her to a wedding.

Chapter 10

In the garage, Stephen dropped the phone back on the cradle and glanced up to see Kenzie dressed for her waitressing shift at the club. Things had been a little awkward, at least on his side, since they'd slept together. Natural, basic needs, he reminded himself. They were consenting adults and clearly compatible in and out of bed. Still, he should probably make time to *talk* about it. Maybe she'd be open to...what?

Although it felt wrong to suggest they hook up whenever the mood struck, he believed sex could remain a fun distraction for them both, as long as they weren't adding in elements of a relationship. He *liked* Kenzie; he just couldn't go down that road again. She might understand if he found the guts and the right words to explain it.

So why did he keep hesitating?

"You okay?" she asked, her head tipped to the side.

"Lost in thought," he said, patting himself on the back for the clear communication. "You're closing tonight?"

"Hmm? Yes." Her gaze darted around the office. "Are you heading out, too?"

"They need a wrecker on the Schuylkill Expressway. Big accident."

"Is the vehicle coming back here?"

"Not from the sound of it," he replied.

"All right," she said. "Be safe."

With everything going on, those two words had become their form of saying goodbye.

"Thanks. You, too." Should he kiss her? He wanted to, had been missing her lips, the soft curve of her cheek under his palm. The last time they'd kissed was after the dinner he'd arranged with Mitch and Julia. Good grief, with Kenzie around, he felt more like an insecure teenager than a capable adult. If he asked a friend for advice he'd only be setting himself up for those subtle, hopeful glances that silently asked if he was finally moving on with his life.

"Ah, one quick question," she said, trailing him out of the office. "Daniel Jennings is getting married on Sunday."

Stephen paused. Whatever he'd hoped she might say, that wasn't it. "They're getting married on the Fourth?"

His fiancée had been gone three years and still weddings creeped him out. Mitch's wedding had been the only invitation he'd accepted in all that time. Thankfully, his brother had put the best man duties at the reception on their younger brother's shoulders.

"Would you go with me?" She stepped closer as the words tumbled out in a rush. "I know it's July Fourth and last-minute, but with Murtagh skulking around, I really don't want to drive out there alone. Mitch offered to let me ride with them, but I'd rather not if I can avoid it. If you're willing that is. Please?"

When she seemed to run out of words, or oxygen, she stared at him, her blue eyes wide and hopeful and her lips clamped together. How, exactly, was he supposed to say no when she looked at him that way? He doubted any man with a pulse could resist that appeal.

"You just want me to drive you over?" *Please just need a driver*, he thought.

"Well, I was hoping you'd stick around as my plus one."

"As…as your date?" He couldn't remember the last time he'd let a woman ask him out. He stared at her, wondering what she was thinking. Being flattered and confused was his problem.

"Would that be so terrible for you?" she asked.

He pulled himself together. Another woman might have posed the same question like a cornered cat, hoping to save face. Not Kenzie. She was genuinely concerned that he couldn't handle it.

"I'll take you." He told himself it was simply to erase that furrow of worry between her golden eyebrows.

Relief washed over her face and she bounced a little on her toes. "Thanks so much. We don't have to stay long—"

"It's fine." He felt his lips curve as he watched her. "We should both get going."

"Right." She started forward, then rocked back on her heels. "I'll just, um, go now."

He gave in to all that sweet, fiery energy bubbling from her and luring him in. Reaching out, he caught her elbow, drawing her back so he could press a quick kiss to her lips.

A jolt like heat lightning speared through his system and he took the kiss deeper. When he released her, a dazzled smile spread slowly across her face. Yeah, that's what they both needed, an affirmation of this desire thundering like a distant storm.

"Be safe," he reminded her. They walked out and he hit the gate for her to leave ahead of him as he climbed into the cab of the tow truck.

Given a choice, he'd follow her to the club first, but he was needed at the accident site and trailing her would only undermine her fragile independence.

He could see Murtagh's sneaky antics were taking a toll on her. Although nothing new had happened for almost forty-eight hours, everyone was on edge, anticipating who knew what. The man hadn't done anything sensible since she'd pulled him out of that fire.

Stephen wished there was a more direct solution that would allow Kenzie to get her life back on track. In a perfect world, she'd never be out of his sight until the police had Murtagh contained. Hardly a perfect solution, as it would make them both crazy. She had too much energy to be cooped up even in a place as busy as his garage. And he was used to being alone, coming and going as he pleased without any concern for anyone else.

It surprised him to realize he was going to miss her when she eventually went back to her place. That was for the best, he reminded himself. He wasn't the man she needed. He wasn't the man any woman needed. His business and family were plenty of life for him.

Once Kenzie left he could get back to honoring Anna-beth's memory by keeping an eye on the community center. He thought of those pictures of Kenzie with the bartender that been plastered on social media sites with derogatory comments. Subtract the nasty side of it and Stephen could see them together. A guy like that, outgoing and friendly, suited her better than Stephen ever could.

So why did he feel anger bubbling by the time he caught up to the traffic jam near the accident site? He had no right to be possessive or jealous over her. They were a couple of people riding out a tough situation. Better to keep it at that.

He liked her because she was a great person. End of story. She knew her cars inside and out, which was as fun as hell. They worked well together, which was rare for him. She tolerated his music, didn't try to talk constantly, and when she had something to say, she said it clearly.

He enjoyed doing things for her. She was always so pleased and a little surprised. So what if he hadn't done those things for anyone in three years? She deserved it, the way she did so much for others, including him.

She was beautiful and sexy with all those subtle curves. That laugh. He felt himself grinning just thinking about her. Man, he never got tired of that sound. His hand flexed as he recalled that quiet triumph when he'd finally got that braid loose. He could weave his fingers through her hair all night. Would she like that?

He was relieved when the police guided him around the stopped cars to the wreck. Stephen swallowed hard, trying to ignore the signs of lives forever changed. Three cars and an 18-wheeler were crumpled as if a giant had thrown a tantrum. He could avert his eyes from the blood on the shattered windshield of a sedan, but the scorched metal and recently extinguished gasoline fire assaulted his nostrils.

One fire truck pulled away as Stephen positioned the tow truck to collect a minivan the same color as Megan's. It had been crumpled like an accordion. It wasn't her car, he knew it wasn't, yet his heart hammered in his chest at the sight of a child seat in the second row.

One of the police officers on the scene was Bob Greely, an old friend from the neighborhood. "Did anyone make it out?" Stephen asked him when he walked over to say hello.

"Only the one fatality," Bob replied. He aimed his chin toward the 18-wheeler. "According to witnesses, the idiot on the bike was zipping in and out of traffic and misjudged the cutback in front of the semi."

Stephen hadn't noticed the motorcycle wedged into the front wheel well of the truck's cab. "Damn."

"Guy wasn't wearing a helmet, didn't stand a chance when he was thrown clear." Bob shook his head. "I think the others will all survive, though there were some serious injuries."

"Good to know."

Stephen hooked up the minivan and secured it on the bed. "I've got room for the sedan if you want," he offered.

"That would help. Everything's going to evidence first," Bob said. "You know the address."

He dropped plenty of cars at the evidence lot.

"Thanks, man." Bob came to the door as Stephen climbed up into the cab. "Hey, is that Kenzie Hughes really staying with you?"

"She is." Stephen braced himself, determined to keep his cool no matter what Bob said next.

"Good. I saw some of that crap on the news. Your security is tighter than Fort Knox, and sounds like she needs it."

Stephen paused. "What do you mean?"

"Just having a rough time, is all."

"Yeah." For a minute Stephen had hoped Bob might know something more "Can't the cops do anything about Murtagh?"

"Not my beat, but you know we try to watch out for our own. Can't believe he went after her that way with the interviews and the, ah, other stuff."

Based on his reddening face, apparently Bob thought the pictures were real. Stephen bristled, barely suppressing the urge to explain that the steamy nude shower photos plastered on the internet weren't actually Kenzie. It wasn't Bob's business. Technically, it wasn't Stephen's business either, and he needed to remember that.

He drove over and loaded up the sedan, then maneuvered out of the area, waiting patiently for the state troopers to make room for him to join the flow of traffic.

He used the voice command to dial Megan's number. Her husband answered, and in the background he could hear his sister and the kids playing. It set his mind at ease and loosened the ache around his heart. He managed some small talk for a minute or two and then ended the call. That was something his family would surely analyze and dissect over Sunday dinner.

He was kind of glad he would be at the wedding so he wouldn't be there to hear it.

While he was behaving oddly, he went ahead and called his mom to let her know why they wouldn't be at dinner. He intended to keep the conversation short and to the point, but her answer derailed his plan.

"Stephen, is Kenzie all right?" she said, as soon as she picked up.

A cold lump formed in Stephen's gut. "As far as I know. Why?" He checked the clock; she'd left for the club two hours ago. If she hadn't arrived, Grant would have called.

"Reporters are all over the pier. Down near the Escape Club," Myra said.

They always were, Stephen thought darkly. It seemed the media was determined to make Kenzie lose her cool. As if being a woman plagued by a bitter old man was somehow her fault.

"The club was evacuated due to a bomb threat," his mom announced.

"Murtagh."

"That's what your father said," Myra agreed. "It's too early for any proof. The fire department and police are still assessing the scene."

"I'll head that way as soon as I can," Stephen said.

"There's more. Murtagh confronted Kenzie outside, during the evacuation. With so many reporters around, it was all on camera and quite ugly."

"What the hell?" Why hadn't anyone called *him*?

"Grant stepped in, and others, too. Murtagh hasn't left yet. Preening for the cameras, trying to claim he's the victim again, being accused of things he didn't do online."

"Shouldn't they be covering the bomb threat instead of pandering to his agenda?"

"You'd think so," his mother agreed.

At this rate the man would cost Kenzie her job. What Stephen wouldn't give for another big drug bust or major car theft, anything to shift attention from Murtagh's campaign against Kenzie. In his mind Stephen entertained violent, satisfying attacks on Murtagh that he'd never be able to carry out in reality. It took the leading edge off his temper.

"If you go down there, be careful."

"If? I can't leave her to deal with this alone." Someone should have called him. He was supposed to be protecting her.

"Well, at least keep your face away from the cameras," she said.

He laughed. His mom had a way with priorities for her children. "I promise."

"We'll be grilling out on the Fourth," she reminded him. "Bring steaks or brats or whatever you'd like to share."

"Oh, right." The reason he'd called. "We won't be there."

"It's the Fourth of July," she said.

"And a Sunday," he added, before she could. "I remember the family traditions, Mom. One of Kenzie's friends is getting married and we're going to the wedding."

For a long beat of silence he could imagine his mother gaping at the phone in shock. "Is that the Jennings wedding?" she said at last.

"Yes."

"Mitch and Julia are going, too. They promised to stop by beforehand. Maybe the four of you can all ride together from here. Your nieces and nephews will be crushed if you don't stop in."

He wanted to call her on the silly, miserable-child ploy, but her heart was in the right place. Myra Galway couldn't suppress her urge to mother people. After this mess on the news, she would want to see Kenzie and reassure herself that everything was fine.

This was the real risk of taking a woman to Sunday dinner: his mom got too interested in the guest. In Kenzie's case, Myra knew her better than Stephen did. Being an attentive, caring mother, she probably had delusions that somehow Kenzie could put an end to Stephen's hermit tendencies.

"I'll let you know how the timing shakes out," he hedged. "I need to unload the wrecker now."

She wished him luck, asked him to tell Kenzie they were thinking about her, and told him she loved him.

"Love you, too, Mom."

He supposed love was the real Galway tradition. It was the cornerstone of the steady foundation Sam and Myra had given their children. Building on love, they'd instilled respect, responsibility and a solid work ethic. With all that in his genes, drummed into his sense of self, he shouldn't be surprised that he felt a need to stand between Kenzie and anyone bent on hurting her.

Chaos swirled around Kenzie. The bomb squad was inside the club with canine units, searching for any sign of explosives. Patrons milled about, pressing the safety perimeter the staff and police had set up. No one wanted to miss a thing. The lights from various media teams flooded the area, washing out the flashing lights of first responder units. Under any other off-duty circumstances, she would go over and visit with the firefighters or offer to help. Tonight, Murtagh had effectively blocked that path. With the right camera angle, she knew it would look as if the PFD welcomed his presence.

Kenzie turned away from his creepy stare, doing what she could to blend in with the rest of the staff, avoiding the harsh lights and judgmental speculation. She'd never been one to shy away from noise or a crisis. Right now, she was anxious for the relative quiet and absolute privacy of Stephen's garage.

Leaving the club wasn't an option; Grant had made that clear, even if the Charger Stephen insisted she continue to use wasn't blocked in. There wasn't anything for her to do.

Jason walked over and rested his arm across her shoulder. "How are you holding up?"

The question made her eyes sting with tears she would not shed in front of Murtagh. She dug deep for cold anger instead. "He's an embarrassment. Why can't he crawl back under a rock?"

She, Jason and Grant had been the last out of the club, making sure the patrons were safely clear. The three of them came outside to find the bands and the rest of the staff had organized the customers back from the club, making way for the first responders.

The media, already documenting the evacuation, had caught everything when Murtagh ambushed her with his false apologies. His appearance at the club had instantly made him the prime suspect in the bomb threat, though she could never voice such an opinion.

"He's slime," Jason said. "Just hang in there."

She was trying. "Do I have a choice?"

Jason gave her a little shoulder squeeze and glanced past her. "Things might be looking up," he said cryptically.

Before she could ask, he turned her shoulders and she was facing that scowl she found far too appealing.

"Stephen?" She glanced around. "I wasn't expecting you. The reports on the accident were dire."

"It was ugly."

For a split second something flashed in his hazel eyes, a shell-shocked emotion she recognized from her mirror after a particularly grueling call. Then he spotted Murtagh and his gaze iced over with lethal intent. She loved him for it.

"We're leaving," he said. "Now."

"I—I can't." At his sharp look, she decided not to argue. "Just let me tell Grant."

"Already did."

That irked her. He couldn't continue to simply *handle* so many things on her behalf. Housing, car repairs, food and transportation, too. At some point she'd have her life back and she needed to take care of herself. "Presumptuous much?"

When he stepped closer she noticed the unmistakable scent of smoke and burned gas clinging to his shirt. He had soot and dirt on his skin and a smudge along his jaw that she wanted to reach up and wipe away.

"You *want* to stay?" He folded his arms over his chest. "Fine."

If there hadn't been so many cameras around, she would have hugged him. "False alarm or not, Grant will need help with this crowd."

Stephen's hard gaze took in the scene around them. "You don't leave people hanging. I get it." He aimed a far more intimidating version of his relentless scowl at Murtagh.

He did get it, she realized, grateful. He hadn't fixed her car because she couldn't; he'd done it because, like her, he needed to stay busy when things got tough.

Sometimes visual, tangible progress was the best defense against all the other uncontrollable stuff in life.

"Thanks."

He glanced down at her, his expression softening. "Had to try."

"I know." She wanted to hug him, and hooked her thumbs in her back pockets to keep her hands to herself. "Look at that." She nodded toward band members clearing a space in the center of the crowd. "Only here," she said with pride. Grant had built something special, and though her part in his business was small, she felt like she mattered.

"Are they setting up to play?" Stephen sounded as impressed as she felt.

She nodded, reluctant to move closer to the music because that would put her—and Stephen—closer to Murtagh.

They didn't have power or full instrumentation, but the headliner band had pulled acoustic guitars from the equipment van and were basically leading a sing-along to keep people distracted. The drummer made do with his sticks and a tambourine.

"Ridiculous," Stephen said.

"Yes it is," she agreed, laughing. "But it's working."

"It's a grown-up version of summer camp," he muttered.

"All we need are s'mores." She glanced in the direction of the car, which was still blocked in. "How much time do you think we have before they let us back inside?"

"You aren't seriously thinking of going to the store for graham crackers, chocolate and marshmallows for this crowd."

"We could take your car." She batted her eyelashes in an overdone and obvious ploy.

His eyebrows flexed into another frown. "I doubt the PFD would let you have an open flame anywhere around here."

His logic popped her fantasy balloon. "True. Still fun to think about."

"If you say so."

Everyone around them was otherwise engaged with the issues inside the club or the impromptu entertainment outside. Though Kenzie and Stephen were surrounded, they might as well have been alone.

"You didn't like summer camp?"

"Not the kind you're talking about," he admitted.

"Why not?"

He shrugged and tucked his hands into his pockets. "It just wasn't my thing."

She wondered if he'd been homesick or if he just wasn't into all the outdoor classic recreational stuff. "No go-cart camp?"

He shrugged. "Fishing with Dad was one thing. Going camping with the family was fine when we did that."

So it was about being on his own. Interesting that he was so comfortable with solitude now. Although his family was rarely more than a few blocks away at any given moment. She caught a gleam in his eye. "You put stuff in your sisters' sleeping bags, didn't you?"

He smirked and she fought the urge to kiss that sly expression right off his face. "Nothing was ever proven."

She smacked his arm lightly. "You were guilty."

"How can you be sure?"

"First of all, the smirk is a dead giveaway. Second,

I'm also an oldest child. Did you use the plastic worms or live bait? Frogs, maybe?"

"My sisters squealed over everything. I can't recall exactly what Mitch tucked between their sheets."

"Mitch, right. And if I ask him, he'll blame you. Or Andrew." She folded her arms, reluctantly impressed and a little envious. "You were so lucky to have a worthy accomplice. I had to create watertight alibis for my pranks."

His smirk smoothed into a smile, but just when she thought he'd laugh, his eyebrows snapped together and his lips went hard.

She twisted around, following his gaze, and caught a glimpse of Murtagh walking toward them. Stephen stepped in front of her and his fingers curled into loose fists. "You don't need to come any closer."

"I just want to talk to Miss Hughes."

"That opportunity passed," Stephen said. "If you have something to say, write a letter and send it to her attorney."

Murtagh's face bunched into a sneer and she braced for another insult. He must have remembered they had an audience, because his demeanor changed abruptly. Too bad for him his hangdog look wasn't very convincing.

"Her indecisive actions hurt *me*, if you recall," he stated in a voice that carried.

Kenzie could feel the nearest cameras aiming toward them. Only a few days of living under this media microscope and she was exhausted.

"She's playing you, Galway," Murtagh continued. "Yeah, I know who you are. She's got you wrapped around her pinkie, fighting her battles. Because she can't win on her own."

"Battles you started," Stephen said, with far more calm than Kenzie could muster.

She didn't say a word, didn't rise to the bait as he tried once more to convince her he was innocent of the online trouble. It wasn't in her nature to hide behind anyone or anything, but right now Stephen was shield and shelter. Murtagh had put her through enough; why wouldn't he leave her alone?

Standing behind Stephen, she could feel the strength radiating through the solid muscles of his back. He'd fight for her if he had to. While part of her thrilled to that idea, she knew it would be worse for everyone if he thrashed a retired firefighter.

"Still can't handle any trouble without a man for backup. You aren't good enough for the PFD."

She slipped her hand into Stephen's and dropped her forehead to his shoulder. Let the media interpret that however they pleased; she didn't care anymore.

"The PFD is a team," Stephen said to Murtagh. "Have you forgotten that's where the real strength lies?"

"A team weakened by females," Murtagh shouted. "If she did everything right, why is she hiding behind you?"

With his encouragement, Kenzie came around to stand at Stephen's side. "Because she can *trust* me," he said. "The real question should be why there's no one standing with you while you continue to attack her."

She saw that strike a nerve as Murtagh started to bluster. Even in the less than ideal lighting, she could see his cheeks turning red. The media was catching all of this.

Stephen turned his back on Murtagh and guided her ahead of him. "I'm sure Grant can handle this without you," he murmured, when they were several paces away.

"The jackass won't leave while you're here. He doesn't want you stealing his spotlight."

"So the answer is for me to step aside and let him have it?"

"Hell. I don't know." Stephen rubbed a hand over his face. "Tonight? Yes. Let me take you home. Please. My gut says that's the right move under the circumstances. No one here will let him malign you."

"I'm not a coward," she insisted.

"Isn't discretion the better part of valor?"

"You may have a point," she replied. There wasn't any workable solution here. Logic wasn't effective against the bitter messages Murtagh was trying to sell. Maybe leaving would give the man enough rope to hang himself, as he'd done in the civil suit.

"Let me find Grant."

"Call or send a text from the car." Stephen aimed her toward the parking lot across the street. "He'll understand. Especially after he sees the late news."

"We don't have to watch it, do we?"

"No. We have something better to do."

She shot him a look, wondering if that was some sort of innuendo that they'd be sleeping together, but he didn't elaborate.

He waited in the parking lot only until they got a reply from Grant. Then he left the club behind and took a convoluted route back toward his neighborhood. He stopped at a small grocery store and held her hand as he darted through the aisles, picking up ingredients for s'mores.

"You're kidding," she said, as he paid the cashier.

He grinned down at her and the butterflies in her

belly soared. Maybe he didn't grin often because he knew how deliciously devastating it could be. Better to use that kind of power sparingly.

When they reached the garage, he set up two long folding lawn chairs and started a fire in the grill. She unwrapped the chocolate bars and graham crackers and soon they were roasting marshmallows on the tines of the grilling fork.

Though it wasn't quite the same as camping, the s'mores picnic was quickly becoming the highlight of her day, a close second to his agreeing to take her to the wedding.

They stuffed themselves on the sweet treats, laughing about the pranks they'd pulled on their younger siblings back when they could get away with it.

"You miss them?" he asked, as she licked sticky marshmallow goo from her fingers while assembling another s'more.

The chocolate was melting and she caught that drip, too, before it splattered on her work apron. "Every day," she answered. "Mom needed a change of scenery, though."

"You should give her a call," he said, squishing another s'more together.

"I check in regularly."

"I meant because of earlier."

She'd intended to, but had let herself get distracted with this whimsical side of Stephen. As she polished off the s'more and went to wash her hands, some of that Murtagh-induced tension crept into her shoulders, but it lacked the sharp bite and infuriating intensity she'd felt earlier.

She called her mom and gave her a heads-up that she, the club or both might feature on the news.

"I saw a breaking news headline of some trouble at the club," her mom replied. "I knew you'd be okay. You always are."

"Thanks. Grant handled the evacuation well."

"It was a false alarm?"

Kenzie realized she didn't know. "Pretty sure. I left early because Murtagh got belligerent."

"If you didn't sound so calm about it, I'd encourage you to file a restraining order."

Did she sound calm? She felt calm, thanks to Stephen. "Grant's encouraging that, too," she said, trading her waitressing tennies for flip-flops.

"He was a good friend of your father's. I'm glad he's in your corner."

Kenzie agreed, but she was peeking through the camper door, admiring another man who was in her corner. "Just don't believe everything you see or hear on the news, Mom."

Her mother laughed, that rich sound that had always made Kenzie smile through even the worst circumstances.

Feeling better after the conversation, Kenzie took off her apron and dropped it on the bench seat of the camper. Grabbing two beers from the refrigerator, she went back out to the makeshift campfire.

Stephen was pulled from his thoughts when Kenzie waved a beer in front of him.

"Something to cut the sugar," she said.

The soft smile on her face made him want to pull her close and keep her safe from Murtagh and every other threat lurking out there in the world. "Good talk?" he asked instead.

"It was. Thanks for reminding me to do it."

"No problem." He took a long pull on the beer. She seemed restless, standing there watching the fire rather than sitting back and enjoying it.

"Need to talk about it?"

She shook her head, that long pale braid rippling softly down her back. He couldn't quite get his mind off how silky that hair had been spilling over the pillows.

"Mom wants us to come by the house on our way to the wedding on Sunday," he said.

Kenzie turned to face him, finally sitting down sideways on her chair.

Her lean legs were bare from the hem of her khaki shorts on down, and she'd ditched her tennis shoes for flip-flops. He wondered what she'd do if he stroked the bend of her knee the way he wanted to.

"At some point I have to go home," she murmured. "To my apartment."

He wasn't ready for that, even if it was safe. "File a restraining order against Murtagh and I might let you."

"Let me?" She laughed. "You realize I'm a grown woman?"

He twirled the beer bottle back and forth. "A detail I haven't missed."

She blushed. At least he wanted to believe he'd made her blush. Hard to tell in the weak lighting, so why not assume the positive?

"You've been great…"

He heard the "but" and mentally finished the sentence several ways, all of them unfavorable. "Murtagh clearly isn't done," Stephen said. "It's okay to rely on me until the cops can pin something on him and keep him out of your way. I don't want anything to happen to you."

She stared at her beer bottle. "Thanks." Her voice cracked on the single syllable.

It was as close as he'd seen her come to actual tears. "Come here," he said, making room for her on his chair between his legs.

"I'm fine."

"Maybe I'm not?" It would be nice to hold her close and relax in the knowledge that they were both alive and well. "I could use some company watching the fire die out."

"If only we knew of a way to put it out safely, right now."

He chuckled, the sound startling both of them.

"No fun in that." He patted the chair. "Spoils the ambience."

She moved over to perch at the end of his chair.

"Scared?" he asked.

"Not of you."

"Good." He drew her back against his chest, his legs bracketing hers. He was almost afraid to breathe until she finally relaxed against him.

It was a quiet intimacy he hadn't shared with anyone since his fiancée, and he suspected they both needed the comfort after the things they'd dealt with today.

"Was the accident as bad as it sounded?" she asked, in little more than a whisper.

"Worse," he admitted.

She linked her fingers with his and they didn't talk anymore as they watched the fire die down. He felt like he was going in reverse with her, giving her his home, sleeping with her to burn off adrenaline, and now, resting easy. Maybe it made sense in the context of their odd and sudden friendship. They had so much in common, loner tendencies among them.

The other night, they'd simply found each other, used each other, and now...

Now what? he asked that voice in his head. This was temporary. Kenzie wasn't meant to be a permanent fixture, no matter how well she seemed to fit into his life and business. She was right; at some point she had to go back to her life.

He didn't want that day to be any time soon.

When she was nearly asleep on his chest, he roused her and nudged her into the camper.

He stirred the coals and dumped the last of his beer over them. Certain the fire was out, he retreated to his makeshift apartment in the office. He splashed water on his face and changed into a T-shirt and shorts, but as he made up the bed, he changed his mind.

Returning to the camper, he knocked lightly and waited for her invitation.

"Come in."

He walked inside and caught her standing at the bathroom door, toothbrush in hand. "The office is too far away." He moved to the dinette and started changing it to a bed. "I'm sleeping here tonight."

Her smile was slow and beautiful and loaded with gentle understanding. "Okay. Grab what you need."

He helped himself to a pillow and blanket and stretched out while she finished brushing her teeth. When she came out, she didn't go to the bedroom, she curled up beside him, her back to his chest. When he stiffened, uncertain, she drew his arm over her waist.

From one breath to the next she was asleep. Well, hell.

Breathing in the warm citrus scent of her hair, he decided he wasn't going anywhere before morning. He wouldn't abuse this trust. He might just be the luckiest broken man in the world.

Chapter 11

He'd been there when she woke up on Friday. The overwhelming peace of that just rolled over her, easing the anxiety that had been building until she thought she'd break. Her first thought had been to kiss the burnished gold whiskers shading his jaw, to wake him up slowly with sensual caresses so they could thoroughly enjoy each other.

She'd never be able to keep things light, friendly or simple if she made that move. Her heart was perched, ready to fall into his strong hands. She wasn't sure she could walk away whole if she gave him all she felt right now.

They slipped into a comfortable routine through Friday and Saturday, staying close to the garage and working on the Nova. *Together.* He'd closed the garage for a long weekend in honor of the holiday and they were alone in a cocoon of car parts, tools and music. She loved every minute of it.

Of course, she knew they stuck to the garage in part to dodge the media and to keep her out of Murtagh's sight. It was only Stephen who had to cope with her rant when the PFD moved her back to full administrative leave on Friday afternoon. And only Stephen knew how hard she clung when he pulled her into a reassuring embrace.

On Saturday morning the Camaro came back, and it was stunning with the silver-and-black paint scheme. They took a quick trip around the neighborhood to test it out, and satisfied, Stephen parked it in the fourth bay, where it would safely wait for Matt Riley to pick it up.

On Sunday morning they shared coffee and muffins she'd baked, while they admired the completed Camaro and work-in-progress Nova. In the afternoon, they enjoyed a few leisurely hours at the Galway house, getting silly with the little ones, giving her time to convince Myra she was coping with the latest debacle. It was all so happy and normal, so easy.

She and Stephen didn't touch at all in front of his family, but she felt his eyes on her and knew he felt her watching him, too. At some point they were going to have to talk or risk exploding from the desire arcing between them.

Dressed for the wedding, they took the convertible out to Boathouse Row. Stephen was model handsome in his dark evening suit and his eyes were hot when he saw her emerge from the camper in her shimmering strapless dress.

Whatever Shannon and Daniel had done to secure this venue on the Fourth of July paid off big time, in

Kenzie's opinion. The early evening ceremony was intimate and brief, with guests gathered around an arch of ivy where the couple exchanged vows. The only attendant was Shannon's son, Aiden, standing proudly between them.

The reception spilled outside to the dock and a lovely lawn, and the Jenningses had timed it perfectly so everyone could relax and enjoy plenty of food and cake and dancing as they waited for the fireworks display to start at dark.

Kenzie couldn't take her eyes off the sweet family dancing together in the center of the parquet floor, surrounded by their equally delighted guests. Daniel was practically bursting with pride and love for his bride and stepson.

"I've never seen him so happy," Kenzie said to Stephen.

"Daniel or Aiden?" he asked.

"Both." She chuckled. "All three, really," she added.

Daniel had once vented to her after a difficult breakup that he wouldn't date again until after he retired from the fire department. She understood the sentiment. Outsiders seemed to have this warped image of the job—that they were all bravery wrapped up in fitness and sex appeal—until things turned dangerous. Then the adrenaline-junkie accusations would fly, followed closely by pleas and ultimatums.

Her last boyfriend had been shocked she'd chosen the PFD over him. Being dumped for showing commitment to the job was a fairly common theme among her peers. It took a certain type of person to understand the rigors and the joys of the work they did. Firefighters and other first responders saw more than most people wanted to share and way more than others needed to know. Doing the job well didn't mean doing it unscathed, emotionally or physically.

Her gaze drifted over the other guests. Mitch and Julia were having a blast on the dance floor. Her friend Carson Lane was sharing a dessert with his new wife, Lissa. They'd eloped a few weeks ago and returned oozing joy and contentment. Right now, with foreheads nearly touching, they were clearly sharing an inside joke. Kenzie was so happy for the two of them even as a wisp of envy breezed over her.

Someday. With the right man.

Wonderful events like weddings and the memories being made here were all the more precious because they were on the front lines during their community's most stressful moments. Her day to share this kind of affirmation of life and love with friends and family would come. Her heart clamored that she'd found the right man. Her mind and soul wanted to agree, yet she couldn't bring herself to push him for answers. Not yet.

She glanced at Stephen, wondering what to make of these past two weeks, primarily the past few days. Since waking up together they had shared several kisses, a few tantalizing embraces and lots of laughter, but they were tiptoeing around the bigger issues. Neither of them wanted to talk about the next step and both were avoiding another tumble into bed.

For her part, much of it was the pervasive uncertainty of Murtagh, her career, and where she might have to go to keep doing what she loved.

"Kenzie?"

"Hmm?" Her thoughts had drifted well beyond the wedding reception. Even here she'd let Murtagh creep into her mind like an oily fog. She'd fought so hard to stay on the job despite his antics, yet as she watched Shannon slip into Daniel's embrace for a slow dance, Kenzie wondered if going in a new direction professionally would open things up personally.

Maybe she should talk to Jason about how he'd made the transition.

Stephen covered her hand with his. "Would you like to dance?"

Her body responded to that gentle pressure of his callused palm. Warmth flooded over her from that first point of contact and butterflies fluttered through her belly. With a smile, she stood and walked hand in hand with him to the dance floor.

A serene peace enveloped her as he drew her close, buffering the persistent, sharp desire she felt whenever he was near. That longing had her on edge constantly. Every day was a new test of her willpower to keep things light, when she wanted to explore every hard inch of his body and reclaim that spectacular pleasure they'd shared only once.

His hand rested lightly at her waist, his shoulder firm under the fine fabric of his suit. She remembered the feel of that shoulder, the heat rolling off him as he'd braced himself over her in the bed. It was all she could do not to press her body into his.

Not a good idea to reveal so much with her friends and his brother watching, eagerly hoping for something romantic to develop between them.

"Are you blushing?" His voice was soft at her ear.

"I hope not." She lifted her face and offered him her brightest smile. "It's been a lovely evening."

"It has," he agreed.

The moment stretched and swelled, full of romance and potential with the music swirling around them, the lights twinkling overhead, the scent of lilies in the air. Somehow she managed to keep her lips away from his.

"Thanks for being my plus one," she said, as they swayed together. She found him as enticing in his suit and tie as she did when he was elbow deep in an engine at the garage.

"I didn't think I'd enjoy it," he admitted. His eyes were hot when they met hers and his fingers flexed at her waist. "This makes the effort worthwhile."

She knew the ceremony had been tough on him, but he'd soldiered on with that stoic expression he applied to every uncomfortable task. If he'd been at Julia and Mitch's wedding, she didn't recall seeing him.

"Were you at your brother's wedding?" She regretted the question immediately as his body went tight all over.

"Of course."

"I was at the reception." She leaned back, pretending to leer at him. "I can't believe I overlooked you in the sexy older brother tuxedo."

As she'd hoped, teasing him eased the strain she'd inadvertently created.

"I ducked out early," he replied.

"My loss." She smoothed her hand over his shoulder, offering a small comfort.

He tugged her close. "You think so?"

His husky tone sent goose bumps racing from her hair all the way to her toes. He guided her through a final turn, gave her a squeeze as the band switched to a more lively song. She had to stifle her frustration. She wasn't ready to move on from this more fascinating side of Stephen.

They strolled from the dance floor toward the champagne table and he handed her a glass, taking water for himself.

One more example of the caring, thoughtful nature he frequently hid with a scowl. He'd been generous with everything, going above and beyond to help her. He'd expressed great care for her safety and offered comfort in her lowest moments. They'd even had mind-blowing sex they couldn't seem to talk about. It shouldn't have meant anything, except it did to her. The more time she spent with him, the more she wanted to know what it might have meant to him.

Just ask, she told herself.

She sipped her champagne and tried not to blush again. Her past was peppered with a few short flings to go along with the two serious relationships. She'd been borderline delusional, or possibly too needy, to believe she could keep her emotions out of whatever this was with Stephen.

Maybe the scent of a working garage had gone to her head. That factor didn't hurt, but it was the man who pulled her attention, made her feel safe enough that she could let her guard down and sleep, or shout, or laugh with abandon.

"What are you thinking about?" he asked.

"The Camaro," she fibbed. *Chicken!* "Do you think we can take it out one more time before the buyer picks it up?"

"I can't make any promises. Riley told me he has all of next week as vacation and will try to get up here to pick it up."

"Bummer."

"There are other cars out there." Stephen drew her

away from the champagne table just to the edge of the lighting, where they couldn't be overheard. "Tell me what you were really thinking about."

"You," she answered, deciding to stop being a coward.

He cocked an eyebrow, waiting for her to elaborate.

If they were going to delve into feelings, it would be wonderful if he could go first. Too bad she didn't see the conversation going that way.

"You think this atmosphere is getting to me?" he asked.

"No. From my vantage point you're managing just fine." Could he see that for himself, or was his vision still too clouded by his loss?

"You don't sound particularly happy about it."

"On the contrary." She rubbed a hand over his arm. "I'm thrilled. I'd been feeling guilty for dragging you here. All my claims about independence and still I needed a friend to hold my hand for a trip across town."

He took her free hand in his, gave it a gentle squeeze. "I'm glad you asked me."

They both knew it was a cheesy half-truth and she laughed despite the sensations his touch stirred.

A rash of "if only" thoughts went through her mind like a stampede. If only they'd met earlier. If only he could stop blaming himself for the past. If only he was ready to move on and try loving someone else. Someone like her.

Loving.

Yes. That sounded perfect. Her heart gave a kick while her mind flooded with images of what loving Stephen would look like. That was probably light years ahead of where they were tonight. It might even be impossible. Still, it was love, and her heart would not allow her to believe otherwise. She knew it as surely as she knew her name.

Under the spotlight of that truth, her courage crumbled. It was the one thing she wasn't sure she could tell him without hurting them both.

"I should go say hi to Julia." It was a lame and ineffective diversion and she couldn't decide if she wanted him to let her off the hook or not.

"In a minute."

His gaze fell to her lips and her pulse leaped as he leaned in and covered her mouth. The kiss went from tender to blazing in the span of a heartbeat. She tasted the tart lemon of the wedding cake as his tongue stroked boldly across hers. With their joined hands trapped between them, she nearly dropped the glass in favor of holding on for dear life. She wanted to get closer almost as much as she wanted to get him alone.

Stripping him out of this suit would be an erotic pleasure. Her palms were tingling already, anticipating another go at his sculpted body.

Nearby, fireworks began with a heavy *boom* and she gave a start as bursts of gorgeous color sparkled through the trees, danced in the reflection of the river.

His mouth trailed along her jaw and he nipped her ear. "Can we go home now?" His breath fanned the sensitive flesh of her neck and she shivered. "Please."

"Yes." She was wound so tight, she hoped they could get out without having to speak to anyone.

"Don't move." He kissed her, lightning quick, and slipped the glass out of her hand.

A moment later he was back and he tucked her under his arm as they moved around behind the party toward the parking area. He paused several times for deep, lingering kisses, as if he couldn't go two minutes without a taste of her.

She knew just how he felt. The sweet anticipation mounted in the car when they could only hold hands or sneak a kiss at a stoplight. She nearly suggested stopping at the next motel they passed, but checking in would likely take longer than finishing the drive to his place.

When the garage gate closed again after he pulled through, she was tempted to dive on him.

Last time, they'd fallen on each other so fast, all that heat and need. Now she wanted to take her time and savor the process. Savor every lean, sexy inch of him.

He parked the car at the camper steps. Swiveling in his seat, he wrapped his hand around the nape of her neck and pulled her in for a kiss. She kept herself from falling into his lap with one hand on his muscular thigh. Maybe the car could work for round one this time. No, no. She wanted to take it slow.

He shifted, rapped his knee on the steering wheel and muttered an oath against her lips. She laughed. "I'll race you to the steps." Throwing open the car door, she was impressed her quivering legs were up to the task. But Stephen hadn't run for the door. He'd turned toward her and, halfway between the car and the camper, caught her in his powerful embrace, pressing her body to his. His arousal was evident and her hips flexed in an almost painful eagerness for the pleasure ahead.

He groaned, his hands squeezing her hips.

Her lips found his and she slid her hands under his jacket, crushing his perfectly pressed dress shirt as she tried to tug it free of his waistband.

"Kenzie…" He murmured her name over and over as

he nuzzled the length of her neck. He leaned her back and trailed more of those provocative kisses lower, along the skin bared by her strapless dress.

"Stephen," she breathed, as the summer breeze and his touch played havoc with her senses. "Inside." Protected by his security system or not, she'd rather not run the risk of this private moment getting caught on a camera.

He didn't hesitate, nudging her toward the camper. His warmth and scent surrounded her as he reached around and opened the door. His fingers skimmed under the hem of her dress, along the backs of her knees as she started up the steps. She froze, mesmerized by those rough fingers.

"Inside," he reminded her, his palms sliding the fabric of her dress over her hips and back down.

She darted into the camper and immediately turned to him, using his tie to bring his lips to hers. Oh, the way he kissed left her breathless and obliterated her self-control.

Her heart racing, she forced herself to slow down as she pushed his jacket off his shoulders. He ran his fingertips back and forth across the top edge of her dress while desire pooled low in her belly. Neither of them spoke; they just watched each other, as if any word would shatter the moment.

She unknotted his tie and started on his buttons, breathing in the clean scent rising from his skin at the base of his throat. When she kissed that vulnerable spot, he groaned again and boosted her onto the tabletop.

Her startled giggle faded as he tugged the fabric back and his mouth closed over her breast. She breathed his name like a prayer. His teeth tugged lightly on her taut nipple and she moaned, shoving her hand into his thick hair.

He wedged his hips between her thighs and she wrapped her legs around his and rocked against him. When at last her hands were cruising along his torso, the slabs of muscle honed by hard work, she remembered why she'd wanted to take it slow.

She drank in the sight of him, memorizing every rise and hollow that defined his body. Burnished gold hair dusted his chest, turning darker below his navel. Her fingers followed the trail of their own volition.

He caught her hands at his belt. "Kenzie. You're too much."

"Same goes," she replied, kissing the hard line of his jaw. "Let's be too much together."

His chin jerked in a nod and he claimed her mouth once more as she reached back and unzipped her dress. The fabric fell to her waist as his hands covered her breasts, teasing and molding her until she was rocking against him, pleading for more.

He lifted her from the table, let the dress fall to the floor, then walked backward toward the bed, bringing her along. She worked his belt loose and he took over, undressing in a rush. No more barriers between them, he fell back on the bed with her sprawled over him.

Oh, this was a fantastic view, and she sat up to enjoy it. To relish all of him this time as she'd promised herself she would. In no hurry now, she feathered kisses over his torso, her hands moving leisurely. This was her chance to give him pleasure, to stoke his passion and hers by reflecting every sensual desire he brought to life in her.

Suddenly, he turned the tables, rolling her under him and kissing her soundly before taking his skilled lips lower over her breasts, down her belly and lower still to her core. The fast climax bowed her body and he soothed her as she trembled on that delicate edge. When he filled her, thrusting deep, she experienced an indescribable sense of unity.

Love makes all the difference, she thought, reveling in every sensation.

The rest of the world faded, her only thoughts for Stephen and this moment, loving him with all she had right here and now. With her body rather than words he might reject. She gazed up at his intense face, stroking the hard ridges and sinews of his arms. She was too lost in him to hide the feelings roaring through her, and she surged up to steal a kiss.

He laced his fingers with hers, filling her body and soul, and driving them both closer to that sparkling peak. The pressure built and built, and when the climax swept through her he swallowed her cries in a hard kiss as he found his own release.

For a long delicious moment their hearts thundered together. Moving to lie beside her, he drew her in close, and her fingers skimmed through the curls of hair on his chest as she tried to fit all the pieces of herself back together.

It was a lost cause, she thought with a private smile. She kissed his chest, wishing her happiness could fill all the spaces of his heart that had been damaged by grief. The words were there, eager to burst free, and she held them back.

She didn't want him to try to explain away her feelings with the excuse of the romantic wedding or post-sex high. What she felt for him wasn't going anywhere.

It was simply a matter of giving him time to discover if he could love her in return.

At just past six, Stephen's phone hummed and chimed. Tangled up with Kenzie in the bed, he quickly silenced it before realizing it wasn't his morning alarm, but a notice from the security system. One of the floodlights on this side of the lot came on, slicing through the dim interior of the trailer. In their fascination with each other, they'd forgotten to pull the curtains.

"What is it?" Kenzie mumbled, tugging the blanket over her head.

"Nothing serious." He knew his security system was making the correct response to whatever had tripped the alarm. Most likely a cat had set off the motion detector. It happened occasionally.

He moved out of the bed as he cycled through the camera feeds, and barely stifled an outburst when he came across the hole in the back fence. It took a precious few seconds to find the angle that showed a man tagging Kenzie's original loaner car with a can of red spray paint.

Stephen pressed the icon to get someone from the security service on the line. He snatched the slacks he'd worn to the wedding from the floor. As he pulled on his pants and searched for his shirt, the service confirmed the silent alarm had been tripped and police were on the way.

The operator advised him to stay in place, out of sight. Stephen wasn't taking any chances. If this was Murtagh, he wanted to provide an eyewitness identification. He found his shirt and slipped it on.

"Stephen?" Kenzie was sitting up now, her hair tumbled. "What is it?"

"Security notified the cops about a breach in the fence. It's handled. Go back to sleep."

"Too late. I'm awake," she said.

"Stay here anyway," he told her. For the first time since she'd kissed him on the camper steps, Stephen wished he'd been sleeping in the office. Then he'd have access to dozens of tools that would make useful defensive weapons.

At the moment, he had only his wits and his phone.

Watching the vandal's progress through the feed on the cell phone, Stephen silently stepped out into the cool morning air. He intended to block the hole in the fence, preventing an escape.

The derogatory message in red paint on the side of the office would have been bad enough on its own. Hearing the vandal attempting to open the bay doors propelled Stephen into action.

No way he'd let anyone destroy client cars, especially not the Camaro that Riley was eager to pick up. Stephen hustled around to the front of the shop, cringing at the sight of wet paint dripping across Kenzie's loaner car.

The message there and on the office wall was identical to the harsh words scrawled across the firehouse, only this time, Murtagh had been caught holding the spray paint can.

"Step away from my property," Stephen said. He held up his phone and pressed the camera icon. Between the phone and the security cameras there shouldn't be any wiggle room for Murtagh.

"If it isn't the boyfriend," he sneered.

"The cops are on their way." Stephen took another step closer. "You won't get away with this."

"Get away with what? I was walking by and saw a kid squeeze out of the fence. Came to make sure you and Miss Hughes were all right."

"No one will buy that. There are cameras covering every inch of the property inside this fence." He'd never been more pleased or satisfied by his decision to beef up his security. "Your lies won't do any good this time."

Murtagh's eyes went wide in his puffy face. "Bull. You have one camera on the gate, that's all."

"Feel free to believe that. Tell it to the cops if you like." He nodded toward the gate. "Here they are now."

Murtagh did an excellent impression of a deer caught in the headlights of an oncoming truck. He froze, refusing to give an explanation or make any comments without his lawyer present. The responding officers had him cuffed and were hauling him to a cruiser when he spotted Kenzie hovering at the corner of the building.

Stephen was close enough to see Murtagh's eyes turn cold and vicious, his face flooding with angry color. Whatever delusion plagued Murtagh, the man wasn't done with Kenzie.

Stephen blocked Murtagh's view, taking the full brunt of the man's hatred.

Two policemen settled Murtagh into the backseat, while another one questioned Stephen.

"Will you be pressing charges, sir?" the officer asked.

"Absolutely."

"Then come on down to the station. I'll get the paperwork started." The officer turned to Kenzie. "Did you see the man tag anything, ma'am?"

"No," she said. "Will Stephen's statement be enough to keep him off the streets?"

"We can hope," the officer said. "Have a good day."

"When can I clean this up?" Stephen didn't want to leave these offensive messages up any longer than necessary, out of respect for Kenzie.

"Thanks to your security system, we have all we need," the officer replied.

When they were alone, Stephen pulled her into the trailer and just wrapped his arms around her. She was safe. His security measures had worked, protecting her and his property.

"Coffee," she said, withdrawing after a moment. She looked adorable in her worn cutoffs, a tank top emblazoned with the name of a band that recently played the Escape Club, and one of the Galway Automotive caps on her head.

"This will hold him," he said, uncertain which of them needed more reassurance.

"Maybe. Depends on what they charge him with," she said, her normally cheerful features grim. "I saw his face when they hauled him out of here. He blames me for everything that sucks in his life."

"He's wrong," Stephen said, rubbing her back. Kenzie epitomized all the good stuff left in the world. "I'll get started on the fence," he said, when she slipped out from under his hands.

He missed the warmth of her lithe body and the softness of her hair falling loose, but he sensed she was looking for more than physical distance.

"I'll call someone to clean up the graffiti."

"You don't have to do that. It's not like you're a real employee."

She sent him a long, inscrutable look from under the bill of the ball cap. "If you're working on a holiday, so am I."

It took him a second to figure out what she meant. With the wedding, he'd forgotten today was a holiday, since July Fourth had landed on a Sunday. "Right. I'll change clothes and take care of the fence."

When it was repaired, Stephen had to decide whether or not Kenzie should go with him to the police station to make the report. He didn't want to leave her here alone and he really didn't want to run the risk of her bumping into Murtagh.

Grant and his crew had their hands full with another concert setup, so that was out. Though she wasn't expected at the firehouse, maybe they would let her visit. Mitch was on duty and Stephen didn't trust many other people with her safety.

If he explained the situation to his dad, Samuel could stay here while Stephen filed the report. Kenzie might never know how worried he really was for her. His dad wasn't available, but his mom offered to come over under the guise of needing more windshield wiper fluid. Myra could make that small task last hours if necessary.

He was just telling Kenzie to keep the gate closed while he was gone when his mom pulled in.

Kenzie aimed an exasperated look at him. "You called a babysitter?"

"No." He shuffled his feet. "Not exactly."

"It's fine," she said. "I get it."

"You do?" He hadn't expected resigned acceptance of his protectiveness.

"Yes," she said, though she didn't smile. "I wasn't

too thrilled about waiting here alone and your mom is great company."

"Kenzie. You should have said something."

She shrugged, leaning back against the workbench. "It was just residual fear. It passes." She'd pulled her coveralls on halfway, gathered at her slender waist in deference to the rising temperature of another bright summer day.

He reached out and curled his finger around the silky end of the braid resting on her shoulder. "It's going to work out," he whispered. He couldn't label the shadows in her eyes as vulnerable, but something was weighing on her. Probably worry, since he'd guaranteed her safety and Murtagh had managed to get in, anyway.

"Why don't I file the report later?"

"If you don't press charges now, his lawyers will have him out within the hour," she said. "Go." She gave him a little shove. He trapped her hands with his and kissed her.

Releasing her, he pressed the button to raise the bay door for his mom's car to pull in. One more layer of protection between Kenzie and the outside world couldn't hurt.

He gave his mom a quick hug and then jogged for his car, determined to make the fastest police report in history.

Chapter 12

Kenzie needed some time and space to process the myriad emotions flooding her system. Last night had been so beautiful, so much more than sex and physical needs. She'd gone into it knowing her heart was already in Stephen's oblivious grip, and yet she'd been overcome by the experience.

Maybe she *was* romanticizing his basic physical responses due to wedding-effect, or she was using her feelings for Stephen to block out her fear of Murtagh. No. That was insecurity talking. She knew her heart and mind; now she just had to figure out what to do about it.

First, she had to accept that if Murtagh was willing to cut through a fence and vandalize Stephen's business, he might never quit hounding her. Would he drop this pursuit if she gave up her career? Maybe they should get that story out there and see if he gave up the hunt.

With all of that in her head, she gave Myra a warm smile. "Does your car need any service?"

"Probably not." Her own sheepish smile was so like her oldest son's. "The wiper fluid might be low."

"I'll take a look," Kenzie said, heading to the sporty crossover.

"I brought coffee cake," Myra said, while Kenzie raised the hood.

"You know Stephen keeps plenty of coffee around."

"Do you have time to chat?" Myra asked.

"Of course." She didn't have anywhere else to go. She checked the level in the reservoir and added more fluid. Closing the hood, she walked over to the shop sink and washed her hands before leading Myra into the office.

"I know Stephen was worried about leaving me alone," Kenzie said. "Thanks for coming by."

"After this dreadful vandalism, I can understand his concerns."

"Me, too." Kenzie set a cup of coffee to brew for Myra.

She was feeling inexplicably emotional and not at all ready to discuss the real issues with Stephen's mom. Yes, she loved Stephen and she was fairly sure the news wouldn't surprise a mother as tuned in as Myra. Kenzie just wasn't sure love would be enough to keep Stephen. He hadn't given her any real indication that he was ready to leave the emotional safety net of his dead fiancée.

"Samuel tells me Murtagh drank heavily his last year with the PFD. They tried to get him help, but he just wouldn't take responsibility for his actions."

"Some people don't want help." Kenzie pulled a chair closer to the desk so they could use it as a table. "Not until they hit rock bottom."

"True," Myra agreed. She sliced coffee cake for each

of them and they sat on either side of the desk to eat. "Mistakes, booze and a bad attitude forced him into retirement."

Raspberry streusel, Kenzie realized, as she bit into the buttery pastry. "This is amazing."

"It's one of Stephen's favorites."

Kenzie took a bigger bite, hoping she wouldn't be cornered into asking for the recipe like a woman planning to stick around. Her wants and hopes were irrelevant if Stephen wasn't ready to make that kind of commitment.

"I didn't make the connection earlier. Samuel reminded me that Randall Murtagh was replaced by the first female firefighter to come into that house."

And then another woman had rescued him. No wonder he'd gone off the rails. "Is he still drinking?"

"I don't know. He's been a loner ever since," Myra said. "The problem with waiting until someone hits rock bottom is never really knowing where that point is."

True. "Are you concerned about someone?"

Myra's lips curved and her eyes, filled with love, crinkled at the corners. "Always. At the moment, I'm concerned you'll get caught in Randall's blind, misplaced hatred."

Kenzie brushed the crumbs from her fingertips. "Stephen is confident pressing charges will help."

"Good. What are *you* confident about?"

"That I won't let him win. His showing up here was definitely a shock," she admitted. "I've wondered if I should announce my resignation from the PFD."

"Do you want to quit?"

"No." She traced the rim of her coffee cup. "My thought was if he thinks I've quit, he'll stop this nonsense."

"And the people you care about will be safe," Myra observed.

Kenzie nodded.

"Stephen maintains excellent security. He beefed it up when those car thieves were plaguing the city."

Kenzie swallowed a laugh. "Mitch was miserable when two of the cars the guys had rebuilt were stolen from their customers."

"You don't have to tell me." Myra rolled her eyes. "Sunday dinners were borderline morose for a time."

In more comfortable conversational territory, the two women chattered on. The normality of it was as reassuring and fun as if Kenzie was hanging out with her own mother and her sister. By the time Stephen returned, she had almost forgotten why he'd been gone. It had been a wonderful couple of hours.

Stephen found his mother and Kenzie in the office, laughing over something they claimed he wouldn't understand. He managed not to point out that he wanted to understand every intriguing facet of Kenzie. Once they'd both said goodbye to his mom, Kenzie went to change for her shift at the club and Stephen prepared for an afternoon in the shop.

"Thank you for pressing charges," Kenzie said, when she walked back into the office dressed in her Escape Club uniform. "I'm sorry Murtagh's issue with me spilled over on you. The cleanup crew should be here by noon."

"It's not your fault, Kenzie. I'm glad he won't be able to squeak through the cracks again. You'll be able to get back to your life."

Once Murtagh was finally buttoned up she'd be safe. As safe as she could be in her career of choice, anyway.

"Back to my life?" she echoed.

"That's what you want," he pointed out. Since the day he'd towed her car, her every decision and action had been moving her closer to getting back on shift with the PFD.

She looked past him to the shop beyond the door and then her gaze roamed the office, including the couch he hadn't slept on since the bomb threat. Had his mother noticed that detail?

Stephen could tell Kenzie expected him to say something more, but what? Of course he'd miss her when she left. He was addicted to her laughter, and when her eyes sparkled as she smiled, all the tension faded out of his body. He hoped she'd make time to keep working on projects like the Nova. Maybe she'd agree to dinner once in a while.

The woman had destroyed his solitude and he didn't even mind.

"What if it worked out?" she asked quietly. "You and me. We're good together, Stephen."

What if?

Every time she returned from a shift at the firehouse or the club, he felt such a wave of joy and gratitude mixed with relief. When she handed him a cup of coffee or a message about an appointment or a potential sale, he felt her presence like his own personal sunbeam. Strong or not, he wasn't ready to put any of that pressure of his past on her shoulders, and he didn't know how to put any of it into words.

"I love you," she said.

Those were the words.

She tipped her head, watching him. "Did you hear me?"

Yes. Of course he'd heard her. The words were bouncing around and through and over the rubble of the wall that had protected his heart since violence had destroyed all his plans with Annabeth. When had Kenzie knocked it down?

"Kenzie." This was too sudden. He still hadn't figured out whether or not he was up for another relationship. *What if?* What if she went to work and didn't come home? He couldn't survive another tragedy. Not now that his heart was all open and vulnerable to her every word and action.

"You know what?" She plucked the keys to her restored compact from the wall hook.

Joey had brought that back with the Camaro, but Stephen hadn't reached out to the buyer yet.

"Forget I said anything," she continued, with an eerie calm. "You've been a great help to me during a trying time. I'll always appreciate that." Unshed tears glistened in her big blue eyes. "Take care."

He'd made her cry? He didn't think that was possible; she was so tough. Tougher than he could ever be.

"Kenzie." She was long gone by the time he jerked himself away from that paralyzing fear and moved to follow her.

He swore and was turning back to grab his keys when his eyes latched on to movement on the security monitor. As Kenzie drove away, Murtagh got into his car and followed her.

Why wasn't the bastard in police custody?

Dread surged through Stephen's system. He snagged his phone and his keys and set off after Murtagh.

In the car he called Kenzie's cell phone, but she didn't

pick up. He hadn't held out much hope that she would. Clearly, she was furious and rightly so. He'd screwed up everything. He called Grant next, only to hear another voice mail message. At the tone, he gave Grant the basic information and then he called the police, reporting Murtagh's plate number along with a description of the car.

He stayed on Murtagh's tail, grateful Kenzie was several car lengths ahead of them. If he couldn't do anything right in a relationship, at least he could distract the jerk hassling her. Stephen should have been doing a better job of that all along, per Grant's original request.

He'd gone and fallen in love with her and then chickened out when she called him on it. For the first time, he realized he wanted her in his life more than he wanted to protect himself from further pain.

He couldn't let Murtagh succeed, whether or not Kenzie ever understood his belated epiphany. Although she deserved far more, stopping Murtagh was the first step to keeping her.

They were almost through the cramped streets downtown when Kenzie turned for the club and Murtagh turned the opposite way. Stephen followed him. Using the hands-free commands, he kept calling Kenzie's number, though she continued to ignore him.

Ahead of him, Murtagh sped up and took turns at the last second, clearly trying to lose him. Fortunately, Stephen's street racing skills were still sharp. Murtagh wasn't breaking any laws, though his aggressive driving and Stephen's efforts to stick with him earned them both plenty of honking horns from other nervous and perturbed drivers.

Murtagh gained some space by running a red light, and Stephen chose to stop rather than risk a serious accident. By now Kenzie should be safe at the Escape Club anyway, likely getting an update from Grant that the police had let Murtagh walk.

Stephen tried to pick up the trail again and when he couldn't find any sign of the man or his car, he eventually turned toward the club.

Midday, it was early enough that she had time to talk. Well, time to listen. She'd had the guts to speak plainly and it was his turn. His heart stuttered as he practiced the words he'd never thought to give to another woman. "I love you, Kenzie."

It sounded right in the quiet Challenger. He could only hope she'd believe him and forgive his blunder.

There were a couple cars next to Grant's over in the employee area, including the Mustang they'd sold to Jason. Stephen parked next to Kenzie's little sedan at the kitchen entrance. He walked up and when he pulled on the door, found it locked.

"Come on!" He glared at the security camera. "Let me in."

A moment later the door swung open to reveal Grant, his mouth set in a grim line. "Got your messages."

Stephen shoved his hands into his pockets, his fingers curling around his car keys. "Hopefully, the police will pick him up soon."

"Agreed." Grant's stocky build blocked the doorway. "Is that all you needed?"

"I need to speak with Kenzie."

"She gave me the impression she doesn't want to speak with you."

"Then she can listen," Stephen snapped. "This is personal, Grant." And urgent. He couldn't let her wonder about him any longer.

Grant's salt-and-pepper eyebrows lifted and he stepped back so Stephen could enter. "My guess is you'll need to do some groveling," he said in an undertone. "She's helping Jason prep at the bar."

An ugly surge of jealousy reared up in him. It was hard to believe at one point he'd wanted to push her toward the assistant manager. He'd been an idiot.

"Is she even on the schedule tonight?" Stephen wondered.

"I'll go check." Grant turned down the hall to his office.

His heart hammering erratically in his chest, Stephen hurried into the empty club. Kenzie sat at the end of the bar, laughing with Jason. Jealousy took another swipe at him, but he ignored it. Kenzie didn't play coy games. She said what she meant, and she'd said she loved him.

He paused, wishing he'd changed out of his grimy garage clothes. Next to Jason, he looked like…well, exactly what he was, a mechanic. "Can I talk to you? Privately."

She tipped her head toward the front doors, which would be open soon. "We need to finish this prep."

"The band isn't even here yet," Jason muttered. "Give him a break."

"I have," she whispered fiercely as she slid off the bar stool.

Stephen soaked up every nuance as she approached, grateful to have another chance. Her eyes were bright, with temper now instead of tears as she stared up at him.

She folded her arms over her chest. "So talk."

"Did you listen to my messages?"

"I deleted them."

"Good." He didn't want her to think he was here only

because of Murtagh. "You mean everything to me, Kenzie. I didn't expect to feel this way again."

Her jaw set and her fingertips flexed into her upper arms as if she was trying to keep herself in check. *Again* was the wrong word. His feelings for her were beyond the scope of his experience. He pushed a hand through his hair.

Suddenly, he tugged her into the shadow of the hallway, out of Jason's view. He couldn't do this with an audience. She was stiff under his hands and he released her immediately.

"*Again* is the wrong word, but it's right, too. I did love Annabeth."

"I should hope so," she snapped.

"This. Us." He cleared his throat. "What I feel for you is so much more that it scares me. You are so tough, so vibrant." Wishing she'd let him touch her, he plowed on. "I didn't think I deserved a second chance after…" He left that unfinished.

She blinked, her gaze on the ceiling and her teeth biting into her lip. "It wasn't your fault."

He shook his head. This wasn't about the past; it was about the future. Their future. What could he say to convince her to stick with him? "I screwed up back at the shop," he said, starting over. "I won't make excuses for it and I'll probably screw up a hundred times more by the end of next week."

Her lips quirked up, though she caught the smile before it broke free.

"Only this matters." He tucked a wayward strand of her hair behind her ear. "I love you, Kenzie."

Her lips parted on a startled gasp.

He hated that the ghosts of his past had left her doubting. "I love you so much that I tried to deny it in some ill-advised attempt at self-preservation. Being safe isn't living all out. You reminded me of that essential lesson. Forgive me?"

"Stephen."

That was all, just his name. Those two syllables were as sweet as any touch of her amazing hands. He started to say something more, when an explosion rocked the kitchen.

Shouts of "fire" came a moment before the first belch of smoke hit the hallway. She started toward the kitchen, but Stephen caught her and pulled her behind him.

Murtagh stalked toward them from the emergency exit and the gun in his hand was pointed at Stephen.

"Get out of here," Stephen said to Kenzie. "Go."

"Look, I created a crisis, Hughes. Go fix it," the man dared. "Be the pretty hero if you can."

Stephen felt Kenzie shift behind him. "You picked the wrong target," he said.

"If female firefighters can do anything, prove it," Murtagh shouted. "Prove it!"

"How in the hell do you keep getting into my club?" Grant's voice roared above the sound of the fire and the clanging alarm as he charged up behind them.

Too late, Stephen saw Murtagh's finger squeeze the trigger, and he shouted a warning. The lethal black muzzle of the gun flashed and Stephen tried to shelter Kenzie. He didn't care about her training, only about getting her out of here alive.

Grant swore, skidding to a stop in front of them, his arms spread protectively as Murtagh threatened to shoot again. "You'll never get away with this. Put down the gun and we can reduce the damage here."

"Hand her over." Murtagh coughed as the smoke choked the hallway. "Let her prove what an asset she is to the city."

Kenzie had been with this man in a fire before. If she didn't do something soon, none of them would be walking away. It took a concerted effort, but she wedged herself between the bigger bodies of Grant and Stephen. "What do you need, Randall?" she asked in that easy-going tone she'd used before. "Let's go outside and talk about it."

"You took my job!" Spittle gathered in the corners of his lips.

She swallowed her first instinct to point out that was a preposterous claim. He was beyond logic. She thought about Myra's assessment of rock bottom. Murtagh kept sinking, finding new lows. She'd seen it in the earlier fire.

"Did you set the fire in the kitchen?" she asked conversationally.

"Yes!"

"Why don't you help me put it out?" she offered. The faint sounds of fire engine sirens were growing louder. "We can be heroes together." She shifted toward the kitchen, relieved to draw his attention from Stephen and Grant. "Think how pleased the PFD will be."

The smoke was stinging her nose, burning her lungs, yet she wouldn't quit. Despite his desperate actions recently, Randall Murtagh had once been a valued member of the PFD and community at large.

He snorted "No female can equal a man in a crisis." He waved the gun at Stephen and Grant. "Once again, two *men* have stepped up to shelter you."

She spread her arms wide. "Randall, I'm right here, out front. Let's go do this."

"You will be." Coughing again, he used the gun to gesture for the three of them to move into the empty club. "Go on."

"Run," Stephen whispered, moving between her and Murtagh as much as he dared.

"No." She wasn't going anywhere without him. Or Grant. At least in the club, the air was clearer as the smoke rose to the rafters.

Grant slowed his steps. "Whatever has you upset, Randall, we can sort it out. Just put the gun down."

"It's too late for that," Murtagh said woodenly. He lined them up against the bar.

Kenzie had heard that tone from him before, through the filter of her turnout gear. Suddenly it all clicked. His deliberate resistance in that fire, his focused pursuit of her ever since. "You didn't want to be saved that day."

"Of course I didn't!" Randall screamed.

Crap. This changed everything. He was willing to die, eager for it, and he had no qualms about taking them along with him.

He doubled over, clutching his head. Grant moved in, but Murtagh stood up. "Back off!" He leveled the gun at Kenzie. "You showed up with your idealistic persistence and made everything worse. *You.*"

"It's not her fault you're an arsonist," Stephen said, distracting Murtagh as he squeezed the trigger again. The bullet went wide, shattering the transom over the club's front doors.

Murtagh pressed the hot muzzle of his gun to Stephen's chest. "On your knees."

"No." Kenzie felt tears on her cheeks as Stephen

obeyed. "Randall, let him go. Let them both go. This is between you and me."

To her relief, he lowered the weapon, leaving a small burn mark on Stephen's T-shirt. They were hardly out of danger. A telltale sound overhead drew her attention. The fire was chewing through the roof. They had to get out of here.

Though Murtagh lowered the gun, he maintained control. If they tried to run, he could shoot at will. There wasn't enough cover between their position and the front door. The hallway was black with smoke, emergency lights glowing.

"Randall, let's go," she said quietly.

"It's too late," Murtagh was saying. "You can't do anything. This will show the city and the world that females should not be trusted to fight fires."

"I certainly can't do anything when you're holding me at gunpoint. Let these guys go. They don't know how to put out this fire."

"No." Murtagh shook his head, then groaned as if that caused him great pain. "They should know they backed the wrong dog in this fight."

Clearly, reasoning with him was out of the question. "You've made your point," she said, willing to plead, to do anything to save Stephen and Grant. "We need to get out of here."

"Are you scared?" Murtagh leaned close.

"Yes." Though not at all for the reasons he probably believed. She was afraid for the people fighting the fire in the kitchen. She knew real fear that Stephen and Grant were being targeted by a man who wanted only her.

"Good." He was nearly nose to nose with her.

Beside her, still on his knees, she felt Stephen's hand

on her calf. The touch steadied her. "What do you want from me?" she asked.

"Just the last few minutes of your life," he said, suddenly calm. "You should thank me for allowing your friend and overprotective lover to join us."

The smoke seemed to be thinning. The firefighters must have the worst of the blaze contained. What would Murtagh do when he noticed? Behind him, she caught a movement at the hallway. Stretched out on his belly, Jason was signaling something to Grant.

"If you want to kill me, just do it," she said, stepping forward, keeping Murtagh's attention on her. "Let these guys go."

Stephen caught her hand in his.

She shook him off. Taking the focus was all she knew to do to give Grant and Stephen a chance to escape. "Come on, Randall. Man up. Let them go and just take the shot. You've tried everything else to get me out of the PFD. This is the last chance you'll have."

"Kenzie, no," Stephen said.

A man shouted from the front doors, identifying himself with the police department, ordering Murtagh to stand down.

"Hostage negotiator," Grant explained. "You should talk to him. Want my phone?"

"There's nothing to negotiate," Murtagh said.

"Sure there is," Kenzie said in a soothing voice. "This can be the end of it. A simple misunderstanding. You and I can start fresh."

Murtagh's shoulders slumped and for a split second, Kenzie thought they were making progress. Then he looked up and she knew he'd gone over the edge. His gaze was blank, his motions stiff as he started shooting wildly.

Stephen yanked her to the floor and covered her body with his. The impact knocked the breath from her lungs. Another gunshot bit into the bar, missing them by inches and sending splinters through the air. Grant swore as one more gunshot sounded. There was a heavy *thud* and then an echoing silence.

She squirmed out from under Stephen, intent on helping whoever had been shot, but it was too late. Murtagh had killed himself.

She didn't realize she was sobbing until Stephen tucked her close to his chest, hiding her face from the gruesome view. "I'm here. Let it go." He let her cling as waves of sorrow and confusion shook her body.

Voices surged all around them, but he held on, sheltering her while she lost it. She couldn't even pinpoint why she was so upset for a man who'd aimed so much vitriol and hatred at her.

Time seemed to slow as Stephen stroked his hand over her head, down her braid, again and again. She breathed in the earthy, honest scents of the garage and the man underneath.

"Are you hurt?" She peeked under his T-shirt, grateful the gun hadn't burned him.

"Not a bit, thanks to you."

She dropped her head to his shoulder as the emotions began to subside. "I love you," she murmured.

"I know," he replied.

She smiled against his chest, hugging him tightly. He was her lifeline, her connection to the bravest part of herself. "You love me back," she said.

He tipped up her face until she was mesmerized by those steady hazel eyes. "I know."

His lips met hers in a kiss sweeter than their first. Laced with the undeniable passion they'd discovered in each other, it was a kiss full of hot temptation wrapped with comforting acceptance.

It was a kiss between lovers with plans for a long future together.

Stephen finally believed it was over when they were safely back at the garage. They were home. The police statements had been made, the news reporters directed to her lawyer and the assurances given to her family and his. Grant had even told them an initial search of Murtagh's laptop proved he was the source of the cyber bullying.

In the trailer Kenzie had showered and changed into those cutoff shorts and a snug tank top sporting patriotic red, white and blue. He'd cleaned up as well, choosing khaki cargo shorts and a loose, short-sleeved cotton shirt, thinking they might both benefit from a long, leisurely drive tonight.

Right now, she was still too wound up to enjoy much of anything. Stephen caught the tremor in Kenzie's hands as she reached for the tea he'd brewed for her. He understood that quaking, as everything inside him still trembled, as well.

"I can't believe Grant has to close the club," she said.

It was hardly the first time since the fire was contained that she'd expressed that concern.

"Grant's faced far worse," he reminded her. "He'll get through it and have the place open again in no time." Stephen thought Grant and Kenzie had that unflagging spirit and fortitude in common. Traits he'd not seen in himself until Kenzie made him take a closer look.

"Probably," she agreed, her smile not quite up to full power yet.

Stephen kept expecting to hear something stupid come out of his mouth about risks and the benefits of a safe distance. It didn't. He wanted to hold her, to sleep beside her every night and wake up with her every morning. To laugh and curse over back-ordered parts and challenging repairs. He wanted to ask her to take the real risk of tying her future to his. For today, for a lifetime.

"You were amazing," he said, not for the first time.

"You saved my life," she murmured, staring into her tea.

"I panicked," he admitted, sliding into the bench seat next to her and drawing her close to his side. "You had it under control."

Her body hitched on a sound that wasn't quite a laugh. She managed to sip the tea and he felt her relaxing into him.

"He didn't have to kill himself," she said at last.

Stephen sighed. "Murtagh was troubled. Beyond the bitterness of any injury or insult that a woman saved him from a fire." He pressed a kiss to her temple. "He was lost in a dark place."

Kenzie snuggled closer. "Sounds like the voice of experience."

"To a point," he confessed. "I never truly considered ending my life, but I did what I could to increase the odds."

"Picking fights and hunting drug dealers is dangerous," she said.

"Says the woman who runs into burning buildings

and calls it a good day." He stopped and stared at her. "Wait. You knew I did that?"

She sat up, brushing his hair back from his face. "I'd been warned about your odd hobbies. Falling willy-nilly wasn't one of them."

Kenzie had set him free, restoring his hope and giving him good reasons to spend more time living his life than haunting his past. Since the narcotics team had moved in and cleaned up the street at last he didn't feel the need to keep up the "odd hobby."

"Grant told you."

She nodded.

"Is that why you stuck around every time I tried to push you away?"

"Please." This time her laughter came much closer to that bold joyful sound. "You did everything except beg me to stay."

"Yeah? Well, I was getting to that when the fire interrupted us." He shifted in the seat and took her hands in his. He really should have a ring, but he didn't want to waste another moment. "Marry me, Kenzie. Be my partner in life and I promise we'll find something to laugh over every single day."

Her blue eyes sparkled and he wanted to kiss her. It took all his willpower to leave her mouth free to give him an answer.

She glanced to the ceiling before meeting his gaze. "If I say no, you'll probably forget how to laugh again," she said, tracing the line of his finger with her thumb.

"So say yes," he murmured.

"Yes." She brought his face to hers and kissed him soundly. "Yes." She peppered more kisses over his nose and cheeks. "You'll be my husband and give me great cars. I'll be your wife and give you great headaches, kids and cookies."

He laughed, backing out of the dinette space and pulling her along with him.

"Plenty of laughter and love, too," she added.

"We'll put that in the vows," he said, his hands sliding under her top and lifting it up and over her head.

Outside, he heard a car horn at the gate. He muttered an oath as he checked the display on his phone. "It's Matt Riley."

She groaned and scrambled for her shirt.

"You could wait here," he said, halfway out the door. The sooner he made delivery, the sooner he and Kenzie could get back to celebrating their engagement.

"I want to meet him," she said. "I'll get the keys."

"All right."

Stephen opened the gate, then jogged over to open the bay door, grinning at the sight of the 1972 Plymouth Cuda he and Mitch had restored for Matt's father.

The driver parked in front of the bay where the Camaro SS was waiting under a protective cloth cover.

General Ben Riley emerged from the driver's side a fraction slower than his son leaped from the passenger side.

"Is she ready?" Matt asked.

"All set," Stephen replied, reaching out to shake hands with Ben. "I appreciate the repeat business, sir."

Ben leaned back. "Something's different about you," he said.

"Oh, it's the smile." Kenzie joined them, a set of keys dangling from her finger. "He's been practicing more lately."

Stephen slid his arm around her waist. "My fiancée," he said, making the introductions.

Ben offered hearty congratulations and wished them a marriage as long and happy as he'd shared with his wife. Stephen noticed Matt was a little more reserved, most likely distracted by the purpose of the visit.

"Go on," Stephen urged. "She's all yours now."

Matt pulled back the cloth and gave a whoop of joy. "Perfect!" He circled the car, then came around and gave Stephen a manly hug, utterly delighted.

Kenzie held out the keys. "She handles like a dream."

"It would've taken me forever to get her into this kind of shape," Matt said from the driver's seat a moment later. "Dad, look at these details."

"Excellent work," Ben agreed.

"We just worked to your son's specs," Stephen said.

Matt started the engine, his face as bright as a kid at Christmas.

"I hope you have a place to run her wide open once in a while," Kenzie said. "It's a great experience."

Over the top of the car, Ben grinned at them. "We know of a few places to open her up."

"Good." Stephen felt Kenzie lean in, her finger hooking in his belt loop.

He accepted the check for the final payment and waved the Rileys and their muscle cars through the gate. He hoped they kept their word to send him even more business. The restorations were a challenge he enjoyed.

Though not as much as he enjoyed the woman beside him.

He reached for Kenzie. "Now, where were we?"

She scooted away, walking backward to the trailer, gathering the hem of her T-shirt, giving him an irresistible glimpse of her midriff. "We might have been celebrating that I said you could be my husband."

Her sassy grin lit him up. "Oh, that's right," he said, chasing her down and sinking into the kiss when she let him catch her. She'd healed him, brought him back into the world, body, heart and soul. Whatever life tossed at them tomorrow or in all the days to come, he knew he could face it with laughter and courage, because Kenzie had taught him how to love.

* * * * *

Don't miss other books in Regan Black's
Escape Club Heroes series

Protecting Her Secret Son
A Stranger She Can Trust
Safe in His Sight

Available now from Harlequin Romantic Suspense!

ROMANTIC suspense

*Carrie Price's ghost-hunting boss has been kidnapped—
on camera. Now it's up to her and New Orleans cop/
navy SEAL Bastien LeBlanc to find him. Will Carrie
dare reveal her own violent past and trust Bastien
when that past comes calling for her? Or will she lose
everything...including him?*

*Read on for a sneak preview of the final book
in the Code: Warrior SEALs miniseries,*
Navy SEAL Cop
by New York Times *bestselling author Cindy Dees.*

A flash of lightning outside was followed by an almost
immediate crack of deafeningly loud thunder that made her
jump. She thought she caught a glimpse of a shadow outside
her window, a human-sized shape in the tree, as if someone
had climbed it and was peering inside.

Ohmigod.

She bolted out of bed and flew out of her room, shooting
across the hall to leap into Bastien's room in about one second
flat. She plastered her back against the door, breathing hard.

Bass was out of bed and standing in front of her in about
the same amount of time. Crud, that man could move fast.
"What's wrong?" he bit out.

"I thought I saw someone outside my window. It was
nothing, I'm sure, but it spooked me."

He touched his throat with a finger and ordered tersely,
"I need someone to check out Carrie's room, inside and out,

ASAP. She thought she might have seen someone outside her window."

"Who are you talking to?" she asked.

"My men. We're all wearing earbuds and microphones."

"You went full commando in a bed-and-breakfast? Isn't that a tiny bit of overkill?"

"What if there really is a guy outside your room?" Bass responded.

Oh, God. There went her pulse again.

Bass gathered her into his arms as if he sensed her panic. "I've got you. You're safe. No one's going to hurt you."

She mumbled against his chest, "I feel so stupid."

"No need. You have every reason to be jumpy." A pause, then he added, "You're freezing. Come get under the covers and warm up."

He deposited her in his bed, which was still warm from his body. Heat wrapped round her like the hug he'd just given her, comforting and secure. She was disappointed when he didn't join her. Instead, he continued to stand over by the door, listening at the panel.

Without warning, he slipped outside, leaving her alone in his room. Great. Now she could freak herself out in here.

She stared fixedly at the alarm clock on his nightstand, her tension climbing with every passing minute. What was going on out there? Why had he bolted out of the room like that?

The door flew open and she froze in terror, her gaze darting around frantically in search of a weapon.

Find out who just burst in the door in
Navy SEAL Cop *by Cindy Dees,*
available August 2018 wherever
Harlequin® Romantic Suspense *books and ebooks are sold.*

www.Harlequin.com

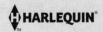

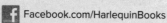
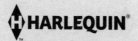

LOVE
Harlequin
romance?

Join our Harlequin community to share your thoughts and connect with other romance readers!

Be the first to find out about promotions, news, and exclusive content!

Sign up for the Harlequin e-newsletter and download a free book from any series at **www.TryHarlequin.com**

CONNECT WITH US AT:

Harlequin.com/Community

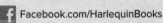 Facebook.com/HarlequinBooks

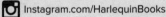 Twitter.com/HarlequinBooks

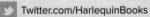 Instagram.com/HarlequinBooks

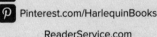 Pinterest.com/HarlequinBooks

ReaderService.com

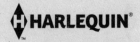 **HARLEQUIN**®

**ROMANCE WHEN
YOU NEED IT**